Bro

Betsy Reavley

www.bloodhoundbooks.com

Print ISBN 978-1-912986-10-1

Also By Betsy Reavley

Carrion
The Quiet Ones
The Optician's Wife
Frailty
Pressure
Murder At The Book Club
Murder In The Dark

For Jasper Joffe. Thank you.

Prologue

I have taken more than the recommended dose
And absorbed half a bottle of the honey liquid.
I do not wish to be swallowed up
By my eternal death. Rather I long
To leave this plagued mind tonight
And escape to another realm.
Life flows through me intravenously.
Churning and screaming gargles
In the pit of my stomach:
The place where I find you,
A state of lost love and frustrated dreams.
The loud and the quiet.

Part One

It wasn't always easy being in my head, but I knew nothing else. I wasn't ashamed of my insanity. I didn't see my diagnosis as something reprehensible; it wasn't as if I had contracted HIV from dirty needles. People aren't embarrassed to admit they have cancer, but *my* cancer couldn't be seen; it didn't require chemotherapy. My cancer was invisible to microscopes. My cancer ate away at my emotions. My cancer was called something else: manic depression.

My life had been a series of false starts but my release from the psychiatric hospital set off a spiral of events that nobody could have seen coming.

My doctors had agreed to release me into the care of my family, which comprised of my mother and younger brother. I was twenty-three years old when I left Redwood hospital in Suffolk. I had been there for four months and eleven days. When I was admitted, the doctors told my family I would be there for a long time. I was a danger to myself, they said.

The hospital had been my sanctuary and my prison. I had been sectioned under the mental health act after the police found me freaking out in a department store. I had hidden myself among a rail of clothes in John Lewis. When asked by security what I was doing, I'd told them that the Taliban were after me and I was hiding. The security guard had thought I was taking the piss, and, in his angry frustration, grabbed hold of my arm and tried to pull me out. It was only after I'd screamed and bit his hand that the people watching realised I wasn't well. Unsurprisingly, the staff had been so unnerved by my behaviour they called the police.

I hardly remember any of this. Most of what I know is second-hand, coming largely from my mother and the doctors. It is all a distant memory. I remember very little of what I did or thought during my paranoid, manic episodes. What remains is a blurred memory of a feeling, and it isn't one I wish to recount. Needless to say, it was very easy for the court and mental health professionals to deduce I needed a stint in the loony bin. Much later I learned that *I'd* attacked the guard, who claimed he'd never laid a hand on me; a fact that had been backed up by onlookers.

During my time at Redwood I was kept under heavy sedation until I'd calmed down enough to be able to listen and cooperate. The drugs had left me feeling like a zombie, so doped up that my legs were like jelly, and I'd found it nearly impossible to walk; my head so full of fog it had been no surprise that my paranoid delusions had stopped. I simply couldn't handle both at once so the medicated mist had won out.

After hours of therapy, and a winning cocktail of drugs, I'd begun to return to my old self. It was then, three weeks into my incarceration at Redwood, that the enormity of my situation had dawned on me. I'd been sitting in the communal television room, looking at the other patients, or inmates as I liked to refer to them. That's the first, clear recollection I have of my time spent there, but I wish it wasn't.

It was a grey summer that year. The sun had forgotten to shine. A cold, still sky looked over everything and the space where light should have been had felt hollow. The common room had been dull, as a result of the missing warmth, and everything was a dirty grey-brown colour; the sofas, old and worn, wouldn't have looked out of place in a seventies' nightmare. The faded, sickly orange and tan fabric had shown every speck of dirt and every stain it had accumulated over the years. I'd stared at it for so long it looked as if it were alive with bugs.

In the opposite corner had sat a middle-aged man with wiry salt and pepper hair and wild eyes. He'd been talking very quietly to a fat, young woman who'd kept glancing nervously in my direction. Her gaze had made me feel uncomfortable. Their words were hushed and I'd tried to concentrate on the television to distract myself from the feeling they meant me harm. It had been a relief when one of the nurses casually walked through the room with a clipboard under her arm.

'Alright, love?' she'd asked. She'd smiled and I'd wriggled in my seat. I hadn't been able to bring myself to smile back so had offered a nod and turned my attention to some dust particles that were dancing in the air by the window.

Meanwhile, the whispering had grown louder from the two inmates. I'd heard the man spitting out his words, although what he'd been saying wasn't clear. The fat woman had turned to face him and screamed before bolting from the room with a speed I couldn't have predicted.

'Don't touch me, don't fucking touch me!' she'd screeched as she hurtled down the corridor. Two nurses armed with syringes had run after her. I'd watched her disappear around a corner and turned back to the television, startled by a wild-eyed man who'd been squatting behind my chair, his chin propped on the backrest.

'Dotty as a cuckoo, that one,' he'd said, looking at me with his head tilted. I could feel the warmth of his breath on my cheek and I'd stood up to look at him. 'Don't worry, lass, 'Arry won't do you no 'arm.'

I'd eyed him warily, and again found myself nodding in response. 'You're new, ain't you? I can always spot the new ones a mile off,' he'd continued. I'd chosen another seat and sat down again, facing him this time. He'd jumped over the chair like a sprite and made himself at home; the way he moved had reminded me of a monkey.

'I'm 'Arry,' he'd announced, as though he was introducing himself at a party. 'I've been in and out of here a bit and I know 'ow this place works. If you need anyfing, I'm your man. I know all the nurses; know which ones are gooduns and who you should avoid. Know most of the poor sickos, too.'

He'd leaned closer, looking pitiful, an ingrained sadness in his hazel eyes; I could see how lost he was. This had made me feel less nervous and I'd realised I was grateful for his attention and company. As he'd removed a pouch of tobacco from his faded camouflage trousers, I'd noticed his fingernails were black with dirt. He'd rolled himself a cigarette. The whites of his eyes were as grey as his T-shirt. He'd put the cigarette into his mouth and gripped it with his dry lips as he began a frantic search for a lighter. I'd watched him in a daze, remembering I had one of my own; I'd reached for my packet and the neon green lighter. Timidly, I'd offered him the lighter, not wanting to make any physical contact with my new friend. He'd seemed aware of my apprehension and gently took it from me, smiling with gratitude. He'd lit his rolled cigarette and inhaled deeply, filling his lungs and loudly exhaling.

'That's better,' he'd said, looking calmer. 'So, what's your name then?'

'Annabel,' I'd told him, realising it was the first time I'd spoken to someone other than a nurse or doctor in a few days.

'Nice to meet you, missy. I'm 'Arry,' he'd told me again. He'd smiled, revealing yellow, stained teeth. 'I've got papers to prove I'm mad but can the rest of them prove they're sane? That's what I want to know.'

I'd shrugged, not sure what to say.

'Only jokin', only jokin',' he'd chortled.

A nurse had walked by and frowned at us. I'd immediately felt dirty but didn't know why, and Harry had ducked down in his seat, his knees brought up to his chest. He'd kept his head perfectly still, and I'd watched as his eyes followed her until she'd turned into the corridor.

'Spyin' on me,' he'd said in a hushed, nervous voice. 'They've got their spies makin' sure I don't reveal their secrets.' He'd leaned in again and I could smell his stale body odour. The only thing I could do was nod.

'Old 'Arry knows things, you see. Things the government don't want others knowin'. I was in the Falklands and I know what really went on.' His eyes had darted wildly around the room, looking for evidence of someone else listening.

'I'm not allowed to talk to the doc without them sending in one of their government people. They need to make sure old 'Arry doesn't let slip coz of the Secrets Act. What I know could change everyfing and, you see, I won't tell, but it makes my head feel a bit funny sometimes like, so they put me in here so they could watch me. But I know what their plan is. I know what they want to do to 'Arry.' He'd smoked furiously and edged ever closer to me. I'd felt completely uncomfortable and wished the sour-faced nurse would reappear.

'I won't never tell, but they are real worried about me, about how much I know. I'm a soldier, through and through. Wouldn't never let down my men by revealin' the truth about what really 'appened.' His words had been gaining speed and my head had begun to ache with his insanity.

'They want to keep me here so they can control me.' Self-importance had dripped from his words. 'But I see what they are doin'.'

He'd suddenly jumped up and bolted over to a window that looked out over the green area, where we were encouraged to get some air. He'd pointed his finger at the glass and tapped it loudly.

'See that tree, down there, the chestnut? Well, one day they will find old 'Arry swinging from that tree. One day you will see me hangin' there and you'll all say "poor old 'Arry", but you'll be wrong, coz it won't 'ave been me what will have done it. It'll be them who'll have put me up there and made it look like I did it to myself because they're worried I know too much. One day, missy, mark my words, I'll be found in that tree.'

I'd sat, frozen in my seat, wondering if I could get up and leave safely. His brow had been lined with stress and, although I was scared, I couldn't help feeling pity for him. I'd felt sorry for us all: we were tragic and lost. Every person there was filled with an aching sadness. If I could have saved them all, I would have. Harry was lost in his own delusions – as I'd been not that long ago. As though suddenly remembering his train of thought, he'd spun round to face me.

'But, you'll know, lass, you'll know it weren't me that did it. You'll know it was them but you mustn't ever say. You have to keep it a secret all to yourself, otherwise they'll come after you, too.' And with that, he'd brought his finger to his lips, given me a wink, and walked off, seeming content that he'd unburdened himself and at the same time protected me from 'them'.

I'd stayed in the scratchy chair for a moment or two, making sure he'd gone. I'd been glad to be alone in the common room. I couldn't have handled any more crazy talk. I'd got up and wandered over to the window, looked down at the tree, and wondered how long it would be before the poor soul did kill himself. I'd tried to shake off the image of his limp, dead body hanging from the tree. The picture in my mind had made my head hurt. I'd rubbed my temples and tried to think about something else, but now I was infected with Harry's madness as well as my own. I'd gone to my room, got into bed and curled up under the covers, and cried there for the rest of the day.

***

Waking up in my own bedroom in the family home had taken some getting used to. I had been in the hospital for what had felt like years, and being there had become normality. For the first few days I'd sit up in bed and just look around the room, adjusting to the sight of my belongings, wondering for a moment if I was in the middle of another delusion. What should have been comforting wasn't.

I got out of bed and stared at my pink feet; my legs were pale and thin. The drug-induced sleep had left me feeling detached and it took a few minutes to shake the blur from my skull; I didn't feel confident on my feet until the fog had dissipated. I glugged half a pint of water from a glass on the bedside table and eventually found the confidence to stand up. A head-rush left white spots floating in front of my eyes as I pulled the curtains open. The grey-brown sky was low as I watched Wookie, the family dog, sniff about in the garden below. He went busily from shrub to shrub, sniffing the azaleas and viburnum, cocking his leg on the trunk of the cherry tree.

I could hear the sounds of pots and pans coming from the kitchen: Mother was awake. My old floral kimono was hanging on the back of my door, so I wrapped the silk tightly around my body and it helped me feel more at home. I found my way into a pair of tatty slippers, hesitantly left my room, and shuffled into the bathroom. The noise from downstairs stopped and my mother called up the stairs.

'Annabel, is that you?'

'Yes, Mother,' I replied. 'I'll be down in a minute.'

I pulled the bathroom door shut, opened the cabinet and removed my toothbrush and toothpaste. My mouth felt dry from the medication. I watched myself going through the motions of brushing my teeth. I saw myself in the mirror and didn't recognise the person staring back at me: a girl with greasy blonde hair and a long fringe over her empty blue eyes, her face puffy and miserable. Once upon a time I was attractive. I heard a tap at the door.

'Are you in there, darling?' asked my mother. 'Is everything alright?'

'I'll be out in a minute!' I sputtered through a mouthful of foam.

'OK, great, just checking that everything is alright.'

I pulled the lock back and swung open the door to find my mother standing there, wringing her hands.

'Can't I go to the sodding bathroom without you worrying?'

'Of course you can, darling,' she said, looking ashamed. 'I just wanted to make sure . . .'

'"Everything is alright", yes, I know,' I said. 'It's fine. Everything is fine. I'm not slitting my wrists with a razor, I was just cleaning my fucking teeth.'

I pushed past her and made my way to the stairs. My mother opened her mouth to speak but thought better of it, so simply nodded and followed me down into the kitchen.

Settling back into home life with my family was proving harder than I'd first anticipated.

Our village house had stopped being home a long time ago. But, to an outsider, it looked like the perfect family residence. Photos of sports days and smiling kids on beach holidays stood proudly in brass frames. The country kitchen was clean and homely, painted in muted shades of duck-egg blue and cream. The sitting room was peach and my mother's collection of scatter cushions made it inviting. The seventeenth-century rooms were large but not well lit. We had a dining room and a separate study that had become a TV room for my brother and me. The house had six bedrooms and three bathrooms. We were some of the privileged few.

I could remember a time when we'd been happy. It was so long ago it seemed like somebody else's life. My mother did her best to jolly us along, but the sadness within her couldn't be masked.

When I was ten, my seventeen-year-old sister was killed in a car crash. Late one January evening, Lucy had been driving along a winding country lane when a deer had jumped out in front of her. She'd only passed her driving test two months earlier. To avoid hitting the deer she'd swerved on the slippery black road and collided with an oak tree; she died on impact, and killed the deer.

My parents had adored Lucy. Not only was she extremely pretty, she'd also been kind, generous, and smart. I'd always felt like the less-attractive version of her. She did well at school, had rarely got into trouble, and was a popular girl. Everyone had loved her, and so had I – even if she had been an intimidating role model for me.

Mother and Dad met when they were in their twenties at a friend's party. Three months later, Mother became pregnant with Lucy. Dad proposed, and they had a small, shotgun wedding in Hammersmith, weeks before Lucy was born.

I'll never know if my parents really loved each other at the time, or if duty had forced their hand, but, whatever the reason,

Lucy had brought them together and kept them together; until her death, they were good parents. Dad worked hard and provided for us all, and Mother looked after us in her role as housewife. We were an unremarkable family, but we were happy.

After the crash, my parents fell apart. My mother started drinking and my father buried his head in his work. Three years later, my father abandoned us and moved in with a much younger woman he'd met at work. My brother, Will, and I never saw my father after that. He and his new wife had a baby, and no time for us. I was hurt then, and still am, but it gave my mother the kick up the bum she'd needed. After a long, miserable grieving period she stopped drinking. Will and I were able to return to some kind of family normalcy. We'd looked out for each other during that time and had become very close. Now, years on, my Mother is happy and stable and I am the train wreck.

The death of my big sister resulted in the loss of two members of my family. I don't think I have ever properly mourned either of them. At least that's what my psychologist tells me. It seems this is the cause of all my problems, never mind the fact that manic depression is hereditary and my maternal grandmother was famously as mad as a box of frogs. But, so-called professionals are uncannily able to ignore certain facts if they think they are right.

Despite my mother insisting she recognised my symptomatic behaviour, her opinion was ignored. My psychologist decided cognitive therapy alone was the answer, leaving my poor mother to beat herself up and think somehow that she was the cause of my instability and should have done more to protect me. This couldn't have been further from the truth, and it wasn't until a sensible psychiatrist had concluded I was suffering from my first manic-depressive episode that she was able to let herself off the hook.

Now, a few weeks after my release from the nut house, I could see the effect my illness had had on her. I felt guilty, just as she had. Guilt is a funny thing: it's infectious, it spreads like a disease and our home reeked of it; it oozed from my bedroom.

My existence was monotonous. I spent my days in my pyjamas, staring at the television while American talk show hosts tried to solve the problems of the masses. One hillbilly moron merged into the next as the words floated past me.

***

Autumn blanketed the countryside around our house and I became frustrated by my non-existent life. I watched the leaves outside blowing to and fro, the wind lifting them into the air, suspending them in time before dropping them somewhere else. I realised I needed a change of scenery.

I flipped open my laptop. Before I knew what was happening, I found myself on a website booking myself into a small hotel on the coast. I couldn't think clearly at home with my mother watching my every move, and I felt I was in danger of becoming agoraphobic. A break would do me good. Explaining my sudden urge to escape wasn't going to be easy and was likely to alarm both my family and my doctors.

For the first time in days I found myself wanting to wash. I ran a bath and filled it with lavender bubble bath and jasmine oil. The scents filled the room and a sweet steam clung to the walls. With my radio tuned to Classic FM, I pulled down the roman blind, lit a number of cream candles, and turned off the lights. I slipped out of my kimono and into the soapy water. Immersing myself in the bubbles, I floated on a quartet of violins.

I lay dreaming in the old Victorian bathtub for three quarters of an hour, washing my hair repeatedly with rose hip and cotton-scented shampoo. After rinsing my hair, I stepped out of the cloudy water and onto the white tiled floor. A chill ran through me, making the hairs on my arms stand to attention. Patting myself dry and wrapping a powder-blue towel around my chest, I ran conditioner through my long hair before I dared to look in the mirror. I looked a bit better, although dark shadows remained beneath my solemn eyes. My skin was pale. The touch of summer sun I'd caught a few months earlier had now abandoned me. Straggles of dripping hair hung around my face and clung to my neck and shoulders. Staring at myself left me feeling numb: I looked pathetic. I turned away and went back to my bedroom, where I dried my hair, slid into bed and turned off the light.

Lying in the cocooned darkness of my duvet, I hatched a plan that would explain my sudden departure and allow me to break away from the confines of my family without a bombardment of questions. I knew if I told them I was going away alone it would set alarm bells ringing, so I concocted a story that I was going to visit Toby, my best friend from school, who now lived in Oxford. Once I felt confident I'd be able to get away without raising suspicion, I drifted into a dreamless sleep.

***

The next few days passed uneventfully, but offered me the chance to lay the groundwork for my escape. Initially, my mother was wary of letting me go, but I assured her I'd be in safe hands with Toby, who she knew well and she trusted. As predicted, her shoulders dropped and I was relieved to have been able to put her mind at rest. Thanks to a white lie, I felt guilt free.

Early Thursday morning, I pulled out a worn leather suitcase that had been collecting dust in the back of my wardrobe and packed a number of warm sweaters. It was impossible to forget the vast number of pill bottles covering my bedside table. I scooped them up, dropped them in, and dragged the surprisingly heavy case downstairs.

The wind had already picked up; a branch scratched against the windowpane. The greyish-yellow early morning light made a pattern on the oak floor. The house felt eerily quiet. I went into the kitchen, popped some bread in the toaster and made myself a mug of tea, before sitting at the old farmhouse table to inspect an Ordnance Survey map I'd found on the sitting room bookshelves. It practically covered the entire table and I struggled to unfold it, battling with crisp corners and folds that refused to bend.

In between drinking the sweet, milky tea and taking bites of hot buttered toast, I lost myself in the map. Looking down at the expansive Suffolk coastline, I realised how unfamiliar I was with my own part of the world. The hotel I'd booked was in a little seaside town called Southwold. It was rumoured to be very pretty.

The previous night I'd asked my mother if I could take the dog with me. Raising an eyebrow, she'd asked if Toby would mind having him to stay. I explained that Toby worked, and during the day I was going to be alone. I wanted Wookie for company. (Will and I had spent many childhood hours enjoying the Star Wars films and it just so happened our big, scruffy brown mongrel of a dog shared an uncanny resemblance to Chewbacca.) My mother agreed to let me take him and asked no more about it. As I bundled my suitcase, wellington boots and dog into the back seat of my car, I began to feel something that echoed excitement. I was hardly setting off to conquer Everest, but my trip was an adventure of sorts.

It was about quarter to ten when I got into my red Fiat and headed down the driveway. My mother stood on the gravel, watching and waving; I gave a hoot as I drove through the gateway and set off through our village. I watched in my rear-view mirror as the house got farther and farther away, thinking that it no longer felt like home, and sadness pulled at my brain.

I drove through 'Constable Country'. The landscape resembled one of his famous paintings with its vast and changing sky. Suffolk is a quiet, low-lying, under-populated county of few towns. Among its gentle hills and arable fields is the occasional grassy pasture where black and white, or brown, cows graze. The landscape is dotted with picturesque gabled farmhouses with terracotta tiled roofs, their plastered walls painted in whites, soft creams and yellows, faded pinks, and the occasional washed-out garnet colour known locally as 'bull's blood'. The crops had been harvested, and most fields were now ploughed or palest green with newly planted winter wheat. It was a scenic drive, despite the gathering black clouds above and the ominous wind clattering the trees.

The road wound through little villages that had been forgotten in time, and I thought it unlikely that anything very interesting ever happened in them. Each village had its own pretty church and tidy green, with the verges and gardens neatly manicured. People took pride in the appearance of their streets. You could almost smell the community spirit.

There is only one road in and out of Southwold; when I reached it I slowed right down and took my time to observe the streets and buildings. The houses were a mix of red brick Victorian and older cottages, plastered and painted in subtle pastel colours.

I passed a number of nice looking pubs and a few greens before reaching the coast road. With no plan, I crawled along the road looking at the neat, colourful beach huts and the pier. The Suffolk Coast and Heaths is an Area of Outstanding Natural Beauty. I saw a lighthouse standing proud in the distance and I couldn't help feeling that it was my undiscovered secret.

I felt I'd come to the right place and that fate had somehow led me there. A single raindrop landed on the windscreen. I pulled the car onto the verge and turned off the engine. The wind howled and whistled all around and the waves jumped and tumbled onto the shore. Seconds later, buckets of water began to pour down from the sky. The drops pelted the roof of the car and made a tinny noise above my head. In the back seat, Wookie watched with detachment. The raindrops snaked their way down the glass. Then the downpour ceased, almost as quickly as it had started. I examined the scrap of paper on which I'd written the address of the hotel. I made a U-turn and headed back towards the town.

It wasn't hard to find the Swan Inn – a large, cream, detached pub just a street back from the main promenade. I pulled into the gravel car park where there were only two other cars. I got out, stretched my legs, and let Wookie out. He sniffed about and cocked his leg on an unsuspecting dustbin. As the wind whipped my hair, I grabbed my bag and whistled for Wookie to come to heel.

Inside the pub I waited in a cosy room that had a lit fire and smelled of home cooking. The ceiling was supported by heavy beams; copper pots and pans from days gone-by hung on hooks over the bar. The walls were decorated with turn-of-the-century photographs. It ticked all the boxes. From behind the bar a woman smiled at Wookie and greeted me. She was short and round with a kind, plump face.

'Can I help you, love?' her broad Suffolk accent resonated around the room.

'I've got a room booked. Annabel Livingstone.'

She nodded and reached for a key.

'Follow me,' she said.

We went through the bar and restaurant and up a narrow staircase to a brightly lit corridor.

'I've put you in number five.' She turned the key and pushed open the door. 'I think it's our nicest room.'

It was a charming room with a large bed and a window that looked onto the street below. There was also an antique dressing table, a flat screen television and two nice pencil sketches of the surrounding area. There was an armchair by the window, and a side table with a potted plant on it.

'It's lovely,' I said, patting Wookie on the head. He sat by my side, waiting for attention.

'The TV has all the Freeview channels. There's a hairdryer in the drawer and tea and coffee making facilities on the table by the door. We have free Wi-Fi and in your en suite there are towels – plus some complimentary toiletries. If you need anything else just ask. I'll be around all day.' She cheerfully dropped the keys into my open palm before disappearing out into the corridor.

I threw back the covers and flopped onto the crisp white sheets, taking a long, deliberate breath. Now I was here I wasn't sure what I'd been planning to do, or why I'd come. I sat up and searched through my suitcase for the book I'd packed. I hadn't been able to concentrate on reading for months and months, but

I figured it was worth having another go. I propped myself up against the feather pillows and opened my Stephen King. Wookie flung himself down on the floor, knowing his walk would have to wait for now.

About an hour later, I looked at the clock and realised I was hungry. It was nearly one o'clock, so I decided to brave the weather and search the town for something to eat. Filled with the satisfaction of reading again, I put my book down, pulled on my wellies, clipped Wookie onto his lead, and left my room.

Stepping out onto the street I was greeted by drizzle. I pulled my collar up around my neck and decided to turn left and see where it led. After ten minutes' ambling I came to a small bakery advertising freshly made baguettes. I hooked the dog lead around a lamppost and ducked inside to escape the wet. A pimple-faced teenage boy was sitting on a stool behind the counter, fiddling with his mobile phone. He glanced at me and waited for my order as I inspected the options on the chalkboard.

'I'll have a ploughman's baguette, please.' I checked my pockets for some money.

'Want mayo wiv' it?' He stuffed the sliced bread with chunks of cheddar.

'Please,' I responded, in the same curt tone he'd used.

I paid for my lunch and left the shop, pleased to see the rain had more or less ceased. The road remained deserted and I wandered along the seafront looking for a bench. Before long I found myself perched on a low, damp wall that separated the pavement from the beach. I couldn't see anyone walking on the sand, or the street, and only one lonely car drove past, its windscreen wipers waving slowly. Things had worked out as I'd hoped: apart from a wet Wookie, who sat by my side, begging for a piece of my lunch, I was completely alone, and I liked it.

I let Wookie roam free on the beach while I ate. When I'd finished the baguette, lemonade and chocolate bar, I called Wookie and put him on his lead. The waves were grey and rough so I resolved to explore the town further and save the coastal walk for the following day. As I traipsed along the damp streets, admiring the houses and shops, I grew increasingly aware of my solitude. I knew the autumn weather wasn't inviting, but I seemed to be walking through a ghost town and had begun to find it spooky. I turned the corner and spotted a shop with a newspaper board outside. The headline read:

Second murdered girl found on beach

I stopped dead, realising that the small town was in the centre of a national murder investigation. Caught by a sudden, strong urge to smoke, I nipped in to buy some cigarettes. A man in his sixties greeted me.

'Yes, miss?' He looked over the top of his glasses. His face was weathered.

'Twenty Silk Cut, please.'

He took a pack from the shelf behind him and rang in the amount on the till.

'That'll be seven pound seventy. Anything else I can help you with?'

'No, that's it, thanks. Dreadful about these girls.'

'Are you press?' he hissed. 'Because I've told you lot I'm not going to talk about it. It's morbid and disrespectful. I refuse to indulge in idle gossip!'

'Oh, Christ, no, I'm not press,' I said, tripping over my words.

He softened. 'Well you don't live round here, so where are you from?'

'I've just come to escape for a few days.'

'Odd place to come at this time,' he said warily.

'I didn't realise it was here. I mean, I just wanted to come to the coast for a few days, and ended up booking a room in one of the pubs here. I don't pay much attention to the news.'

'You mean, you didn't know?' he said sceptically.

'No, I did, I mean, I just kind of ended up here without realising.'

The man cocked his head to one side and slid the packet of smokes over the counter towards me.

'Well, it's a bit odd to come and do the tourist thing at this time of year.' He looked at me with suspicion. 'Let me give you a friendly piece of advice, if I may: watch where you go. It's probably best not to mention the news to the folks you meet in town. People are awful sore about this business.'

I nodded, thanked him, and hurriedly left the shop. My heart was beating hard in my chest as I took quick strides along the pavement, back to the sanctuary of my room. He was right: it *was* odd that I'd ended up in a town where a live serial killer investigation was taking place. Or was that what had pulled me there?

Before heading inside I got an old blanket out of my car and attempted to towel-dry Wookie, who wriggled and rubbed himself against the fabric. I entered the bar and made a beeline for the stairs. I made an effort to avoid eye contact with the small number of people who were sitting on stools at the bar, talking in hushed tones to the landlady who'd shown me to my room earlier.

I spent the rest of the day in my room. I sat for tireless hours at my laptop, looking into the murders that had enveloped this quiet part of rural Suffolk. The first body had been found in April. At that time, I had been so out of control I'd not been able to concentrate on anything other than my delusions, let alone a news story. A morning jogger had come across the naked, broken body of a young woman, washed up on the beach. The police announced later that she had been there for a few days and hadn't been discovered due to the cold, stormy weather that had been battering the coast and putting off ramblers. The woman had been reported missing by her family two weeks earlier.

The second body had been discovered only ten days prior to my arrival. A twenty-four-year-old student nurse had disappeared a week before the discovery of her remains. Her boyfriend had appeared on the national news to make a teary appeal for information, and the media had whipped up a storm speculating that a serial killer was on the prowl. The police neither confirmed nor denied that they were working under that assumption, which led to further wild tales being bandied about by the tabloids. No one official was prepared to say 'serial killer'. One police chief had admitted a similarity in the victims' ages but, as yet, there was no evidence to connect them, other than the means by which they had been 'brutally killed and sexually assaulted'.

Slamming the laptop shut, I sat back in my chair and let out a long sigh. I began to wonder if I had chosen this place out of a subconscious urge to be close to the investigation. The morbidity of my recent thoughts left me suspecting that that was the case. For some reason, I wanted to be close to death, to feel its cold presence around me. It was a gloomy realisation and I decided I would avoid the story from then on.

Glancing out of the window, I saw the street lamps were on, their gleam reflecting in the wet tarmac. A rich blue evening sky sat above the rooftops as the last of the birds returned home to roost for the night. I decided to go out and look for some fish and chips – I had no desire to sit alone in the pub eating dinner. I grabbed my keys and wallet and made a decisive exit in search of some hot food.

The next morning I was woken early by the buzzing of my phone. I felt about for it and read the message:

Hope all is well darling. Give me a call to let me know
you are alright.
Love Mum xx

I grunted and buried my face in my pillow, dropping my phone on the floor. Wookie, who was on the bed, looked at me with one eye and puffed out his cheeks. He didn't appreciate being woken up either, it seemed. If I didn't reply I would continue to be harassed by messages. I leaned out of bed and retrieved the phone. I texted back that I was fine and would call her later on. With the speed of light, she responded saying she was relieved.

I tossed and turned in bed for an hour or so, trying to lose myself in the heady sleep I had been enjoying. It was no use. I could hear the faint hum of a vacuum cleaner in the bar beneath me, and pale light filtered through the curtains onto the cream walls, hinting that a nice day was ahead.

I switched on the television and watched an early morning news program aimed at the less discerning viewer. It was about the right level for me at that time in the morning, and I propped myself up against a number of pillows and slumped back. Just as I thought I might finally be able to drift off to sleep again, the dog stretched his legs and decided it was time to get up. It was nine o'clock, so I gave in.

The room, which had been immaculate when I had arrived, now looked chaotic. Clothes were strewn over the chair, a dirty teacup sat on the table, along with my book, laptop, wash bag and a number of other bits I'd brought along for the trip. The bedspread was crumpled up on the floor, along with two cushions that had been on the armchair.

After a cursory tidy, I threw open the curtains to see what the day ahead might have to offer: it was nice to see a clear sky. The rain that seemed like it might never stop had ceased, and had left behind a clean-looking world. The calm reminded me that I needed to take my tablets. I took a handful of pills and went into the bathroom to wash them down. I jumped in the shower, then dressed, before heading downstairs to let Wookie out for a pee in the car park. As I headed back into the bar I was met by the friendly landlady.

'Hello, love, come to have a bit of breakfast, have you?' She bent down to ruffle Wookie's hair and I smelled her sickly vanilla perfume.

'I have.' I was shown to a table near the fireplace.

'Right, so, tea or coffee?' she asked.

'Um, tea would be great.' I fidgeted in my seat, feeling self-conscious that we were the only two people in the bar.

The stout woman paused behind the bar to turn on the radio, then disappeared through the door into the kitchen. I sat alone, waiting for my breakfast, grateful for the comforting hum of a familiar tune that floated out of the retro stereo. It seemed to take forever before my hostess reappeared, looking somewhat flustered, carrying a tray that was laden with food and drinks.

She put down the coffee, having forgotten I'd ordered tea. Next came a glass of orange juice, a basket of cold toast and a hot plate of beans, sausages, egg and bacon. Unfortunately, the fried egg was a wobbly mass of leaky yolk and resembled frogspawn. Proud of her culinary achievement, she smiled and poured me a cup of coffee while asking if Wookie needed something to eat. I said he'd be thrilled with any leftovers she had and she happily scuttled off to look. Quickly, I scooped the egg off my plate, along with one of the sausages that was so burnt it looked like a petrified dog turd, and fed them to Wookie, who gobbled them up leaving no trace of their existence.

After Wookie and I had filled our stomachs, we left the breakfast table and wandered over to a display of tourist leaflets, which sat pride of place on the windowsill.

I was studying a guide to Suffolk coastal walks when a pair of scruffy-looking locals came in.

'Hello, Sal,' said one, 'a pint of my usual, and whatever Jude 'ere wants.'

He pulled up a stool at the bar and manoeuvred his bulky frame onto it. His companion, who was much younger and slimmer, watched me with keen interest. I could feel his eyes burning into me as I tried to focus on the glossy map. Panic hit me out of nowhere and tiny beads of sweat formed on my brow; my hands quivered and I felt my cheeks flush. An insatiable urge to escape this man's scrutiny ran through my body and, without even looking up to see the stranger better, I dashed out of the bar without so much as a 'thank you' to the landlady – whose name I now knew was Sal.

When I reached the car park I bent myself over the low wall, gasping for breath, shaking like a leaf. I felt hot and cold at the same time and my breakfast churned in my stomach. A panic attack had hold of me and it was a good fifteen minutes before I regained my composure. Once the worst of it had passed I sat on the wall trying to steady my nerves and regulate my breathing. Wookie came and sat beside me, pawing at my thigh. Anyone who has lived with a dog knows they have a sixth sense when it comes to the welfare of their owners. I suspect they can smell panic and fear.

My eyes felt dry as I stumbled back in a dizzy haze. The sky seemed bluer than ever and the clouds were luminous with 3D brilliance. I felt euphoria coursing through my veins and the world took on a surreal glow. I sat staring at the gravel in the car park, and noticed tiny splinters of light coming up through the cracks in the ground. The blood coursed around my body, and every beat of my heart seemed to echo through my skull. I felt like I was living in a Vermeer painting, with the colour turned right up, and I barely noticed as a couple of teenagers wandered past me on the street, giggling to themselves at what must have seemed a very strange sight. But, as hard as I tried, I couldn't tear myself away from the wall. I got on my hands and knees and began parting the gravel, searching for the pool of white light that I was sure lurked below.

It didn't occur to me that scrabbling about on the ground was abnormal behaviour until I was interrupted by a hand on my shoulder. It was the man who had been looking at me in the bar. He was tall, broad shouldered, and was wearing a dark green wax jacket and round-toed boots that were grubby and well-worn.

'Are you OK?' he asked. His eyes were the darkest, richest brown I had ever seen. I shook myself from my daze and stood to answer him, brushing the gravel marks from my knees.

'Oh, yes, I'm fine,' I said gaily. 'I was just looking for my bracelet that I dropped here yesterday. I still haven't managed to find the fucking thing.' I was surprised how easily I had made up the lie. He nodded and smiled, his lips almost disappearing into a thin line.

'Do you need help looking?'

'No, no, it's fine,' I said, tripping over my own lie. 'It didn't mean that much to me, it's just annoying, you know?'

'Sure, OK. Well, in case I happen to come across it, what does it look like?'

I began to panic. *He knows I'm lying.* I was convinced he was trying to catch me out. Again, my cheeks flushed.

'Oh, oh, um, silver, a silver chain . . . link bracelet. Silver with um . . . a star on it,' I told him, avoiding eye contact.

'Right, well, I hope you find it.' He inspected the ground for the fictitious object. 'I'm Jude, by the way,' he added, extending a hand, 'see you around.' He disappeared down the street.

I stood glued to the spot for a moment, flummoxed by my own behaviour. I decided it wasn't a good day to go for a walk on the beach alone – given what had just happened, I couldn't trust myself – so I went to a convenience store to stock up on supplies that would keep me going for the rest of the day, without having to leave my room.

Moments later I was in Costcutter, basket in hand. The world was a blur. People barged past me, grabbing their daily groceries, while I pottered at a snail's pace. Insanity gripped me as I struggled to identify the items I wanted. Gradually, my basket filled; this mediocre task felt like I was living in a computer game, trying to complete a level. As I queued to pay, I came across one of the mandatory obstacles: a very small, elderly lady, who smelled of urine and dusty books. She had thin grey hair and was wearing a lavender coat made from scratchy wool. She kept dropping her change on the floor and muttering to herself. When I finally reached the checkout, a fat, middle-aged Asian woman, sweaty and scowling, greeted me.

I returned to my room at the Swan, closed the curtains, got into bed and turned away from the world. I lay enveloped in the duvet for what seemed like hours. I felt safe there, protected from my mind and the dangers I was exposed to when I stepped into real life. Lying there, wrapped up and protected, I found that I couldn't think about anything other than the man from the car park. I thought about his face, obsessing over each detail; the memory of his eyes and his smile intoxicated me. He was tall and handsome. He had clear, pale skin, and pink lips that seemed to curl around each word he spoke. Beneath a granddad cap, curls of fiery ginger hair protruded, glinting like copper when the sun hit them.

It had been a long time since I felt someone had really noticed me. His apparent interest, however brief, made me feel human again. I couldn't get him out of my mind: there was something special about him, something mysterious, and I wanted to see him again. Finally, my limbs relaxed and I fell asleep.

At about half past eight I woke up to hear music coming from downstairs. After spending the rest of the day in my room, sleeping, eating, and watching mind-numbing daytime television programmes, my head felt more lucid and I decided it was safe to leave my room for a while. I got out of bed and applied some make-up. Ordering Wookie to stay, I closed the door behind me, locked it, and listened: he only whined once before settling down to wait for my return.

Downstairs, the bar was busier than it had been earlier. There was a guy with a guitar singing a country song and three tables were occupied with people watching him. The bar was crowded with folk nursing half-drunk pints. I found a quiet corner and sat down. I remembered it was Friday night – that explained the influx of customers. It was the first time since I'd arrived in Southwold that I'd seen more than a couple of people together, and I supposed the macabre events that were currently surrounding the seaside town would keep the locals mostly indoors.

After enjoying a rendition of 'Mustang Sally', and watching the barmaid, whose name was also Sally, sing along with tuneless enthusiasm, I approached the bar and ordered a double gin and tonic and a whiskey chaser. Two middle-aged men paid close attention as I knocked back my shot. One of them gave me a cheer and a wink, to which I responded with a blank stare. His pal laughed and prodded him in the ribs. My rejection had been noted. I was only in the mood for one thing: getting drunk.

I returned to my table and sipped the cool drink. It was a bad idea to mix alcohol with the hefty number of pills I was on, but my turn had left me needing to escape myself, if only for a few blurred hours; the headache would be worth it.

After a few more rounds, I began to feel the effects. I started to enjoy the singer and before long was rocking to and fro in my seat as he belted out 'Walking in Memphis'. The song finished to my rapturous applause and I got up and teetered over to order a bottle of bubbly. My mood had lifted and I didn't mind that I was alone. My own company was treating me very well.

I turned to find Jude standing there, smiling. I gave a drunken nod of acknowledgement and returned to my corner with the bottle and one lonely glass. He stayed at the bar for a while, chatting, before approaching my table. He asked if he could join me, I told him it was fine and suggested he helped himself to the champagne. He sat back in his chair and removed his cap, politely declining my offer.

'Did you find your bracelet?' he asked, leaning forward to engage me.

Self-conscious in his presence, I silently shook my head, wriggling in my seat. I refilled my glass and drank it in one go.

'Thirsty?' he said.

I still couldn't speak, so I shrugged, looking into the bottom of my empty glass.

'I'll be back in a mo.' Jude stood and pushed his chair away as he spoke, and left the table. He returned a moment later with a pint of water.

'I hope you don't mind, but I thought you could do with this.'

He pushed the glass to me, with a kind but sad expression.

'Jesus, am I that bad?' I asked. I took a sip of water. He seemed satisfied by this and sat back to watch the musician, who was by now half-cut himself. We sat together, not speaking, for a few songs.

'Why are you here?' he asked.

Taken aback by the question, I felt compelled to be honest. I opened up to this stranger about my life and the spell I'd spent in the psychiatric hospital. It poured out of me with frightening ease. I unburdened everything that had been swimming around my troubled head since my release, and with each confession the weight on my shoulders felt lighter. Jude listened, his eyes fixed on mine, nodding with understanding, not interrupting.

Instead of feeling judged, I felt like a Catholic in the confessional. The more I spoke, the less I cared whether he understood or not: the release was what I needed. I'd been so lonely and trapped within my own head, it was a blast of freedom and enlightenment to talk to someone else.

After my monologue I felt like a new person. I looked around the bar to find it was nearly empty, and the man with the guitar had given up and gone home. Sally was behind the bar, polishing glasses and chatting merrily to a gentleman who was clearly trying to get away.

Jude looked down at his hands; I could tell he was deciding what to say.

'You needn't say anything,' I told him, 'I'm not after pity or advice. I just wanted to get it all out. Don't worry, I'm not dangerous or anything.' The statement sounded eccentric.

'I was a lost soul, once,' he said, pulling his chair closer, 'but I've since found happiness. It's late now, but I'd like to talk to you about it sometime, if you'd let me?' His words slid over me like butter.

'Sure.'

'Tomorrow,' he said, getting up. 'Meet me tomorrow at eleven, in the bar, and I'll tell you all about my journey.'

'OK,' I agreed, also standing, and feeling more sober than I deserved. 'My name is Annabel, by the way. Guess I'll see you then.'

With that, the mysterious Jude left the bar and walked out into the night. I stood, stunned, wondering what on earth had just happened; Sally broke my reverie.

'Seems you have an admirer, my love. Word of advice though, he ain't exactly normal.'

'Neither am I,' I said, smiling as I stepped out to light a cigarette. I set off walking and followed the winding tarmac from the pub towards the shore, as the lights from a truck came creeping up behind me.

Part Two

My head is pumping. Blood trickles down my brow and into my eyes. I cannot see through the red fog. I blink over and over. I need to see. Where am I? I try to move my arms. They are bound behind my back. I can feel cord cutting into my skin, tight around my wrists. My knees are tucked tight up under my chin. The skin on my chin stings. It feels like carpet burn. My ankles are bound too. Everything aches. My head is fuzzy. Am I in a car? There is a smell of petrol. I feel very nauseous. I can feel the rough carpet floor against my cheek. I am being thrown around. Yes, I am in a car. I am in a metal tomb, travelling in red darkness. I am panicking. My breathing is strained. I cannot catch my breath. How did I get here? I hear other cars moving in tandem with me in my prison. The vehicle brakes and comes to a standstill. The car jerks forward, throwing me against the cold, hard interior of the boot. My jaw aches and a metallic taste fills my mouth; is that blood? My tongue searches my mouth; one of my teeth is missing. There is a raw, bloody gap, empty. Where has it gone? I feel sick again. I gag. Vomit erupts out of me. It tastes of blood and alcohol. I am lying in my own sick. The stench seeps into my nose, mixing with the smell of petrol. I am sick again. The gap where my tooth was is so tender. I wriggle violently, trying to free my hands and feet. If I can slip the restraints I might have a chance. I pull as hard as I can. The rope tightens around my wrists. They are aching even more now. I feel the veins in my wrists throb, trying to get the blood to my hands. Panic returns. Stay calm. Think, for fuck's sake. Think. Listen to the sounds. The traffic seems far away now. I am bobbing about more. Helpless. I am sick again. It is wet and slimy against my body. I try to turn away from it but I am trapped. Trapped in misery and pain. Terrified. My whole body is shaking. There is less blood coming from my head now. I can feel it clotting, forming a thin layer over my face. I am so cold. Am I dying? I need to wake up. Wake up, I tell myself, wake up . . .

***

The next morning I woke wondering what had happened the previous night. It was a blur and my head was thick with fog.

The first thing I noticed were his cowboy boots. Their faded tan leather looked so out of place with the midnight-blue velvet jacket he was wearing. He was chewing a long piece of grass, thoughtfully rolling it about in his mouth from left to right, while he stood in the doorway waiting for me. I felt tongue-tied.

Wookie ran up to him, wagging his long tail. I didn't know what any of us were doing there, or what I expected to come from this meeting. Without a word, Jude pointed his head towards the door and we walked together in silence. The dark clouds had silver-yellow edges and they moved with slow intent out to sea. We stood on the shore watching the waves curl their white frothy hands into the cold sand and pull it back into the water. Many minutes passed until the silence was broken.

'There is a beautiful walk if we head south along the coastline,' he said.

I looked at the sky. 'Fuckballs, I think it's going to rain.'

With unnatural certainty, he said it would not and he led me along the beach. His unwillingness to engage made me feel uncomfortable: I didn't want to walk for hours in silence, he had promised me something and I found myself doubting his intentions.

'What are we doing here?' I said.

He stopped, and turned to look at me, blankly.

'We are going for a walk.'

'No offence, but I don't want to go for a bloody walk. I hardly know you.'

'Oh, I see,' he said, dragging the words out. 'It's perfectly safe, you know. I won't hurt you.'

I laughed.

'I'm not frightened of you, I just don't understand what's going on here. Yesterday, like a madwoman, I poured my heart out to you – a stranger – and now we are standing on this sodding cold beach and you want us to go for a walk . . .' My words trailed away and I felt I'd made a show of myself once again.

'That's strange: most people *are* afraid of me. I'm glad you're not. Come for this walk and I will explain everything.' He held out his hand for me to take. 'I promise, I mean you no harm.'

In my ordinary life, I would have run a mile, but for some reason I believed him and took his hand. I didn't have the foggiest idea why, but I was going to follow him, wherever he led.

'You have taken the first step,' he said as we made our way along the coastal path, 'now, let me show you freedom.'

I looked around and realised we were completely alone; I was with a virtual stranger and I had no idea where he was taking me. It was impossible to know if I was safe or if he was sane, and I wondered if he was one of my hallucinations.

After walking for a mile or so, we came to a high wall, which looked like the boundary of an estate and had a large, dark oak door with a cast iron lock. Jude removed a rusty old key from his coat pocket and opened it. As we stepped through he said, 'Welcome to my world.'

He closed the door behind us with a loud thud and locked it from the inside. I looked around the walled garden. We were standing on a paved path that had weeds growing in between the flagstones. On one side of the path, long grasses and small, native wild flowers were growing; insects hovered among the long stems that were blowing in the breeze. On the other side there was a well-ordered vegetable plot, and beyond this I could see tomato plants growing in a greenhouse.

Jude led me along the path, pointing out the different vegetables they were growing. I had never seen anything like it.

'I bet you never need to go to the supermarket.'

'We don't,' he said, as he bent to pick the last remaining beans from a tired-looking plant.

We passed a man in his fifties, tending to the patch. He stopped and smiled at Jude then returned to his digging. I also noticed some beehives as we went through an arch and left the kitchen garden behind us.

An open lawn lay ahead of us, beyond that, a noble red brick house. It had a wonderful paved terrace, where a few people sat at a rickety wooden table, with steps that led between established lavender and rose bushes. On the far side of the garden I saw an orchard bursting with apples and pears. Among the trees a pair of tethered goats munched happily on the long grass at their feet.

'This is my home,' Jude said as he led me through the wonderful estate. 'Around the other side of the house there's a lake stocked with fish. We keep chickens and pigs, some sheep and three cows. I am proud to say we are more or less self-sufficient.'

I walked with him, taking in all the things there were to see. It was like a miniature world of its own. As we went round the front of the house, I noticed it was in a bit of a dishevelled state. From a distance, it looked well-kept, but up close it was clear that the roof was missing some slates and the windowpanes were badly in need of a coat of paint. Despite this it had a mesmerising charm; had the house been highly maintained, it would have seemed too grand, too daunting.

Clothes hung from a long washing line, flapping in the breeze. Behind them was the lake, with two collapsing sheds nearby – one sheltering a number of rusty-looking bicycles. On the water's edge a rowing boat knocked against a thick stake; the sound of wood on wood was comforting. The more I looked, the more there was to see. On a patch of ground, which acted as a roundabout on the gravel driveway, there were all sorts of herbs growing and the scent of purple sage carried through the air.

Wookie, who had been bounding about, dashed to my side; he eyed a male peacock, who was strutting across the gravel, with suspicion.

'This is Ralph,' Jude said. He doffed his cap as the beautiful bird wandered past.

'This is an amazing fucking place,' I said, staring at a wind chime hanging from a silver birch. The place imposed itself on me, and everything, from the birds and the trees to the house, was larger than I was used to.

'Would you like a cup of tea?' Jude asked.

'Got anything stronger?'

Ignoring me, he strode over to the front door and pushed it open. As I entered, I felt as if I were going back in time: an oil painting of some hounds chasing a fox hung in the entrance hall, the ornate gilt frame was dusty; a few spiders' webs clung to the corners of the room, and burgundy velvet curtains hung in the massive, leaded windows that looked down onto the garden below. Our footsteps echoed on the wooden floor as we went through into a dimly-lit sitting room. I saw the people on the terrace again, and I wondered what their relationship was to Jude.

Suddenly, I noticed a strong smell of roast meat.

'Lunch!' Jude exclaimed, rubbing his hands together, Fagin-like, and sweeping open another oak door that led into a grand dining room.

A long wooden dining table with beautiful carved legs dominated the room; it had carver chairs at each end and benches at either side. On the wall, there was an antique tapestry, and cast-iron candelabras hung from the ceiling, the cream candles half burnt down. A worn Persian rug covered most of the floor, and against one wall stood a grand sideboard with bowls of fruit on it. It was like a Jacobean film set.

The smell of lamb filled my nostrils as we went into the kitchen and I immediately felt hungry. A woman was standing over a green Aga, stirring a pot of vegetables.

'Hello, Maggie,' Jude said to the woman. He planted a kiss on her sun-beaten cheek.

'Hello, my Lord,' she replied with a twinkle.

I guessed she was probably in her late sixties. Her hair was tied back with a handkerchief, a few silver wisps escaping. Light flooded in through another window, bouncing off the yellow walls and lighting up her face. She wore a long, brown, cotton dress and a green crocheted cardigan. As she stirred, bangles jangled on her wrists and her beaded earrings swayed. She gave me a warm smile but said nothing, concentrating on her task.

'A cup of your finest chamomile tea for our guest,' Jude said. He sat down and put his feet up on the kitchen table.

'Of course.' Straightaway, Maggie abandoned her cooking and filled the kettle.

I stood awkwardly in the middle of the kitchen, not knowing whether to offer help or sit down. I wasn't used to being waited on.

Jude was picking at the remains of a baguette on a breadboard on the table. Brushing crumbs off his lap, he got up and told Maggie that we would like the tea under the pergola.

'And when it's ready, bring a tray with two plates of the lamb, please,' he added.

The way they behaved together was curious. He wasn't rude to her, but he spoke with authority and she seemed to jump at his every word. I supposed this was the way people spoke to staff. I smiled a thank you to her and followed Jude outside.

I knew that, later on, I'd write a poem about that moment.

Saving my life
You accidentally saved my life
With the words you spoke
But didn't plan to say.
Underneath your rough skin
Lies a melancholic requiem
Written in messy blood.
You might be someone
To love, though controversial.
And, although
You may never know,
I will owe you my life.
But all that I have to offer
Is an intrusive headache.
For now.

***

Back at the Swan, lying in a hot bath, I went over the day's unexpected events. The Hall was a remarkable and enchanting place. I had been bowled over by it; it seemed happily removed from the modern world. There, it seemed, the human condition was accepted and embraced, not fought against. I loved the philosophy of the place.

Over a long, lazy lunch, Jude had explained to me exactly how it had all come about: he'd inherited the property from his grandparents, who had raised him after his parents had chosen to go and live in the wilds of Africa. According to Jude, they had decided it would be best for him to remain in England and go to boarding school. He had only seen them briefly during the school holidays, and had had a fairly distant relationship with them before their deaths.

Jude had revealed that during his time at Cambridge, where he'd studied History of Art, he'd become an alcoholic, and had whiled away his existence in a drunken haze. He hadn't elaborated, but simply said he'd 'had a moment of clarity', and decided to pack in his boozing habit and 'go back to basics'. He'd gone home to Christie Hall, found the house and land in much need of love and attention, and set about building what he called a 'family' to live there. It had started with two of his friends, and had grown into a community of eight people who lived permanently in the house and to whom it was home. Jude had explained that there were a few others who came and went as they saw fit, but that the 'family' remained small and tight-knit.

I'd asked him how he went about extending invitations to new members, and he'd sat back in his chair, put his arms behind his head, and looked up at the sun streaking through the pergola. He 'heard about people', he'd explained, 'people who needed it'. I hadn't really understood what he'd meant and went back to eating the lovely food Maggie had prepared.

There were, apparently, a number of unwritten laws at Christie Hall that everyone adhered to. Jude had said it was a democracy and that people were free to come and go as they pleased. Under his breath, he'd muttered that it had been referred to as a cult, and then dismissed those claims as nonsense. They encouraged each other to be creative and to embrace all aspects of what it was to be human. At the time, I'd felt sceptical about the hippy-dippy spin he'd put on it, but, soaking in the bath, I began to see what an idyllic set up they had created.

There was still much I didn't understand about Christie Hall, and I was looking forward to another opportunity to quiz Jude that evening. We had made plans to meet at an Indian restaurant for supper. I wasn't really sure what it was that I found so intoxicating about his company, but somewhere inside me he'd lit a flame, and it was the first time I had felt alive in a long time. For reasons I didn't understand, Jude had awoken something in me: hope. His nonchalant attitude to society's rules and his dogged faith that we can each be the master of our own destiny were appealing. I needed to see him again and dinner couldn't come quick enough.

In the back of my mind I was already beginning to dread the idea of going home. My three nights in Southwold were speeding by and I thought about extending my stay. I knew my shrink was expecting to see me later that week and I tried dreaming up an excuse to put my appointment back. It was obvious that my mother would voice her concerns, but I felt confident I would be able to persuade her I was safe and well with my friend, Toby.

I hated feeling like I had people to answer to. I wanted to be left alone to work through what had happened, without the interruption of other people's opinions. Thinking more about my situation, I reflected on what I'd told Jude. The fact that he hadn't shied away or seemed concerned by my instability was a breath of fresh air. It had taken a total stranger to make me feel normal again, something my prescription hadn't managed.

Putting all thoughts of returning home to the back of my mind, I applied some make-up and fixed my hair. It had been so long since I'd paid attention to my appearance and it felt strange. I still found it hard to look at myself in the mirror: my face didn't match my head. I half expected to see a monster staring back at me. Instead, the reflection of a young woman looked back at me. Once upon a time I was popular with the boys, but now I can't imagine why: I look lost, and any sparkle my eyes might have had, has gone. It was difficult to imagine that I might ever be that girl again. Picking up on my flat mood, Wookie came over and sat looking at me with his kind eyes, slowly wagging his tail. I ruffled his head and made a conscious effort to shake the glumness away. I had made a fascinating new friend, I told myself while I was getting ready, and, remembering the dead girls and how they had suffered, I appreciated that things could be much worse.

***

After a long dinner, we left the restaurant and sat on a bench where we gazed at the stars in the dark blue sky. Below us, the sea roared and the waves crashed on the black sand with restrained anger. I had learnt so much about Jude in such a short time and I felt as if he knew me well too. He took something out of his pocket and told me to close my eyes and put out my hand. I did as instructed. Seconds later I felt something small and cold in the palm of my hand. When I opened my eyes, I saw a silver bracelet with a charm attached.

'I found it in the car park. I guess it's yours,' he said, still looking out over the sea. I was speechless; it was exactly like the bracelet I had described to him. But it wasn't mine because I'd made up the story of the lost bracelet. I suddenly felt queasy and found it hard to swallow. I didn't know what to say. I came to the conclusion he had bought it out of kindness, and I felt warm and grateful. I didn't want to lie outright by pretending it was mine, so I simply thanked him and put it on. I was glad to have something tangible that would remind me of him. I held the charm between my fingers and looked up at the canopy of stars.

'You will come back and visit again?' he asked.

'Hell, yes. Very soon,' I said. I knew then my life had changed.

Night flight

The evening was light as a feather.
Pinpricks in the autumn blanket
Reflect the quiet twinkle of eyes.
Vertical landscapes, hushed and deadly
As the silent mamba, hunting.
There is a haunting stillness so brutal,
While tonight you have me.
A wet, grinning moon watches over
While the silk night is sliced
By a single shining arrow.
Lying on the midnight sand,
I watch your soaring arrival go by
Overhead, interrupting my birth tonight.

I was alone, downstairs in the family home, as dawn began to creep up. The noise from the television had become an irritation, like the buzz of a mosquito. I reached for the remote control and pressed the off button. The house was like a tomb. Claustrophobia ran through me as I went to the kitchen, convinced that tea would drown the odious feeling. The silence remained suffocating until half past ten, when Will came downstairs in his black flannel dressing gown. Rubbing his grey-blue eyes, half smiling, half yawning, he wished me good morning. I decided not to mention that I hadn't slept.

I sat in front of the blank television clinging to my mobile phone – Jude had promised to text me and I was waiting for his message with great anticipation. I missed being by the sea, and since arriving home had felt hemmed in.

I'd seen my doctor who'd told me I was doing well but needed to keep taking my pills. He assured me they would kick in very soon and, when they did, I would be back to my old self in no time. The funny thing was, I didn't want to be my old self any more. I longed to be someone else, someone new. In Southwold, I'd rediscovered part of me I'd forgotten had existed. My true self had been lost some time ago, and I'd become foreign.

Staring at the screen, I decided I needed the distraction of something mind-numbing. I flicked through the channels, but Will came in and snatched the remote control from my hand. He wanted to watch a DVD he'd received in the morning post. I didn't argue. I'd had enough depressing reality to last a lifetime.

Will fiddled with the cellophane wrapped around the DVD, as I went over the images of Christie Hall in my head. The place had left such an impression on me, it felt like I was carrying its spirit everywhere I went. It made being at home worse and the longing for escape all the greater. I didn't know when I would next visit Jude and his commune, but I hoped it would be sooner rather than later. I'd had enough of my current existence.

For a few hours at Christie Hall I'd freed myself from illness. It was as though I'd left it at the gate, along with my other demons. The place was alive with love and happiness and I thought it might be the only place on earth I could find contentment. For most of my life I'd felt like a nomad, constantly looking for somewhere to feel at ease; it seemed like I'd been waiting all that time to reach Christie Hall. I stared hard at my phone, willing Jude to make contact.

Never is a promise
Till the day you die.
Never is a promise
Never is a lie.
Promise is a never
Promise till I die.

Will cursed at the DVD's wrapping and silently handed me the case, allowing me to have a go at getting it off. I ripped the wrapping with my teeth and gave the box back to him with a grimace. He rolled his eyes in amusement and slotted the disc into the player, passing me the box.

'It's meant to be really good. Based on a true story, apparently,' he said.

I read the blurb on the back. The film, *Into the Wild,* told the story of a young American man who grew sick of the rat race and opted out. He'd sold everything he owned and had gone on a journey of discovery. It sounded captivating, so I stayed put in the armchair to watch it with my brother. I didn't have anywhere else to be and I liked the idea of whiling away a few hours, immersed in someone else's story.

We weren't disappointed: it was a remarkable film. The main character had abandoned the life his family had wanted him to lead. He'd been brave and adventurous, but tragically his journey ended with his death. The film made me feel like there was a splinter in my brain that I couldn't remove; I was left feeling reflective about my own reality. All my thoughts led me to the same conclusion. I decided to take the dog for a walk. I needed to blow away the cobwebs.

Stepping outside, I was greeted by the cool October air. The leaves in their autumn colours rustled in the breeze that threatened to strip them from their branches. Wookie bounded down the garden to the old wooden gate and waited for me to open it. We stepped through into a field of long grass and headed down towards the river. I felt better being outside again, and enjoyed the wind that nipped at my nose and cheeks. My hands felt chilly and I plunged them deep into my cardigan pockets. Wookie was searching for a stick for me to throw. He sniffed about in the reeds, his nose glued to the bank, his tail waving about like a rudder. The water bubbled below and looked cold and clean. After finding a rather pathetic twig, Wookie bounced over to me and dropped it at my feet, stepping back and cocking his head to one side. His predictability was comforting and I threw the stick into the flowing water. Leaping without grace, he splashed in and swam with determination towards the stick. And then my phone beeped. My heartbeat quickened as I removed it from my pocket to read the message:

28 October. Art Party. You can stay at Christie Hall.
Jude.

It was a strange text, but excitement bubbled in me: I had a date to look forward to. I whistled for Wookie and set off home, rubbing my aching wrists, which appeared bruised.

***

I'd turned a corner. I was able to look forward to the future, and although I took life one day at a time, things were improving. I began to believe I was on the mend, but my dreams were still haunted by my experience in the hospital, and I found it difficult to shake the memories. If anything, I found I could remember more about my time in there. My starkest recollection was of a conversation with a schizophrenic called Paul.

I had been sitting on a bench outside in the grounds, smoking a cigarette and soaking up the hot summer sun that beat down on my shoulders. An ant had made its way through the dry jungle of parched grass near my feet. With determination and focus, it had scuttled through the long stalks, its tiny black body glistening in the sunlight. I remember thinking that life as an ant must be reassuringly simple. From the corner of my eye, I'd caught sight of a man in his late twenties, walking casually over to me, whistling a tune; he was skinny and had mousey hair that needed washing. He was in faded jeans that had hung loose around his waist and were worn at the knees. His blue T-shirt was so large it had swamped him. He'd grinned at me, revealing ugly, crooked teeth. I'd felt uneasy but managed a cursory smile as I slid over to one side of the bench to make room for him. He'd sat himself down and crossed his legs.

'A beautiful day,' he'd said, closing his eyes and tipping his face up to the light. 'You're Annabel, right?'

'Yes I am,' I'd replied, chewing a fingernail.

'I'm Paul. I'm the Keeper.'

He'd opened his eyes and leaned forward so his elbows were resting on his bony knees. I'd wondered what on earth 'the Keeper' meant, but was reluctant to ask, wanting to engage with him as little as possible. I had seen him screaming at one of the orderlies and had heard other patients talk about him. He had a reputation for being creepy and, sitting there beside him, I'd been able see why: he reeked of insanity. It had clung to him and infected everything. I hadn't wanted any of what he had, and I'd felt that, just by talking to him, I was putting my own mind in danger.

'Well, I wanted to introduce myself. I've seen that you don't really speak to anyone here, and I thought you should know that I'm your friend. You can come to me whenever you like. I don't

judge. God doesn't judge. Salvation is just around the corner.'
He'd fixed me with a stare, his eyes had danced with illness.

'Thanks.' I'd wished I was anywhere else.

'The gates of Heaven are open to the righteous. You can get to
Heaven through me. I will guide you to the light. I am the light.
We enter Paradise together. Only there will we be really free.' He'd
spoken with deluded certainty.

On a good day, I am agnostic, but since being hospitalised
I had become more of an atheist. I'd been able to see no sign of
God in my life, or the unstable world in which I'd been living,
but thought it best not to get into a debate with a madman. So,
I'd simply told him, 'That's good to know.'

'I have told you my secret. You must not share it with others,'
he'd said. He'd put a finger to his lips and whispered, 'When death
is near I shall come and tell you. I will lead you through death and
out to the other side where we shall live forever. Through death
we will find our eternal peace. We must die. God has told me so.'

'I see.'

I'd looked around to see if there was anyone who might have
saved me should he have attempted to kill me there and then. My
pulse had quickened and terror had taken hold of me.

'We will die together soon. God will tell me when it is to be.
I will find you when he gives me my instructions. I will help us
get to Heaven.'

I hadn't been able to take any more and so thanked him for
sharing his secret with me, and told him I looked forward to going
on the journey with him. I'd excused myself, saying I had a group
meeting to get to. I'd wanted to run away but thought if I'd shown
my fear, he might have given chase. Once inside, I'd realised I was
shaking and started to look for Harry, who I'd figured was slightly
safer to be around. I hadn't wanted to be alone so spent the rest
of the day in the protective shadow of the old soldier, until Paul
had reappeared and sat next to me, so close I'd felt suffocated. I
could smell his breath and the stale stench from his dirty clothes.
Hygiene wasn't a priority for a lot of the hospital patients. When

he'd brought his lips to my ear and began to whisper I'd turned, terrified, and scratched his face, dug my nails into his cheeks. When he'd screamed with pain it had only taken a few moments for two nurses to appear and drag me into an isolation cell.

Now, sitting alone in my bed, I wondered if either of those men were still in Redwood, or even alive. The thought brought me crashing down to earth and I felt my stomach knot. Redwood seemed like a distant nightmare and I wanted it left in the past, where it belonged. I got out of bed and decided to pack my bag for the weekend ahead at Christie Hall.

I pulled on some faded jeans and a black sweater, and slipped my feet into a pair of brown suede boots. The bass from Will's speakers burst into life next door. Although my little brother annoyed me sometimes, I was so pleased he was at home. I didn't think I could have coped had it been just my mother and me. She'd recently been getting better about leaving me to my own devices, but the pressure of her concern still lingered. I understood that it was natural for her to be worried, and I knew things would be much worse if she didn't care. But, I was a young woman, trying to carve out my own existence, and my mother seemed to fail to understand that I needed time and space in which to do this. I'd never felt I belonged anywhere in this world, and that included home.

The visit to Southwold had come at a good time. Again, I lied to her about where I was going, using the same tale as I had previously. She had bought my story the first time, and did again. I didn't enjoy deceiving her, but I couldn't tell her the truth without causing her concern. It was best for everyone if Christie Hall remained my secret for now.

I packed my bag with enough clothes to last me a couple of days, and hunted out an old book of poetry I liked. I found a set of Derwent pencils and a pad of water-colour cards at the back of a drawer. Not knowing what to expect from this 'art' party, I thought it best to go prepared.

Downstairs in the kitchen, I found my mother reading her newspaper. She was shaking her head and muttering to herself.

There was a cafetière of coffee on the table, so I poured myself a cup. Mother had left some bacon in the pan for me and I fried myself an egg. The smell of bacon fat and the bubbling egg filled my nostrils, whetting my appetite. I'd been unusually hungry recently.

Mother was engrossed in the article she was reading and we didn't speak for a while. I was happy to enjoy my breakfast in silence. Folding the paper and pushing it across the table, my mother sat back in her chair and took her glasses off the end of her nose.

'It's awful this business with these young girls. They are about your age and I can't imagine how the poor parents must feel.'

I chewed and said nothing. I could feel a violent headache coming on.

'I hope they catch the beast responsible soon. Serial killers are unusual in this country. We don't expect them to remain under the radar these days, I mean, there is CCTV and DNA and all that sort of business. Science is meant to protect us. It's like the Yorkshire Ripper or something. It feels so horrible knowing it's happening in our county.'

She got up and went over to the sink to wash up.

'You're talking about the bodies on the coast?' I asked, reaching for the paper to see what she'd been reading.

'I am, darling,' she said, pulling on her rubber gloves.

Though I hadn't been watching the news since my return from Southwold, I wanted to know what was happening with the case. The newspaper article rehashed the details of the murders so far, and was full of speculation about the killer's psychology, but there was little new information. Either the police were playing their cards very close to their chest, or they had no real leads.

'It's like the old days. It's been a while now and the police don't seem any closer to catching the person responsible. By the sound of things, they seem to be waiting for another rotting body to show up, hoping that it might reveal more about the killer. Not very reassuring for young women who live in the area: they must be shitting themselves.'

'Language, Annabel! I'm sure the police are on the trail,' my mother said, trying to sound upbeat.

'You're probably right, Mother. I just hope more young women don't have to meet the Almighty first.'

She scrubbed away at a frying pan. I knew she was thinking about Lucy. How could she not? The death of any girl reminded her of her own loss. I decided to change the subject.

'I'm going to leave after I've walked Wookie.' I pushed my chair under the table and took my dirty plate over to her.

'That's fine. I hope you have a nice time in Oxford, and say hello to Toby. You won't forget your pills, will you?'

'No, Mother, I won't forget the bollocking pills.'

As I left her alone in the kitchen to lose herself in the washing up, my nose began to bleed.

My heart fluttered as I pulled into the long driveway of Christie Hall. The remaining leaves on the trees leading up to the house were beautiful, autumnal shades, and the gentle sunlight filtered through the half-bare branches; some pigs snuffled in dirt in a field to my right. I was soothed by the sound of the gravel crunching beneath the tyres of my car.

There were a few cars parked outside that hadn't been there on my first visit. I pulled up under a chestnut tree and turned off the engine, trying to steady my nerves. I had been looking forward to the weekend and had built it up in my mind so much, I was concerned it might not live up to my expectations and that I would make a fool of myself – my self-esteem was still not back to an agreeable level. My palms felt clammy and my breathing was shallow. I closed my eyes and leaned my head back against the headrest while I got a grip of myself. I didn't feel like myself; everything felt strange.

Seconds later there was a rap on my window and I nearly jumped out of my skin. Jude stood there, looking as calm and cool as I remembered him, and for a split second something about his features made me think of Paul from the hospital. I was haunted by a face I couldn't quite put my finger on. Something felt off.

He opened the car door and beckoned for me to get out. It made me feel special.

'Welcome back,' he said in a more formal tone than I was prepared for. I smiled and reached for my bag on the passenger seat.

'Follow me.' He led the way up to the house. 'I'll show you to your room.'

We went into the foyer where trestle tables were laden with food. The room smelled of cheese and over-ripe fruit. The scent of fresh bread mingled with the distinctive smell of homemade lemonade. It was like being at a luxurious harvest festival. Jude's cowboy boots echoed across the wooden floor, the sound held familiar comfort. We went upstairs and the distant sound of guitars floated through the house. I could hear voices and wondered just how many people were there. We passed a number of decorated doors along a wide corridor, until eventually, Jude ushered me through one with daisies painted on it.

'You will stay here,' he said, indicating one of the two beds in the room. 'Ella is happy to share with you. I'll introduce you when we go down.'

Jude pulled a book off a shelf and flicked through the pages.

'Oh, right,' I said, unable to conceal my uncertainty.

'It's not a problem, is it?' He eyed me closely.

'Erm, no, no. Not a problem at all,' I said with false enthusiasm, putting my bag down on the bed.

'Great. Let's go down, then.' He slammed the book shut and bounced towards the door.

Walking quickly through the house and talking at a rapid pace, Jude explained what the weekend held in store. A number of 'like-minded' people had been invited to stay and join in the party. He said that each person had a gift or talent and would share it with the rest of the house while we feasted together.

My heart leapt into my throat and again I began to feel panic rush through my veins. I stopped and found myself unable to speak.

'What's the matter?' He spun round to see me frozen to the spot.

'But, I don't have anything to offer.' I felt like a little girl who had forgotten to do her homework.

'Do you know a song, or a poem, or anything?' He put a hand on my shoulder. 'It doesn't have to be anything original, just something you like that you want to share.'

I remembered the book of poems I'd put in my bag and a wave of relief flooded me.

'I don't know anything off by heart . . .' I confessed.

'That's not a problem.' He smiled encouragingly. 'Come and meet everyone.'

We wandered through the house and towards the sound of music. The sitting room was packed with people. Some sat on brightly coloured silk cushions on the floor, others were crammed onto the sofas. A man and woman strummed playfully on their guitars and hummed a song I didn't recognise. The room smelled of vanilla joss sticks and marijuana. Beneath one of the tall windows, a number of paintings leaned against the wall.

'You remember Maggie, don't you?' Jude asked as he pulled the woman over to us. She smiled at me while puffing on a joint.

'Hello again,' I said.

She slipped her arm around Jude's waist.

'Welcome to our little gathering.'

The older woman studied me with bemusement. I started feeling self-conscious, and wondered why I had come. The room suddenly felt hot and stuffy. I couldn't bear her eyes on me. I felt like they were burning into my soul and all I wanted to do was escape.

'Here,' said Maggie, taking a long, hard drag from the joint and handing it over to me. I felt as though I was being tested and happily took her up on her offer. Jude winked at me as I took a harsh breath and held the hot, herby smoke in my lungs. Then the pair laughed.

'Come along, girls.' Jude smiled and put his arm across my shoulder. Maggie and I were either side of him and people parted to make way for us as we floated through the room and over to a table with bottles on it.

'Fancy a drink?'

Maggie poured herself a glass of something from an unmarked bottle.

'Sure,' I said. I was trying to work out what was on offer.

'We've got homemade cider, lemonade, elderflower wine, and my personal favourite . . . moonshine.'

I looked over to Jude and remembered he'd told me he was on the wagon. I didn't understand how he could have alcohol anywhere near him.

'Go ahead,' he said, waving an arm over the table and taking the joint from my lips. I pointed to a bottle of something that I thought might be cider just as someone began playing the bongos.

Jude jumped onto a chair and cleared his throat loudly. The room fell silent and everyone turned to face their host.

'Welcome, people of the free world!' he exclaimed. 'It's that time of year again, so please, fill your bellies with the foods nature has provided, and your souls with imagination! Be merry and creative! Be one another's muses! Go forth and love.'

A cheer erupted from his disciples; an old man played a banjo and women bashed tambourines with their palms. The room took on a new energy and it burst into life. I had never seen or experienced anything like it. It was almost like being at a festival, surrounded by people who were all there to see one particular rock star.

Jude remained standing on the chair, his head thrown back, his arms outstretched, his foot tapping in time with the music. I watched in awe, and within seconds found myself joining in with the merriment, losing all inhibitions and feeling at one with the people in the room. I danced and twirled round in the crowd. A young woman I hadn't met before tucked a joint behind my ear, then we linked fingers and formed a circle with the others, surrounding the people playing instruments. It felt like a dream.

***

It was clear that the people who'd left behind their normal lives to live at Christie Hall were all trying to escape ghosts of their own. This seemed like a place where that was possible. All the rubbish that had cluttered our minds was trapped in a dream catcher that hung near the front door.

Before I drifted off to sleep that night, I remember thinking we were safe there from the outside, and safe from ourselves.

In honour of Ted Hughes
Swept off my feet, unable to swim.
'What you fear will kill you',

The scream echoed too long.
He stayed and poisoned my pleasure,
Frightened the life into me.
Because I dared to love him,
Neptune wanted me drowned
And I didn't refuse his death.

***

I blacked out for a minute but I am conscious again. My teeth are chattering. My hands are numb - I think I'm moving them but I can't be sure. There is that bitter taste in my mouth again: bile and blood. I need to be sick. Every part of my body is trying to repel this. No, wait, fuck, the car is stopping again. Where are we? I listen to the sound of my tapered breath. I cannot hear anything else. I strain harder. What is that sound? Voices? No, music. Yes, that's it. Music. Is it coming from inside my own mind? I try to calm down. Blood is still in my eyes. All my senses are bombarded with unfamiliar sensations. This is too much to bear — I am going mad. This is not happening. It can't be. I need to focus on something. I try to hear the music again, listen to the words. The tune, I'm sure I've heard it before. I recognise it, don't I? Another sound: footsteps. Yes, definitely footsteps. On gravel, getting closer. Oh fuck, I can hear keys jangle. Someone has stopped. They are about to open the boot. I'm not ready to leave. Don't open it. I won't struggle. I'll stay still and not make a sound, just don't open it. I need more time. I'm not ready . . .

I left the house with a spring in my step. Jude and his friends had embraced me without judgement or question, and I felt as if I'd finally managed to escape the horror of being trapped inside my own head, until I remembered one of the lows I'd experienced before I was hospitalised.

I was at university in Newcastle, living in a student house. One April morning, after handing in an important essay, I'd walked out into the street still wearing my pyjamas. I'd stared out over the green park, opposite where I had lived.

It was dawn and sun was beginning its climb in the sky. I'd found a spot on the pavement, fifty yards down the road, and sat cross-legged, aware I wasn't properly dressed.

I'd concentrated on the dew, sprinkled like crystals in the park. Taking a number of deep breaths, I'd managed to slow my heartbeat from its furious thud and stop myself from shaking. I'd felt a wave of emotion working its way up from my chest to my throat: an emotional explosion had been due, but I'd controlled it, allowing only one tear to fall. I had sat on the cold, hard ground, trying to calm myself, for at least twenty minutes. I'd spotted a scruffy-looking man, lying wrapped in a dirty old blanket on a bench. I'd watched him for a while, shivering and half muttering to himself in his sleep.

I don't know why it happened or what it was that had struck me, but staring at him helped me find some clarity. I'd wiped my eyes and marched back into the house with purpose. I'd remembered how I'd managed to turn my life around when I had first moved to Newcastle, and realised I needed to find that feeling again. I didn't want to end up cold, sad and lonely on a bench. Instead, a few weeks later, I would end up sitting beneath a clothes rail in John Lewis, terrified and about to be sectioned.

I remembered walking up the path that led to the lecturer's office, a printed-out, half-finished version of an essay gripped beneath one arm. I'd cut through an immaculate lawn, which a notice told us not to walk on. The sound of my footsteps had echoed off the beautiful, creamy, stone walls around the garden courtyard. I'd felt the history of the place come alive around me and imagined the thousands of students who had trodden that same path over the last hundred years. I'd passed two lecturers, deep in discussion, who would not have looked out of place a hundred years ago.

The nerves had bubbled inside me with each step I'd taken. Out of the corner of my eye I'd caught sight of a black crow sitting, hunchbacked, watching me from one of the slate roofs. It hadn't blinked or moved. It had looked like a gargoyle on a cathedral. I'd seen its dark, shining eyes watching me and I felt like prey. Taking it as a bad omen, I'd knocked quietly on the heavy oak door.

My lecturer's office had always smelled strongly of lilies: that day was no different. There, in a cream vase, was a bunch that had seen better days. Their scent had filled the air, disguising the smell of dusty books that neatly lined the shelves. I would forever associate that smell with my teacher and that place. I'd always longed to explore the book collection in her study. In those days, my idea of bliss was spending an uninterrupted afternoon in a bookshop.

The leather-bound volumes took up an entire wall of her office. Some of them must have been worth a fortune. They looked as old as the university itself. She'd barely noticed me as I'd put my essay on her desk. Immersed in a book, she'd only glanced up for a second, just long enough to glare at me. I'd left the office knowing all I could do was hope, and wait for my results. As highly as I rated education, I remembered a quote from Oscar Wilde: 'Education is an admirable thing, but it is well to remember from time to time that nothing that is worth knowing can be taught.' It had comforted me as I prepared for failure.

I studied English literature at University. My A-level results had been impressive and my teachers told me I had a bright future ahead. I enjoyed learning when I was well - it helped to keep my mind busy. Up until I'd begun to get ill, my lecturers thought I was on course to get a First. If I loved something, I was good at it. It's true for most people: we rarely strive to do well at something we detest.

When I'd dropped out of my degree, I resented failing my education more than anything. It pained me that it was something else I'd had to give up, along with the prospects of a normal life. That feeling still haunts me.

Now I am determined never to go back to being that person again.

***

When I got back from Christie Hall I stood outside our house for a while, trying to find that feeling of home. It eluded me, but, just as uncertainty was settling in, I spotted my beloved Wookie in the window. His ecstatic wag made me feel better. I opened the front door and sat on the wooden floor to let Wookie jump all over me. I stroked his soft brown coat and spoke to him in a bizarre voice I was sure he understood. For a minute or two I felt like a child again; I felt safe and able to lose myself in a daydream.

Daydreaming was part of my escape. I'd done it since I was a child. I used to imagine myself as a grown-up, having found my place in the world: the place where I belonged. It was a dream that I still clung to, even in my darkest moments.

I knew there was a better world waiting for me and I knew where I wanted to be: I longed to get back to Christie Hall and make it my home. All I had to do was convince my family to let me go, and hope that Jude and *his* family would welcome me into their fold, permanently.

***

Time had passed since the party and winter had a firm grip on the land. The world was dark and I was lucky to see two hours of light each day. My insomnia was raging. I would finally get some fitful sleep by about three in the morning, to wake again a few hours later when my alarm buzzed. When I did sleep, my dreams were plagued by horrifying images of blood and pain.

I lay in bed for hours while my mind whirled, flitting from thought to thought like a butterfly. Ideas zipped through me, none of which materialised – I couldn't settle on one long enough to put it into practice. The winter gloom outside was of little consequence.

I hadn't had much contact with Jude, or any of the Christie clan, and was beginning to think perhaps they were just a fantasy I'd dreamt up. Jude, who had been so kind and interested, was now an elusive memory. I was haunted by recollections. I pictured them all, sat round the fireplace, laughing and joking, singing and telling stories, and I longed to be there.

As I struggled to hold on to my sanity and remain positive, I found a part of myself I had long since forgotten: I started writing poetry again. It was something I'd done as a teenager when I was going through the usual adolescent angst. I'd used it as a way to work through my father leaving and my delayed grief over Lucy's death.

Now I spent the dark hours sitting at a desk in my room, writing page after page. The words poured out of me. Images became language and feelings fuelled my creativity. I put down all my dark thoughts on paper and found a way to channel my insecurities and fears. It was nice to have some tangible evidence of my turmoil, and I had Jude to thank for it. The weekend of the party had reawakened my love of words. Jude told me he could see it was 'in my soul'.

It was one in the morning and I had been huddled over the desk since ten o'clock. I was losing all hope of hearing from Jude when a message came through:

> This weekend. Winter solstice celebration. Bring festive offerings. Jude.

Overcome with relief, I burst into tears. I texted back immediately and accepted his invitation. This was what I had been waiting for –

an opportunity to return to Christie Hall to see if they might accept me as a permanent member of their family.

***

Arriving in Southwold I was greeted by miserable winter weather. Grey fog covered everything and my headlights fought to find the road. I crawled along; the Christmas crackers I had made were lying on the passenger seat next to me. As I wound my way along the coastal road, the waves clawed at the beach, angrily crashing onto the sand. The sea bubbled and spat with fury. Nature was on the warpath. Finally, I sighted my destination.

Christie Hall stood proudly on a slight hill. It had changed since my last visit: the trees along the driveway were now naked and stark. Lights were on in the windows and, despite its size, the house looked inviting and warm. I felt I had come home despite the downpour.

Joanie opened the door and helped me in as I shook the raindrops off my nose. I'd met her on my previous visit and she seemed great. She was in her early thirties and had a long neck and dark hair that hung low down her back. She moved with elegance and grace and I felt intimidated by her quiet beauty. She was pregnant, and wearing a long white skirt with a loose brown sweater, which clung to her bump. I wondered who the child's father was but didn't deem it my business to ask.

The kitchen was a hive of activity. It smelled of Christmas spices and sweet fruit. Maggie was at her usual spot, standing over the Aga. Sophie, Fran and Ella were seated round the big farmhouse table, peeling, chopping and kneading. They each welcomed my return with warm hugs before returning to their tasks. I put my offering of Christmas crackers on one of the cluttered work surfaces and asked the whereabouts of the other residents. Fran said that Jude had gone to slaughter one of the pigs for the feast. My face must have revealed my horror, since she looked at me quizzically. Ella explained that Celeste and Charlie were out foraging. Before I could offer to help in the kitchen,

Joanie slipped a long, slender arm around my shoulders, which ached as if the weight of the world was on them, and guided me up to the bedrooms.

Expecting to be sharing a room with Ella again, I was surprised when I was shown into a room of my own.

'This is the Bluebell room,' Joanie said, stroking her belly. 'You should be quite cosy in here.'

The room looked like something out of a magazine. The wallpaper was embossed with posies of blue flowers. A cast iron fireplace faced the double bed, with a gilt mirror above the hearth, and a threadbare Persian rug covered the old, smooth floorboards. The room had a distinctly Victorian feel. On a dressing table stood a jug and washbasin. Cornflower-blue velvet curtains hung in the tall window that looked out over the garden; in the distance I could see the sea.

'This is really pretty,' I told her, putting my bag at the foot of the bed. 'I'm unsure exactly what the plans are for this weekend, but I'd like to do something to help.'

'How sweet of you,' she said, tucking her hair behind her ear. 'Jude told me to get you settled in first. He has something planned for you when he gets back.' Joanie turned and glided towards the door, turning to say, 'Make yourself comfortable. Jude will fetch you soon. I'll be in the living room if you need anything.'

After she had closed the door, I stood motionless in the room, looking out of the window. Despite the abysmal wetness and the heavy slate sky, the view was beautiful. It was unspoiled by anything modern. The people who had lived in the house hundreds of years ago would have gazed over the same scene. It was a nice thought that left me daydreaming as Jude came striding in.

'Here she is!' He marched over and embraced me. I held on to him for longer than necessary and inhaled his scent. He smelled of the elements and his closeness was soothing.

'I am so happy to be back.' I beamed.

'Back where you belong.' He held my chin in his hand for a moment, before letting go and making his way towards the door. I didn't move. Did I really belong here? Did I really belong anywhere?

'Are you coming?' There was now a significant space between us. I nodded enthusiastically and followed him down the staircase.

'Do you like your room?' He came to such an abrupt stop that I almost walked into him.

'It's lovely. Like a princess's chamber that little girls dream of.'

He seemed pleased by this as he sauntered on down the stairs, whistling a tune. *What has he got in store for me?* My mind switched between feeling at peace and worrying I was somehow in danger.

'So, what's the plan?' I asked, sensing a task ahead. He put his finger up to his lips and silently led the way. The mystery that surrounded this man fascinated me.

We went into the sitting room, where Celeste and Charlie were standing over a pile of ivy, holly and mistletoe. They waited for Jude to speak.

'Get decorating!' he said, and clapped his hands together. Celeste broke into a smile and skipped over to the gramophone to put on a Miles Davis record. The music soared around the room as we sorted through the jumble of sprigs.

'Very good,' Jude murmured to himself as he went into the dining room, pausing to say, 'Meet me in front of the pig shed in an hour, Annabel.'

I gave him the thumbs up and returned to my sorting.

We made real progress decorating the room: Celeste cleverly plaited the ivy and hung it across the tops of the windows, while Charlie tied mistletoe to the candelabra and twisted some around the iron candlesticks. I was left to deal with the holly and I chose to decorate the mantelpiece.

It was nice spending time with the two people I knew the least. Celeste was a gentle, mild-mannered girl, probably about my age. She had mousey brown hair and small eyes that peered through round glasses. She was friendly but shy.

Charlie was a different kettle of fish altogether. She was direct and self-confident. She had short, cropped hair, dyed vivid pink. I learnt two things about her that afternoon. First, she was an old friend of Jude's and one of the first residents of Christie Hall; second, she informed me she was bisexual. I didn't flinch as I suspected she'd thought I might. She seemed satisfied by my reaction and I felt I had passed the test.

After finishing indoors I stepped outside into the drizzle, and pulled my sweater up over my head as I made my way towards the pig shed. A gale was blowing in from the sea, shaking the naked branches of the trees and threatening to blow me over. By the time I got to the shed I was drenched.

It wasn't really a shed, it was a dilapidated barn that made a great home for the pigs. As I walked in I was hit by the smell: a mixture of dung and something else that I couldn't put my finger on. Jude was sitting on a hay bale, waiting for me. He looked at me with amusement as a pig came wandering over, its tail wagging and ears twitching.

'She thinks you've come to feed her,' said Jude, looking at the sow fondly.

I stroked the end of her snout and her tail wagged faster.
'She's lovely.'

'She is indeed. She's a happy old girl. We've had lots of litters from her. She's a wonderful mother. It's lovely to share one's existence with the animals. We provide for them and in turn they provide for us. It's the circle of life.' His tone grew sombre. 'I want to show you something.'

We went through a rickety door, which squeaked on its rusty hinges, and into a room that appeared to be a sort of store cupboard. The mystery smell was revealed. Lying on a workbench was the carcass of a pig. Its throat had been cut and fresh blood pooled on the table and floor. The gaping wound went from ear to ear. I recoiled in horror and stumbled backwards.

'That's revolting,' I said, putting my hand over my mouth and coughing. Jude went over to the carcass and gently stroked the pig's lifeless head.

'I wanted you to appreciate what we are going to feast on. This pig gave its life so that we can eat.'

'I know that.' I felt patronised.

'No, no, you don't understand. We are having this pig as an offering. We kill one when someone new joins the group. This pig is an invitation to you - that is why I showed her to you: it is part of the ritual. You are invited to join our family, there is a place for you here. If you want it, the Bluebell room is yours. You don't need to decide now, but I'd like an answer before the weekend is up. In the meantime, I have a task for you: write something about this pig and what her death means to you. You can read it at the feast tomorrow.'

He placed a dark green leather-bound notebook in my hand. 'Write it in here.'

I took the book and held it to my racing heart.

'Now,' he said, 'you must be hungry. There's vegetable soup for lunch. Go and join the others. I'll see you in there shortly.'

I didn't want anything to have to die so I could live freely; it didn't feel right, but I embraced the strangeness of the situation and allowed myself to get lost in my distorted reflection in the puddle of blood on the floor.

Through a gap in the curtains, the winter sun shone. I heard voices down the corridor and the cockerel's morning call outside. I had gone to my room early the night before to try to write my poem for the pig. I lay in bed re-reading my words. It needed a bit more work but I thought I was on the right track and I felt proud of myself, something I'd been convinced I'd never feel again. I told myself I had Jude and Christie Hall to thank for fixing another part of me, but I couldn't shake the image of the dead animal from my mind.

I snuggled down under the patchwork quilt and enjoyed the safety of the bed. Moments later there was a knock at the door. I told whoever it was to enter, and sat up. Fran came in. She was wearing faded jeans and a big orange woollen sweater. She asked how I'd slept as she drew back the curtains. I felt as if I was at home with my mother. Fran and I hadn't talked much, but it seemed that she was the designated matriarch, even though Maggie was probably older. It was clear that each of the family had their own place and role to play. Nobody stepped out of line or appeared to question their position. Jude was the top dog, followed by Fran, and then Charlie, Joanie and Maggie. Wally, Sophie and Celeste didn't seem to have a position. Wally was Jude's henchman. Although I've identified a hierarchy, it was a free, loving set up.

Fran advised me to get up and have some breakfast, before joining the entire group on a walk around the grounds. Once she had left, I dressed in a hurry and went down for breakfast. My mouth felt dry and my belly ached for food. Maggie had prepared some scrambled eggs and there was a basket of toast on the table. We ate without saying much, enjoying the food.

After breakfast we put on our boots and coats and went out into the frosty sunshine. It was the first time I'd seen the group do something together, besides preparing for a social event. It felt good, wandering with them all across the land. On the walk I discovered Christie Hall had sixty acres – Maggie told me it had once had three hundred, but Jude decided to sell some in order to fund the community who lived there. That was five years ago, and now they were more or less self-sufficient, able to make a steady living off the land that remained.

Before long we came to a copse of conifers. Wally started sawing down one of the largest; its shiny green needles shook with every push of the saw. Bursts of sawdust puffed up into the air and Wally's eyes. It wasn't long until we were told to step back as the tree came crashing down.

'Good job, Wal,' said Jude. 'This is going in the dining room.' We all clapped and each of us took hold of a branch. We carried the tree back to the house, singing festive songs as the frosty grass crunched beneath our boots.

'Who's going to decorate it?' I asked anyone who was listening.

'You can, love,' said Fran. 'Choose two of the girls to help you.'

'Well, if Charlie and Celeste would do it . . . I think we'd make a pretty good team.'

'Wonderful!'

When we got back to the house, Charlie showed me into a room I hadn't seen before, while the others fought to secure the tree in an upright position beside the banqueting table. The room was a mixture of a gardener's shed, an arts and crafts shop and a classroom. She explained that this was where they recycled bits and pieces, made their clothes, did arts and crafts and fixed things. Charlie told me that they aimed not to waste anything. She showed me a number of boxes that contained all kinds of stuff, from foil bottle tops to pebbles and conkers.

We found a few bits we thought would make good decorations and got to work. Celeste fetched us some sandwiches, while Charlie and I painted, strung and glued our odds and ends together.

At two o'clock we stepped back to admire our handiwork: the tree stood proudly, dressed in her jewels. Celeste had turned some old tins into tea light holders and pierced holes in them for the flames to shine through. I told her I admired her creativity, which made her blush.

Charlie went to get the others for the unveiling of our finished masterpiece. Maggie said it was the loveliest tree she'd ever seen and gave us each a congratulatory hug. Jude, who had a joint dangling from his mouth, just smiled. He slid his arm around Joanie's shoulders, playing with her hair between his fingers. I felt a twinge of jealousy.

We went to our rooms to change and get ready for the guests, who were due to arrive. I brushed my hair and applied some mascara and rouge, before slipping into a long blue dress and a deep purple cardigan. I felt attractive but nervous as I folded up the poem I'd written and slid it into my cardigan pocket, ready for the reading later.

As I walked down the staircase, my stomach knotted and my hands trembled. Suddenly I couldn't breathe and my temples throbbed. The room started to spin and I thought I was going to faint. My brow was sweaty and I was sure my legs were going to give way. I lurched towards the front door and made it outside onto the driveway just in time to throw up on the gravel. I spat out the remaining vomit and looked up to see Jude standing in the doorway behind me. My hands were still shaking.

'Don't be nervous,' he said, taking my hand in his. 'You will do just fine.' But it wasn't nerves that were bothering me. Something else was making me feel sick.

He removed a lavender Michaelmas daisy from the lapel of his corduroy jacket and tucked it behind my ear. 'For luck,' he whispered, planting a kiss on my cheek. Again, my stomach churned, but this time in a good way.

'I accept your offer!' I blurted out. 'I really want to stay here.'

I touched the flower in my hair. 'I have to go home for Christmas. It would kill my mother if I just upped and left. She'd probably think I was losing the plot again and have me sectioned.

There are things I need to clear up at home before I move out for good, but I will come back as soon as I can.'

His mouth curled into a Mona Lisa smile. 'Whenever you're ready, we will be here.' He led me back indoors and for a moment my nerves were left out in the cold, along with the contents of my stomach.

Christmas was just around the corner. I suggested to Mother that we break with tradition and that I prepare the turkey. It would be the first Christmas meal I'd ever cooked. One of the few things I shared with my mother was a love of the season. We always decorated the house together, and this year was no different. I began by hanging a wreath on our front door. I'd made it myself from ivy and holly I had gathered in the woods nearby. I completed my creation with a red satin ribbon, which I weaved in and out and tied in a bow. Mother wrapped gold tinsel around the banisters; I cut snowflakes out of paper and taped them to the windows. I also decorated our fireplace, which was modest in comparison with the one at Christie Hall, with a green plastic garland and miniature felt stockings. Earlier that day, Mother had hung a bunch of mistletoe on a hook that had been put there years ago for just that purpose. We then went into the kitchen to make some mince pies. I'd always loved losing myself in the joy of Christmas.

Later, we all climbed into Mother's estate car and made our way to a garden centre on the outskirts of town. The sky was a thick blue-black and drizzle covered the windscreen as we made our way along the road out of the village. The lights were blurred and twinkling and felt like they were rushing at us.

When we arrived at the garden centre, row upon row of sparkling fairy lights and glowing festive decorations greeted us. It seemed everyone else had had the same idea: people filtered in and out of the entrance, some with bulky trees balanced on their shoulders. Children played hide and seek in the forest of cut trees. Dead trees.

Death of a spruce
A decorated corpse stands in the corner.
Rigor mortis branches shelter
The brightly coloured presents.
The tree wears its seasonal costume

Like an old soldier presenting medals.
Rich green needles fade gradually
With the passing of each day –
A slow death for nature's gift.
Waiting for the end to come,
Lights permanently turned off.
Destiny is predetermined
Before murdered crackers are binned.
The final moment arrives.
Carried out into the eternal frost –
Not receiving a civilised burial.

We piled out of the car into the thick, cold night and searched for the perfect tree. Will was surprisingly tolerant while we examined each and every specimen, dismissing those that looked shabby or misshapen. I saw the twisted faces of something evil in them and felt uncertainty return, tightening around my throat.

Eventually we found the ideal spruce. It stood proud, at eight-foot-high, among the less noble, shorter trees. It cost nearly sixty pounds but perfection was worth the money. I wanted this Christmas to be a good one. Two men struggled to hoist it onto the roof of our car and secure it with rope. I couldn't take my eyes off the strands of fraying rope. They intoxicated me, trying to pull me towards something in the back of my mind.

On our way home, the mood was quieter. We didn't play loud music or chat much. Each of us had retreated into ourselves. Reminiscence hung in the air as strongly as the scent of pine. I remembered a time when my family had consisted of five members. Determined not to spoil what had been fun, I speculated about the chances of a white Christmas. Will took the bait, but Mother concentrated silently on the road ahead.

We got home and found two Christmas cards on the doormat. One was for me, the other for Will. Neither had our address or a stamp on them; they had been hand-delivered. We recognised the handwriting immediately: our father's. Every year since he'd left, he'd done the same thing: posted our presents through the door. I didn't have to open it to know there was a cheque inside for two hundred pounds. I threw mine in the bin; Will pocketed his and said he thought Dad owed us. It was the same as always. My mother bit her lip, doing her best to hide her anger. I gave her arm a squeeze. She gave me a smile of reassurance and retreated into the kitchen.

The only decent thing my father had done since he left us was continue his financial support. Mother hadn't needed to work and we'd never gone without. The private education and middle-class lifestyle we had grown up with was never threatened. But the three of us didn't acknowledge his act of decency. The family had been destroyed by Lucy's death but his career had blossomed; he'd used work as a distraction. We'd lost our family but the house remained ours. It was the very least he could have done.

Will lugged the tree in, shedding its needles all over the floor, then scooted upstairs to lose himself in his music. I sat alone in a pensive mood. The card, with a stupid bloody robin on it, had stirred up the past and I hated my father for that. Did he really think a measly cheque would make up for not being there? I got up and removed the card from the bin, went over to the log-burning stove and dropped it in. I pulled a lighter out of my pocket and lit it; flames burst into life, quickly eating away at the card. The bright orange and blue licks curled over it, reducing the money to ash. I watched, hypnotised, until nothing remained and the fire had died. I heard my mother clear her throat and I turned to find her standing in the doorway, watching me.

'Are you alright?'

'Not really,' I replied, 'but I will be.'

She pursed her lips and nodded, wiped her hands on her apron and returned to her chores.

Those who have left

In the light of my eyes
There is your reflection.
Standing by the empty window

I stare at a hollow horizon:
Your daughter.
The card in my hand
I only have what you left behind.
You are the sound –
Listen,
My heart continues to beat.
A memory dances over me
Like flames eating coal
And I reflect the passing
In my liquid eyes.

***

Christmas came and went. My Aunt Fiona, Uncle Mike, and cousins came to stay, as they did every year. It was enjoyable enough. We ate well and managed to have some fun. Uncle Mike drank far too much, as usual, and my mother got irritated. No one mentioned any of the elephants in the room: my father, my dead sister, or my detention in a loony bin. All the elements of our lives that made us real to one another were swept under my mother's perfectly vacuumed rug.

I tried hard to jolly everyone along and keep it light – it was the least I could do before dropping the bombshell of my move to Christie Hall. The dread of telling my mother was matched only by the excitement I had about the future. In between helping to cook, clean and entertain, I spent time in my room going through my belongings, deciding what to take with me and what to bin. Everyone was so distracted by Christmas that my behaviour, thankfully, went unnoticed. I concluded it would be best if I left very soon after making the announcement. I didn't like the idea of giving my mother too much time to think about it. I had decided that I wanted to move into Christie Hall before New Year's Eve. It seemed fitting to start my new life by welcoming in a new year.

I went through the contents of my bedroom, taking a tour of my past. I discovered old photo albums and long-forgotten diaries.

In a dusty box beneath my bed were ticket stubs from cinema dates with my first boyfriend and a necklace of Lucy's that I'd been given. I rubbed the silver locket between my fingers and gave it a kiss before putting it in my pocket. I returned the rest of the stuff to the box and put it back where I'd found it. I wouldn't be taking it with me. It was then that Will came into my room.

'Whatcha doing?' he said, moving a pile of clothes off my bed and sitting down.

'Just going through some old things.'

'Your room's a tip.'

'Coming from you, I'll take that as a compliment.' I pretended to take a swipe at his face.

'Do you want a hand?' he asked.

'Are you feeling alright?' I joked.

'Just bored as fuck. Uncle Mike is snoring on the sofa, the twins are playing Trivial Pursuit, and Mother and Fiona are drinking Baileys in the kitchen, cackling like a pair of old witches. I need somewhere to hide.' The desire to escape was undeniable.

I looked affectionately at my brother, and told him he could stay in my room as long as he didn't mess with my piles.

'Fine,' he said, 'but what are you actually doing?'

I didn't want to lie to him, so I sat down next to him and told him the truth.

'I'm moving out,' I said.

'Where to?' He sounded bewildered and looked at me as if I was mad.

I told him all about my visit to Southwold, the chance meeting with Jude, Christie Hall and the people who lived there. I explained that I needed a change: something new, and somewhere I could forget about the shit that had followed me around for the last few years. He listened, silently, and I could see him wondering if I was having another breakdown.

Finally, he said, 'Have you spoken to Mother . . . or your doctor?'

'No, I haven't. Not yet. I'm going to tell her as soon as everyone's left. I'm moving out on the thirtieth.'

'Fucking hell, that's soon.'

'I know, but once I've made my mind up . . .'

I could see real sadness in his face and I suddenly felt guilty.

'You'll still see me all the time, you know. I won't be that far away. You can visit whenever you like. Bring your friends if you want. It's a cool place, you'll like it. The people are great. It's going to be just what I need.'

'Well it sounds like you've decided,' he said, rubbing the back of his neck.

'I have.'

'Good luck telling Mother. You know the shit is really going to hit the fan.'

'I'd like your support.'

'What for? You're going. I'll look after Mother and we'll be fine. Don't worry about us. You just fuck off into the sunset. It's not like we aren't used to losing people in this family.' He kicked over a pile of my books.

'Will, for God's sake!' I tried not to raise my voice. 'I need to do this. Don't you understand? There are too many ghosts here, too many painful memories. I'll never get well if I stay.'

'Fine! You run away then, just like Dad did.'

'That's not fair,' I said. 'I'm not abandoning you. For fuck's sake, I'm not your parent. I can't stay here forever. I'm twenty-three and I need to stand on my own two feet. If you'd ever visited me in Redwood, you might have an idea why I have to get the hell away from here.'

Will was about to say something but changed his mind. He let out a loud sigh and left the room. I heard his bedroom door slam shut. I sat down on my bed and cried. I'd been so busy worrying about telling my mother that I hadn't considered Will. We had always looked out for each other. Now he thought I was deserting him. I couldn't leave things the way they were. I needed to clear the air. I wiped my eyes and went and knocked on his door.

'What?'

'Can I come in?'

'Suit yourself.'

He was sitting in a chair at his desk. His room was unusually quiet. I went over and crouched next to him.

'Listen,' I said, 'I'm sorry you feel like that. I didn't mean to be a bitch. I'm not doing this to get away from you. Just try and understand that in order to get better, I have to make some changes. You'll still be my little brother. We'll still see each other and speak on the phone.'

His face softened. He put his arm on my shoulder.

'It's OK, I get it. I don't deal well with change. Guess I might miss you, that's all.'

'I'll miss you too, shithead.' I put a hand on his knee and squeezed. 'Oh, and by the way, I thought you'd like to know, there are some pretty nice-looking women I'm going to be living with. Play your cards right and I'll put in a good word.'

'Now you're talking,' he laughed. His music came back on as I pulled the door shut behind me.

***

Sharing my plans with my mother went as I had expected: she thought I had imagined Christie Hall - that it was one of my delusions. I showed her photos on my phone that convinced her otherwise. She didn't think I was well enough to move out on my own yet. I reminded her that I would not be alone, there were eight other people in the house. She voiced concerns about how I would pay the rent. I explained that there was no rent and my contribution would be helping out in the grounds, cooking, cleaning and being part of the group. She thought it was all too rushed; I was leaving too soon. I assured her I could look after myself. She was sceptical but eventually agreed. What other choice did she have?

I only gave her twenty-four hours warning. After a lengthy discussion, she gave in.

That was until she made the link between where I was going and the news stories about the murdered women. She came bursting into my room waving the newspaper. She accused me of being mad for wanting to live near a serial killer. She cried and shouted. She believed I was putting myself in danger. I gave her a hug. She was just doing her job as a parent, I understood that. At least one of my folks was looking out for me.

We went over it all again, this time taking into account there was a madman on the loose. I convinced her that I would be safe. Sharing a house with eight other people would ensure that. After an hour of going back and forth, she relented. She told me that she would always be at the end of the phone and that I should come home often. She made plans to come and visit me the following weekend; she wanted to see the place for herself. Then she said she was proud of me, and it was my turn to cry. I thanked her for being so understanding. I thanked her for trusting me. She stood and left me to pack, muttering that she would put together some things I might need.

When I was sure she'd gone, I picked up the newspaper she'd left behind and scanned the article: another body had been found on the beach. The police now had to admit they were searching for a serial killer. They pleaded for information. The bodies, which had been in the sea for days before they had washed up on the shore, gave few clues. The salt water had washed away any evidence the killer might have left. The corpses were in such a state that it was nearly impossible to identify them without tests to confirm they were the girls who had gone missing. I shuddered and put the paper in the bin. Sometimes what they don't report is far scarier. The lack of details left my imagination spinning. I remembered something that G K Chesterton had written, along the lines of: 'Fairy tales do not tell children the dragons exist; children already know that dragons exist. Fairy tales tell children that the dragons can be killed.'

It was hard to believe that in a few hours I would be on the road, racing towards my new life. It seemed a long time since I'd been at Christie Hall. I glowed with the memory of my previous visit. They had welcomed me into their community even though they hardly knew me. I could be anyone I wanted. The slate was clean and my story was unwritten. It felt good knowing that the past was going to be left where it belonged.

I lugged my cases downstairs and piled them up by the front door. I found Mother in the kitchen putting tins of food into a cardboard box.

'I don't want you going hungry.' She stuffed in a bag of dried pasta shells. 'I can't believe this is happening so fast. I would like to have given you a proper send-off. We could have had the neighbours round.' She sounded disappointed.

'I'm not leaving the country, Mother. You're coming to visit in less than a fortnight!'

'I know, I know,' she said, 'but do you really have to go so soon?'

'Yes, I do. I want to be settled in before the new year begins and . . .'

'Yes, once you've made your mind up . . .'

'Please try and be happy for me, Mother. This is a new start.'

She didn't say a word but went back to filling the box with the contents of her larder. I sat at the kitchen table and watched her. She was a short woman with a round face and broad hips. Her untidy mousy bob kept getting in her eyes, and she would constantly tuck it behind her ears. I was suddenly struck by how much she had aged. I had always thought of her as young and invincible. Now she seemed human and fragile. I wished I could have spared her the pain my illness had caused. Then Will came into the room, interrupting my train of thought.

'I'll be off soon,' I said.

'Sooner you leave, sooner I can have your room.' He pulled out a chair opposite me. I stuck out my tongue and blew a raspberry.

'Do you want me to help you load the car?' he said.

'That would be great.' I swallowed hard, suddenly feeling emotional.

'I'm sorry I have to say goodbye,' I told him, not looking at his face.

The three of us had a cup of tea and some leftover mince pies, then we packed my car and said our goodbyes. I felt sadder than I had anticipated. It was hard to drive away from them. Will stood waving with his other arm was around my mother. She was sobbing, while Wookie sat at her feet, watching me go. I watched in the rear-view mirror as the house got smaller. It had felt so big when I was a child, full of hiding places. As the distance between us grew, I realised I was going to miss them more than I'd ever expected.

***

Oh no! A key is in the lock. I hear it click. This is it. The boot is going to open any second and I am going to meet my abductor. The boot flips open and immediately a rug is thrown over my head. I wriggle and squirm beneath it. I need to see a face. It's no use, I can't move. I buck and twist but my restraints prevent me from freeing myself. I can feel wetness around my ankles where the ropes are cutting in. Blood? I feel hands on my body, tight and strong, pulling me up and out of the car. My head is pounding. Each time my heart beats, my skull aches. My stomach tightens again. I am retching. There is nothing left to sick up. I am an empty shell. I am being carried somewhere. Why don't I scream? Why can't I call out? I can't remember any words. I can't remember how to talk. My mouth hurts. The air is icy on my bare feet. It feels like night. I cannot see but I recognise that chill. A clean breeze is blowing. I am dirty, covered in my vomit, my blood. I can smell something putrid, like burning rubber. There is the crunch of heavy footsteps on gravel. My captor's footsteps. He is strong, holding my body over his shoulder. I can smell him, like wet mud and rotting leaves. I am too petrified to squirm. If I wriggle he will drop me. What does he want with me? I can't run. He is breathing heavily, grunting like a pig. That is the only sound. I am dizzy again. I am going to be sick. My throat is so dry. I cannot swallow. I need water. It's deadly quiet.

He's stopped walking. It's raining. Each drop is like a needle on my skin. I am drowning. Sinking further into the darkness. The creak of a door opening. Where am I? My head is trapped in a hurricane. I have to let go. Everything is fading. Don't pass out, not now. Just stay awake . . .

It took about a week for me to settle in to Christie Hall. I kept thinking I was in the hospital, or somewhere worse. The place had a similar smell and the echo around the corridors was strangely familiar. I couldn't get used to sleeping in a strange bed, and as lovely as the room was, it just wasn't me, but I didn't know if it was rude to make changes to it. I felt like a guest, albeit a very welcome one. My new housemates were lovely. I think Maggie was my favourite. She had no malice, no chip on her shoulder, she was just who she was.

Jude remained an enigma. He had a strange way of being open yet aloof. It was unnerving. I put it down to the fact that we were still getting to know each other. Charlie was the other person to whom I quickly grew attached. In many ways, she was defensive and brisk, but I admired her honesty. Her sexuality clearly caused her problems. She could also be very funny.

I wondered what would happen if any of us discovered love interests outside the house, or if that had ever happened. Nobody mentioned Joanie's growing baby-bump, but I was dying to know the story. I couldn't ask questions without seeming nosy so I bided my time. Joanie floated around the house like the ghost of a gorgeous hippy, but that seemed to be all there was to her: she was beautiful, but boring.

As for the others, time would tell. Wally was a sweet guy but not the sharpest tool in the box. He was the muscle and Jude the brains. Everyone slotted together like pieces of a puzzle. I couldn't see where I fitted in. It didn't bother me – I was happy to remain on the periphery, able to enjoy the benefits of the community.

I quickly fell into a routine. In the mornings, I would lie in bed reading, Maggie would bring me a cup of tea and some porridge. Lunch was a loose affair, with everyone coming and going as they wished, grazing on the food laid out on the kitchen table. Three afternoons a week we were expected to help around the house and grounds. The chores were split evenly and rotated, so no one got stuck cleaning the loos or mucking out the animals for too long.

The animals were what I loved most about living there. Despite the bitter January weather, I sat for a long time watching the chickens peck about in the dirt. It was like watching goldfish in a bowl: therapeutic, soothing.

I was taught how to make bread – a surprisingly easy thing to do. It was a proud moment when my first loaf came out of the oven. It even tasted nice. Maggie was head of the kitchen, she decided what meals we were having and sourced the ingredients she needed. I learnt more about cooking in a few weeks than I had in my entire life. I was surprised to find I really enjoyed it. Christie Hall taught me many things I hadn't known about myself.

The only thing set in stone was that we were expected to have supper together. We would meet at eight o'clock in the dining hall and eat by candlelight; there was something primordial about the ritual. Jude dressed differently each night, this usually involved him wearing elaborate accessories, such as a velvet cap, a cravat or a vintage waistcoat. On one occasion, he came in brandishing a cane. It was as though he were on stage. I watched and listened to him in awe. We all did: he was our leader. We were all indebted to him for offering us a way out. He had allowed us to leave behind lives that had kept us down.

The evening was my favourite time of day. The whole house came together, and after our meal we would go into the sitting room and sing and dance, play music and tell stories. Jude called it 'The Creative Hour'. We were encouraged to indulge our imaginations. The wine flowed and joints were shared. It was liberating and comfortable. Jude, Charlie and I were usually the last ones standing. We bounced off each other. We shared a wildness. Of the three of us, Jude was the one who held back. I think he felt he had a duty to remain in control. I thought it was a shame, but then self-control had never been my strong point.

Afterwards, I would go up to my room and write poetry, sometimes for hours. I felt as if I had finally found my happy place. Once, Jude came up and found me hunched over the screen, tapping away. He said poetry should always be written in one's own hand. I tried picking up a pen instead and soon realised he was right. It was a mystery how he knew these things. He never wrote anything himself but he was a very good painter. Jude seemed to see things others didn't. He was unlike anyone I had ever come across. His mind fascinated me.

My mother's visit came and went. She had lunch with us and I showed her around the grounds. She was suspicious of the place and wary of the people, but at the end of the tour she seemed happier, having familiarised herself with my habitat.

'Well, at least I now know it's not a cult,' she'd said. 'You know, you can never be too careful, Annabel. The world is full of weird people.'

***

We lived in our happy bubble without any interruptions, until one cold afternoon in late January. The house was quiet. I had been in the kitchen garden helping Maggie dig up some vegetables. When we got back to the house we found Joanie, collapsed in a heap in the sitting room, crying uncontrollably. Charlie was shouting the odds at Wally. One by one, everyone gathered to see what was happening.

'They've taken him! The fuckers have only gone and taken him!' Charlie screamed at Fran.

'Just calm down and tell me what's happened.'

'Jude, they've taken Jude in for questioning! And it's all Wally's fault,' she spat in Wally's direction.

'What do you mean? The police?' Fran put her hand on Joanie's shoulder.

'Yes, yes, the bloody pigs!' Charlie fronted up to Wally, who was shaking like a leaf. We all gasped. No one spoke. Joanie sobbed while Celeste stroked her hair and tried to calm her. I looked at Maggie, who just stared helplessly. Fran put an arm around Charlie's shoulder and led her to one of the armchairs.

'You need to sit down, take a breath, and tell us what has happened,' Fran said. Charlie did as she was told and took some deep breaths.

'Start at the beginning.'

'The pigs . . . sorry, I mean the police, came here and took Jude away. They were talking about the bodies on the beach and saying he was wanted for questioning. I told them they couldn't just barge in . . . but then this little worm stepped up and said they wanted his help with their inquiries, and I just laughed and was about to give him a slap . . . but Jude looked at me, you know, how he does, and I thought twice about it, and then they put him in the back of their car and drove off . . .' The words tumbled out. She sank back into her chair.

'Did they say why they wanted to talk to him specifically?' Fran looked sombre.

'No.' Charlie rubbed her head. 'Just something about a witness . . .'

'I see,' Fran said, none the wiser.

I went over to Joanie who was still inconsolable.

'You need to look after yourself,' I said to her.

Joanie rubbed her belly and stopped sobbing.

'Why on earth would you blame Wally?' Fran turned to Charlie.

'Because he's a fucking idiot!' Charlie gritted her teeth. It was wrong but I laughed – I think my nerves got the better of me. Fran threw me a look that said 'don't you dare'. I lowered my eyes and continued to rub Joanie's shoulder.

'Charlie, get a grip on yourself, this is not helping.' It was clear who was Jude's second-in-command.

'What are we going to do?' Sophie bit her bottom lip. She and Ella stood tightly next to one another.

'Did Jude say anything?' Fran looked impatiently at Wally. He shrugged his shoulders and went over to the window, as though hoping Jude would appear any moment.

'Moron,' hissed Charlie under her breath.

'Not helpful,' Fran said, scowling.

'What are we going to do?' Sophie raised her voice.

We all looked to Fran.

'Well, first,' she said, 'Celeste, you are going to take Joanie into the kitchen and give her a glass of water. She needs to compose herself.'

On cue, they both got up and left the room.

'As for the rest of you, I suggest you go back to whatever it was you were doing.' None of us moved. We stared at each other, dissatisfied.

'I'm sure Jude will be back very shortly. This is obviously a misunderstanding. Just wait and see,' Fran said, responding to our mutiny, but her face gave away her uncertainty.

She addressed Charlie. 'It must have been a terrible shock. I understand you're feeling angry, but I need you to go and make amends with Wally. You're not the only one who's scared.'

Charlie folded her arms defiantly across her chest and looked the other way.

Fran's cheeks flushed red and I noticed her tensing one hand into a fist. 'Do it, now,' she said.

Charlie stayed in her seat and looked at me. I signalled that I thought it was best to humour Fran. Charlie rolled her eyes and then got up.

'Wally, I'm sorry.' There was no real feeling in her voice. Wally just gazed out of the window at the driveway. 'Hello? Wally . . .' She pretended to knock on his head.

'It's fine,' he finally said, and took a step back, looking sheepish.

Charlie leaned forward and whispered, 'He'll be back soon, she's right. He said so himself, didn't he?' She had softened.

'He-he-he said he-he'd be back for din-dinner,' Wally stuttered.

'Right then.' Fran clapped her hands together. 'Very well. That's that.' She strode off, leaving the rest of us standing there.

***

When Jude returned, he was in a foul mood. He sat at the head of the table with a face like thunder. The rest of us stayed silent and waited for him to talk. Maggie glanced at me: I needed to stop staring at Jude but I wanted an explanation. He caught my eye and stared me down. I sheepishly picked at my food. I had been looking forward to my omelette but was unable to eat anything. The rest of the table had the same trouble. The only person who tucked in, was Jude. When he'd finished he leaned back in his chair and surveyed us. No one dared to look at him. Eventually, he spoke.

'Are none of you going to ask what happened at the station?'

We stayed quiet. Finally, Fran broke the silence.

'We knew you'd be home in no time. It was clearly a misunderstanding, so we didn't think we should entertain a conversation about it.' She stood and started to clear the plates away.

Jude banged his glass of water down on the table.

'Please, sit down!' he shouted.

Fran hopped from one foot to the other before she returned to her seat.

'Right.' He lowered his voice. 'For the sake of harmony in the house, I am going to tell you why they took me in and why they released me. I owe you that much. This isn't something we can ignore. It's very serious. People are dead.' His words rang in my ears.

Joanie, who sat to his right, stretched out a hand and placed it on his forearm.

'I've been the victim of mistaken identity.'

Without realising, Ella let out a loud sigh of relief. Jude ignored her.

'A local from the town told the police they thought they saw somebody who looked like me with one of the victims, and no, before any of you ask, they wouldn't say who they had got their information from. According to the officer, I was seen with the girl, walking along the coast on the morning of the eighth. As you know, we were together here, all day. It was the day we fixed the garden shed, remember?'

We nodded enthusiastically.

'So that was that. They let me go. No apology of course.'

'I know you didn't do it,' I blurted out. 'I know it wasn't you. It can't be you.' And somehow, I did know. I couldn't explain it, but I knew he wasn't guilty. In the back of my mind, a face was trying to break through and reveal itself. But the face didn't belong to Jude.

He stood up and walked over to one of the candlesticks, and danced his finger through the flame.

'I'm sorry if you were shaken. Their false suspicions have left a mark on us all. Tomorrow morning, we shall meditate. We must heal the damage that idle gossips have caused.'

His voice cracked and we saw a chink in his armour. Without thinking, I spoke, 'I think you're right. It'll do us all some good. We know you could never do something like that. You must've been shitting yourself.'

'Not really. The only thing that scares me is the thought of you all doubting me.'

He turned to face us. We all quickly shook our heads, but the truth was, it had shaken us. Christie Hall was meant to be a haven, safe from the nasty reality of life, but its walls had been breached. It was a good idea for us to try to undo some of the damage.

Jude smiled and left the room, but a feeling of guilt hung over all of us.

It took a few days before things returned to normal. The visit from the police had left a shadow. We did our best to carry on, but the ominous feeling lingered in the back of our minds. None of us had really entertained the idea that Jude was mixed up with the murders, but the investigation had come too close to us and had burst our happy bubble. Suddenly, we had to admit to ourselves that we weren't invulnerable. I think I shrugged it off the easiest. I hadn't been at Christie Hall as long as the others and hadn't yet become so detached from the world outside. The rest of the house seemed afraid of what lay beyond the walled perimeter, as did I. Until then, I hadn't realised that. We were all hiding from something. We had each gone there to escape ourselves. Suddenly, that illusion felt shattered.

One good thing came out of the incident: it broke down the barriers between Jude and I. He was grateful for the loyalty I'd shown at the dinner table. Perhaps he hadn't expected it. That night he'd learned something new about me, and that changed the dynamics in the house. Fran shrank more into the background; she had lost her place in the group. Jude appeared humbler. His arrest had knocked him for six and he realised that Christie Hall wasn't the fortress he'd once thought it was. We spent afternoons together, walking around the grounds and sharing stories from our past. We discussed our dreams and he encouraged me with my writing, while I helped inspire him to paint.

I felt as if I had known Jude all my life. It seemed like I had always lived at Christie Hall. My illness had faded into the distance, and my time in the hospital seemed like a long-forgotten nightmare. I felt better than I had for years. It's possible the medication I took was responsible for my improved mental stability, but it suited me better to believe my recovery was down to my change in circumstances. Whatever it was, at last I felt right. When my mother visited again, even *she* admitted that she noticed a huge improvement. She was relieved to find me happy and stable, and I was glad I was no longer a burden to her.

One afternoon I was churning butter in the dairy. The room was cold and my breath fogged into clouds. My fingers were numb as I stared into the creamy mixture I was stirring. I found the work rewarding. I'd never imagined myself making butter. I'd searched for validation in obvious places and never imagined I would find it in the bottom of a barrel of buttermilk. As I wallowed in that thought, Celeste came running in.

'Oh, it's so exciting! Joanie thinks her labour is beginning.'

'Fuck me sideways,' I said.

Celeste frowned.

'I mean, she's not due for a couple of weeks. Is it safe?' I asked.

'Safe?' Celeste laughed. 'It's not a question of safe. If the baby thinks it's time, then it's time.'

'Right, well, what do you want me to do?'

'Maggie is on the phone to the midwife right now, asking for advice. I left Charlie looking after her. Wally has gone to get the car ready. Sophie is packing a hospital bag for Joanie and the baby. Can you please go and find Jude and tell him it's time?'

'Yes, of course.' I put down the big wooden spoon.

'Great, thanks,' Celeste said, turning to leave.

'Hang on a sec, shouldn't we tell the father or something . . .' I asked.

Celeste stopped. She looked at me blankly. 'Jude *is* the father,' she said, then walked out.

I froze. I couldn't move. Why hadn't he told me? Why hadn't anyone told me? I felt so rocked by the news I had to sit down for a moment. It felt like my world had just imploded. My head began to spin and I was struck by an instant headache. I got up and went to search for Jude. I had a message to pass on and that was all I could think about. I scoured the grounds on autopilot, wondering what else the group hadn't mentioned to me. I felt betrayed by them all, but mostly by Jude. I found him in the wood. He was chopping up a tree trunk that had been uprooted by a violent storm earlier in the week.

'Your baby is coming,' I said. He brought the axe crashing down into the wood. 'Joanie is in labour.'

'Alright,' Jude said, calmly putting down the axe and taking off his gloves. 'I'm just coming.'

I stood, motionless, and stared at him in disbelief.

'How come you didn't tell me?'

'Not now, my Belle.' He put on his coat and strode off in the direction of the house.

I stayed, alone in the cold, watching him walk away into the February mist. He disappeared into the gloom like a ghost.

***

The next morning, news came from the hospital that Joanie had given birth to a boy. Everyone in the house buzzed with excitement. Everyone except me. I felt sick to my stomach. It wasn't just that they had kept the truth from me. Something else bothered me but I couldn't put my finger on it. Jude waltzed in at midday, looking tired and happy. He announced that mother and baby would be kept in for one more night; she had bled more heavily than was usual but she was going to be fine. He asked us to get her room ready for when they came home. We set about doing it as Jude retired to his room for some sleep.

Maggie suggested that Sophie and Ella should make a mobile to hang in Joanie's room. The rest of us busied ourselves. We washed blankets and painted the furniture we had collected in the months leading up to the birth. Charlie whitewashed a chest of drawers and painted the handles blue.

'Why didn't any of you tell me?' I asked Charlie when the two of us were alone.

'It wasn't up to us, I guess.' She refused to make eye contact with me.

I sat in a chair opposite her and folded my arms. I wasn't going to leave without a decent explanation.

'OK, OK.' Charlie dropped her paintbrush into a cup of water. She ruffled her pink hair. 'It's not what you think: they aren't in a relationship, or anything like that.'

'Thanks for clearing that up.' I couldn't hide my sarcasm. 'So, what happened?'

'Well, she wanted a baby. I know it sounds odd, but it was that simple. She's been here for ages and she asked Jude to be the dad. It was an arrangement they had. She is going to be left to decide how best to bring the baby up. The child is going to know that Jude is his father, but that's it. You know how this place works.' She cocked her head to one side and fiddled with an earring.

'Then why not tell me? Why the big secret?'

Charlie puffed out her lips. 'He didn't want you asking questions about the relationship. You see, the thing is, Annabel,' she continued to fidget, 'Jude has slept with a lot of women. At some point or another, I think he's fucked everyone in here.'

'Even Wally?'

Charlie burst into hysterical laughter.

'We aren't all bi!' I felt my cheeks flush pink.

'He's slept with Fran, and Maggie . . . everyone?'

'No, not Fran, as far as I know . . .' She was wistful.

'Is it part of the deal? Are we expected to shag him?'

'No, nothing like that. It's just not off the table, if you know what I mean?'

'I haven't thought much about sex or relationships. It hadn't crossed my mind.'

'Exactly!' Charlie interjected. 'And Jude didn't want to muddle your head with unnecessary nonsense.'

'OK, I get that, but for fuck's sake, it's hardly a small detail. He and Joanie are having, sorry, have *had*, a baby together.'

'But, is it that big a deal, really?'

'Well, I mean, yes, it changes things.'

'What does it change? You knew there was going to be a baby around the place. What does it matter if Jude is the father?' She searched my face.

'It just bloody does.' It was my turn to feel uncomfortable.

Charlie returned to painting the chest. I got up and headed for the door.

'Don't fall for him, Anna.' Her tone was grave. 'You will only be disappointed.'

I pulled the door closed behind me without responding. It was too late for that.

***

I took the road into town. The wind was battering the coastline and I wanted to avoid the biting cold gale. The sky was an uninspiring shade of grey. I pulled my scarf up over my nose and mouth. My breath felt warm against the blue wool. I felt suffused with sadness. Charlie was right: my feelings for Jude had taken on a life of their own. I felt like I'd been run over by a bus. My stomach was churning and I felt dizzy.

When I arrived at the charity shop, I realised I couldn't recall the walk there. I stepped inside and searched for things that might be suitable. Maggie had suggested I buy any curtains they had and I looked for suitable baby clothes. A decrepit woman, who stank of violets, was also busily fingering the rail of clothes. I did my best to avoid speaking to her. A lady in her sixties sat behind the counter, scrutinising us through a pair of small glasses perched on the end of her nose.

I had to get out of there. I sped around the shop and grabbed anything that wasn't pink. I was finding it hard to breathe so I rushed out onto the street and took some long breaths of fresh air. The thought of walking back filled me with dread. It felt colder than earlier; the air blew hard one moment and was deadly still the next. I smelled electricity in the air. A storm was on its way. The horizon over the sea was black and the weather matched my mood. I stuffed the bag of second-hand clothes into my rucksack and headed off in the direction of Christie Hall. It felt as if this baby belonged to all of us. Hunter was a symbol of hope, he represented everything good in life and I wasn't going to let him down.

St Valentine
I cannot write this evening.
Cupid's day has come
And I am lost in the loneliness
Of an unwritten card.
Feeling the tingle of bubbles,
And tasting the champagne,
I am drunk on the sentiment
You never thought to send.

I felt in a particularly strange mood. Everything had changed since I'd discovered Jude was the father of Joanie's baby. She had named him Hunter and he was very sweet. He had his father's hair – a thick mass of auburn curls haloed his head, dark brown eyes and a little button nose. We all fell in love with him, that was fine, but I had to battle my jealousy. I knew it was ridiculous to feel threatened by a new-born, but I couldn't help myself. Hunter represented a special link between Jude and Joanie.

The house held a naming ceremony. We each, in turn, promised to look after Hunter as if he were our own. Then each of us gave him something we had made. It was a nice idea. We all shared the responsibility of bringing the child up. Although Joanie would be the true mother, we would form a network of unbreakable support around the child, in the same way we were for each other.

By now, I had accepted my feelings for Jude: I realised I was in love with him. We had been distant since the arrival of his son and I was surprised that he wasn't particularly interested in the child. When I asked him about the relationship, he said he would bond with the child when it was older. I struggled to understand his lack of interest.

Since Hunter's arrival I'd closely watched Joanie and Jude when they were together. I saw no evidence that they were in love. While I watched them, Charlie watched me. She knew my secret. She warned me against indulging my fantasy – I didn't heed her advice. My feelings were too deep to control. When Jude came into the room my heart danced and I found myself looking for reasons to be close to him. I would breathe in his smell, which reminded me of honey and toast, taking him in as though he were a drug.

I lay in bed at night, hoping he would come and knock on my door. Every sound set my heart racing. I couldn't sleep. I spent my days tired and spaced out. Maggie noticed that I was distracted but didn't press me on it, which I was grateful for. Charlie was a different kettle of fish, though. She was like a dog with a bone. She would not let it go and continued to try to talk to me about it. In the end, I lost my temper and told her to mind her own fucking business. Unsurprisingly, she didn't respond to this very well. She told me I was a fool and that I was in danger of putting the stability of the whole house at risk. I said I would never do that, but she said that by entertaining the idea I was already going down that path. I stormed off. Hours later, when I'd calmed down, I apologised. She said she understood how difficult it must be for me, but that I should stop indulging in my fantasy. She told me that during all the years she had known Jude, she had never seen him with a girlfriend. He had commitment issues, which was why he'd created Christie Hall; he liked the idea of sharing his life with a group of people, not just one. I admitted that her theory made sense and told her I would do my best to control my feelings.

After I'd had it out with Charlie I felt deflated, and retired to the sanctuary of my bedroom. I sat at my desk by the window and looked out over the garden. Snowdrops littered the ground. The sky was thick with the promise of a blizzard. My throat closed up as a wave of emotion hit me. I needed to vent, so did the only thing I knew I could: I wrote poetry.

Snowstorm
I am just a woman standing,
Wearing my mask and your coat.
Against the snow that falls

Are your black eyes,
Searching my counterfeit face.
If only heavy insanity would sink
To below my surface
Like flakes landing on shoulders
And tirelessly melting;
Effortless as my restraint.
In my sleep, a tired madness –
Enough for us both.
If you do not wish to wake it,
You must step back and away,
Vanishing and fading,
In the blizzard of my mind.

I felt like a tragic heroine from a Brontë novel. But the more I felt, the more I wrote.

I was in a mess. I couldn't eat. I felt nervous most of the time and my sleep was so disturbed that I spent my days walking around like a zombie. One evening, when the house was quiet and everyone had gone to bed, I took myself downstairs and curled up on one of the sofas. I lit some candles and lay huddled up in the mellow orange light. I watched the flames dance and flare with each and every draft. Outside I heard foxes fighting. The house had never felt so empty or lonely.

This House
Treading
through the belly
of our house;
a prison
for unhappy souls.
I could hang
from the beams
oppressive
above my head.

Broken

I hear spiders skip
across the floor
searching
for cracks to haunt
under the floorboards.
The undead are here,
their naked feet
pacing
pacing.
Curtains closed
locking out stars
veiling me
from myself.
Dead furniture
scattered around me
in no particular order.
This place
does not resemble
home
and splinters bite
at my bleeding feet
forever pacing.

The grandfather clock in the dining room struck three. I pulled my blanket up around my chin and tucked in my toes. At night, the house took on a life of its own. I wasn't superstitious but the place seemed filled with ghosts. Jude appeared, wearing only a pair of pyjama bottoms. He yawned and stretched. I sat up on the couch and pulled my hair back into a messy bun. He sat down next to me and put his hand on my thigh. I flinched, but he didn't seem to notice.

'It's cold and lonely down here. Don't wallow in your gloom,' he said. 'I'm going to get a glass of water and go back up to bed. I suggest you come with me - you look like you need company. Why not bunk in with me tonight?'

My heart beat so hard in my chest that I thought it might explode. He leaned in to tuck a stray piece of hair behind my ear and rubbed his thumb on my cheek. I closed my eyes to savour the moment. There was a frog in my throat and I couldn't speak. I pulled the blanket back and folded it neatly over one of the sofa arms. Jude went into the kitchen and returned with two glasses of water. He blew out the candle, plunging us into darkness, and I silently followed him upstairs.

I had only been in his bedroom once, and that was to wake him from an afternoon nap. In the early morning hours, the room demanded quiet appreciation. Jude padded over to the four-poster bed and put the water on the bedside table. He pulled back the curtains: the sky was sapphire blue and the silver moon shone through the wispy clouds. I watched the light reflect on his torso and wanted to touch his warm skin. With a smile, Jude got into bed and looked at me.

I didn't know what to expect, or what I wanted to happen. Was this my initiation? Did I want to sleep with him and become another one of his conquests? I didn't know where it would lead but I slipped under the covers with him anyway. We lay in the suffocating darkness and I listened to the soothing rhythm of his breathing. I was as stiff as a board, waiting for his hands to search me out. But they didn't. I lay still for a long time before I realised he had drifted off to sleep. At first, my heart sank. Then I was relieved: I wasn't sure if I could cope with us having sex. I turned to face him and watched him sleep for a while. His chest rose and fell with each deep breath. I lay my arm on his chest. Moments later, I too fell asleep.

***

I can hear the footsteps creaking above me. My breathing is shallow and my chest feels heavy. Pulling at my constraints, I call out, hoping someone will come and save me. The smell of my body clogs my nostrils, making me gag. I'm dirty and unwashed. The scent of my own fear is revolting and clings to the walls of my prison.

Then I hear a scurrying in the corner and turn my head slowly to discover a rat sitting staring at me. I do not move. I stop breathing, hoping the animal will leave me alone, but it remains, its black eyes gleaming as it examines my exposed skin. It is looking at me like I am its next meal, and I swallow before trying to shout and frighten it away. Its small claws look sharp and its pink tail flicks like a knife as it slinks away.

Please don't come back and bite me, I beg, please just leave me alone. And it dawns on me that there is a way out of this nightmare. Somehow, the rat has found a way in, which means maybe I can find a way out.

***

Time passed slowly and the land came to life again while we busied ourselves preparing the vegetable patch and planting. The garden was awash with crocuses and daffodils. The animals had a new lease of life in them too. Sharing Jude's bed had become a regular occurrence. We hadn't had sex. The two of us shared a closeness that would have been muddied by any physical act. Our connection felt pure. I had found my soulmate, but knew Jude would not be tied down and that he belonged to all of us. I was glad to be a part of his life. He loved us all, and that was good enough for me.

It was lovely to have a child in the house. I adored Hunter. He was a happy baby who grinned at anyone who would look at him. We took it in turns pushing him around the grounds in his pram. I would sing him lullabies. It was an unusual arrangement but one that seemed to work. Each of us had something unique to offer the child. I thought he was possibly the luckiest baby in the world, so many people loved him.

I came to terms with my feelings for Jude and learnt to manage them. The only person who knew about it was Charlie, but she kept quiet. I refused to discuss it with her and she did not press me on it. Things were back to normal and I found myself able to enjoy Christie Hall again. I sometimes wondered if it might be the place I was lost in, not the man.

None of us spoke about what was going on outside the walls. The murders in the town seemed like a distant nightmare. We stopped watching the news and reading the newspapers. We were afraid of being infected by the sadness and misery of the other world. Christie Hall provided us with everything we needed. We shut the world out. The people in town crossed the road if they saw us. We knew what they whispered about us. The label 'cult' stuck. Once in a while the police would show up and ask to speak to us, under the guise of routine enquiries. We knew they didn't bother questioning other people who lived nearby. For Jude, it was like water off a duck's back, but the rest of us felt increasingly hurt and isolated as we became more reclusive.

***

It was the best summer of my life. We spent hours outside playing games and laughing while the hot sunshine beat down on our shoulders. We watched Hunter develop, he would lie on his back on a blanket and kick his legs. Butterflies danced around the buddleia. We made jam and collected honey, and sold our produce by the side of the road to passing tourists. Jude and I regularly went out cycling together, winding along the lazy country roads, or to visit the bird reserve.

We extended our menagerie: Maggie and I went with Jude to a farm to choose some chickens to add to the brood. I had suggested we sold the eggs to local shops to boost our modest household income and the idea received enthusiastic backing. We returned to the house with eight bantams and twelve brown hens. It was the cause of much excitement.

From time to time I saw my mother and Will. It was easier for me to visit them than to have them come to Christie Hall. They didn't understand the place or the people. When I visited the house I had grown up in, I felt lost and longed to return to my new home and my other family. I am sure my mother picked up on it. She did her best not to seem offended. After a few months she could see I was no longer a danger to myself. Eventually she relaxed. It must have been difficult for her to let me go.

Will was bemused by the people I lived with, and the lifestyle I had adopted. It made no sense to him but he accepted it as one of the many things in life he would never understand. Will treated everything with the same unquestioning acceptance.

As the summer gave way to autumn, we planned another Winter solstice celebration. It was suggested that we have a bonfire on the beach and we collected wood from all over the grounds. By the time the day arrived we had a pile that stood nearly ten feet tall. It was a particularly harsh winter; the ground was frozen solid every morning. The thought of a bonfire warmed our souls. We decided each of us would burn something of personal significance as a sacrificial gesture of gratitude to the land and the season. My most treasured possession was the book Jude had given me for my poetry.

The morning of the Winter solstice, the house felt alive. I remembered the first party with such clarity. Now I was no longer a stranger, this year it was my party too, and I should have felt elated but my body felt strangely exhausted.

Joanie and Celeste requested a change in the proceedings. They argued that the animals were too precious to be eaten. They said that since they were vegetarian we should alternate veggie and meat-eating years. The house voted in favour of this and a nut roast was prepared. I was looking forward to the feast but it was the thought of the bonfire that really excited me. A tower of hot flames seemed so exciting and I longed to feel the warmth on my skin: I wanted to feel alive.

The act of burning my poems seemed appropriate, especially since so many of them were about Jude. I promised myself that I'd put an end to my infatuation, along with the book's destruction; I didn't want my life to read like a Christina Rossetti verse. And that's what I kept telling myself, up until the evening of the party.

Before we commenced the burning ceremony, Jude took me aside – he knew I had planned to offer my journal as a sacrifice –

and asked if he could read some of it before it was reduced to ashes. Practically every word in it was about him, but I decided to let him read it; perhaps I wanted him to know how I felt. I liked the idea of him understanding it. Without a second thought, I handed the book over. I stood on the beach, hugging myself, watching as his eyes traced the words. As he read, the rest of the world melted away, as if he and I were the only people in the universe.

I watched as realisation sank in. He read one of the pages over and over again. Eventually he stopped reading and closed it; he wouldn't look at me – his brown eyes stared into the flames. I watched the reflection of the night sky on the sea. *He's decided to leave things unsaid.* I was at peace with that. But then he turned and put his arm around my shoulder; I realised I had been holding my breath and I thought my heart might stop beating.

'You know I love you, Belle,' he said. I remained silent. 'I love you all, each of you mean the world to me.' He thought for a moment. 'I am flattered. You're a lovely, attractive woman.' I knew what was coming, I had known all along. 'I just don't see *you,* the way *you* see me. I've never wanted to get involved with someone from the house. I don't think it would be right. We have a great balance. People know what to expect from each other, something like this would destabilise everything we have worked so hard to create.'

His response wasn't a shock, but as I listened to his feeble excuse I was hit with a burst of rage.

'Yes, no, right, of course – I understand,' I said angrily. 'You wouldn't want to complicate things. Fucking everybody is different. Having a child with Joanie isn't at all complicated. Really, Jude, this hippy shit is just a joke. People aren't like that. You can't just put us all in boxes and expect us to act a certain way, to *feel* a certain way. Just because you decide what suits you, doesn't bloody mean it fucking suits me. And besides, you think I want to feel like this, you think I planned it?'

He was taken aback by my outburst. He couldn't think of anything to say. Then I noticed we'd attracted the attention of the others. They all stared at me in disbelief.

'Oh, come on, you lot think so too!'

Fran glared at me, her hands on her hips. I was hit by a wave of embarrassment but remained furious.

'Fine.' I threw my book into the fire and watched as the flames devoured the pages. 'You all stay here and enjoy the fucking party. I'm not in the mood.'

I stormed off. No one said anything and no one pursued me. Moments later the heavens opened and I was caught in a torrential downpour.

I found my way to the main road and set off in the direction of home. In seconds I was soaked through. The alcohol I had consumed was in full effect. I hummed a song to myself as I walked, the rain falling harder with each step, and listened to the night sounds. The occasional car passed - it was nearly midnight and most of the land was asleep. I saw a group of people going into a house on the other side of the road and I buried my head in my shaking hands. Loneliness stabbed my heart with the echo of their laughter. I felt like a fool and regretted my reaction. I sloshed along through the cold puddles, the rain never ceasing. Suddenly, it dawned on me that it had all been a horrible mistake.

I heard a faint cry and wondered if it had come from me, then the night returned to silence, except for the patter of raindrops. Again, I heard a noise break through the quiet. I stopped walking and stood still, listening for it once more. I tried to work out where it had come from – I heard it again and spun round to see Jude in the distance, walking through the rain, alone.

'Wait!' he yelled.

I called back to him. His pace quickened and soon he was standing a few feet in front of me.

'Why'd you leave?' He was slightly out of breath, dripping wet, and his hands were tucked into his pockets. His ginger hair stuck to his face.

'I just wasn't really in the mood anymore,' I shrugged my shoulders, 'so I thought I'd fuck off home.'

'Oh, right.' He had a knowing look. 'Well, I'll come back with you. Let's go.'

'Fine,' I said, brushing my wet hair from my eyes.

I broke his gaze and we started the walk home; my frozen body was flooded with adrenaline. The rain continued to drench the land but its violence had subsided. We took a shortcut through a field and I am not sure what happened in those minutes, but the next thing I knew, my back was up against an oak tree, the bark as rough as his touch. I was no longer cold and don't remember if the rain was still falling. I gripped the back of his neck as he kissed me; I raised my head and opened my eyes and looked up into the black sky through the mass of naked branches. Water was cascading down my face. My shoes had sunk into the slimy mud.

'Jude, take me home . . .' I said as I bit down on my lip.

'Yes . . . yes.'

We couldn't wait: desire had taken hold of us and we made love against the tree. It was spontaneous and passionate and left me in a dreamlike state.

Afterwards, we were in childish hysterics. We dusted ourselves down, pulled up our trousers and decided to go back to the house. Although the rain had dwindled to a fine shower, we were soaked through and clung to each other for warmth. His arm felt strong across my shoulders as we wandered through the darkness. Soon, we found the main road and made our way to the house, but with every passing car came a feeling of uncertainty.

The house was as black as the night when we arrived – no one was back yet. It felt odd being there, alone together after such a monumental deed. We didn't speak. Neither of us knew what to say. I went into the kitchen to pour myself a glass of water and Jude disappeared upstairs. I wondered if he'd gone to bed, and decided to leave things as they were. I returned to the living room and sat on the sofa. The water tasted of chlorine but I needed a drink. I smoked a cigarette and sat back, still damp and shaking. Drops fell from my hair onto my clothes, sending shivers of cold through me. I was pondering on what had just happened when he reappeared, wrapped in a towel.

'That's better,' he said as he dried his hair. 'Don't you want to change?'

'I hadn't thought about it.' My honesty made him chuckle as he sat next to me. Leaving the towel to hang around his neck like a scarf, he leaned in to kiss me. I reciprocated: desire pumped around my body.

'Go and change out of those wet clothes or you'll catch your death.' He leaned back into the sofa.

'The others will be back soon,' I said.

He said nothing, so I took his hand and led him upstairs to his bedroom. I opened the door and told him to sit on the bed. His expression was coy as I peeled off my damp sweater and stood in front of him in my bra and trousers. He slipped his hands around my waist and pulled me down as I ran my fingers through his wet hair and kissed him. Soon we were naked under the covers.

***

Afterwards, we lay as quiet as mice, in total darkness except for the cherry glow of the cigarette we were sharing. Minutes later we heard the bang of the front door and the bass from music began to boom through the house.

'Shit, shit!' I said. I jumped out of bed and scrambled for my clothes. We both laughed and hurriedly got dressed.

'Look, we can't talk about this now, but there are some things I need to say to you,' I said.

'It's fine. As far as they know, everything is normal,' said Jude, very matter of fact. 'So, you can come in with me tonight – no one will think anything of it.'

'But we . . .'

'Stay with me tonight?' There was hope in his voice.

I kissed him and nodded, before suggesting he went downstairs and prevented the others from coming up to investigate our whereabouts. He gave me a grin and disappeared.

I sat on his four-poster bed. *What next*? I kept repeating the question in my head. I could hardly believe any of it was happening.

Quickly, I threw on some pyjama bottoms and a sweater that belonged to Jude; the fabric felt like home. I looked in the mirror: my face was flushed and my hair had a mind of its own. I barely recognised my own reflection. It was as if I were looking at someone else. Pushing the thought away, I dashed into the bathroom, shoved my face under the shower head and washed my hair with lightning speed, returning to my room to blow it dry. I applied some mascara and felt confident I looked human again, as I made my way downstairs to join the party.

I entered the room and caught Jude's eye. He gave me a subtle wink as I greeted everyone, then went into the kitchen, beckoning for me to join him. I followed, like a child who'd been promised sweets. He rummaged in the fridge and pulled out a bottle of rum: I didn't think anything of it. He stood over two glasses, still in his dressing gown, and I placed my hand on his lower back.

'Stay in my room tonight,' he said. I rubbed his upper arm and he smiled.

The living room was vibrant; everyone was talking at the top of their voices and it made my brain ache. Jude and I stood in the doorway sipping our generous glasses of sweet rum. The liquor sent a warm rush down my throat. Charlie was practically shouting as she told the room an amusing story about an argument she'd had with an old boss of hers; Wally sat back in an armchair, smiling to himself, evidently lost in a haze of his own; Sophie chatted animatedly to Maggie, who listened with appropriate interest, while Celeste concentrated on smoking a joint. The smell of the marijuana reminded me of the purple sage in my mother's garden.

I noticed a light bulb was missing from one of the spotlights – it helped to create an intimate atmosphere in which everyone found blissful comfort. Jude spotted an arm of the sofa was free and balanced himself there, taking up residence next to Fran. Cigarette smoke clouded the air, creating a silver cocoon around us. Although I *wanted* to feel safe, I couldn't quite manage it.

I was drunk again from the rum; a feeling of detachment came over me and I watched from an intoxicated distance as everyone interacted. I fumbled about in my pocket for my phone, which wasn't there. Panic hit me like a train.

'I think it's nearly time for bed,' Jude said, looking directly at me for a reaction.

I shrugged and necked my drink. I felt confused, slightly nauseous, as I sat on the sofa, and I thought I might be swallowed up by it. Jude stood in the kitchen doorway watching me. He looked helpless. A minute or two later he disappeared into the kitchen.

I looked over at him, watching me, and wanted to feel at ease but panic still had hold of me.

I felt out of my depth. My mind began to whip itself into a frenzy. Nothing had been confirmed. Things needed to be cleared up. My stomach was full of alcohol and I was beginning to feel sleepy.

Jude put his arm round my waist and I hoped he didn't think we were going to have sex again. As much as I wanted to relive our escapades, I needed to get some things off my chest first.

'Let's go upstairs.' He spoke softly and motioned towards the stairs with his head, grinning, his eyes dilated.

'I'm tired,' I replied, feigning a yawn. He looked disappointed.

'I need to think about this a bit more,' I told him honestly. 'I need to work out what's happening. I don't want you breaking my heart, you fucker.' I poked him in the ribs and tried not to appear vulnerable.

'This is huge for me, too, you know?' He looked coy.

'Sure.' I didn't really understand what he meant. 'What *is* this? I mean, what do you want from me?' I tried not to sound pathetic.

'I'm not sure what I want. I mean, one minute we're friends, the next . . . it's complicated.' He attempted to order his thoughts. 'I don't like to jump in feet first . . . I'm not ready for that. But I don't want anything to be off the table.'

He sat back and watched me try to make sense of what he'd said. I knew he realised he hadn't clarified anything, but at least he was being straight with me.

'I guess I appreciate your honesty. You're lovely, and you know you are - it's just I hate uncertainty, and I—'

He leaned in and kissed me. I was taken aback, but the spontaneity was erotic and I went with the moment. It was strange that no one noticed us, it was as if we were invisible.

'Let's go upstairs,' I said.

'You sure?' He looked at me hopefully.

'Yes, I am, but promise, just promise me, no bullshit.' I stared into his wonderful dark eyes and felt myself getting lost.

'I promise.' He put his hand on his heart and looked serious. Then he took my hand, kissed the back of it, and led me upstairs.

***

I awoke the next morning in his bed, completely disorientated. My dreams were plagued with a recurring nightmare that hung over my days like a shadow.

The winter sunlight shone onto his floor through a gap in the curtains. I wondered who else was at home, and if anyone knew we had slept together. At least I'd had the sense to put his T-shirt on. He was fast asleep with his arm around my middle. I felt a sudden twinge of nerves. *Should I wake him or slip quietly out?* I didn't know what to do. I watched him sleep for a while; he looked beautiful and it was surreal to be with him. I wanted to burst into tears. I felt at home, and at the same time completely lost.

The thought of not being able to touch him again sent a pain into the pit of my stomach. Would he be pleased to find me there? The only way I'd ever know was if I stuck around to find out. I lay utterly still, so as not to wake him. I had no idea what the time was. Minutes slipped by as I anticipated the moment his eyes would open - I knew if I could look into them I would be healed. All of a sudden, I needed to smoke a cigarette. I did my best to gently slide away. Just as I thought I could make a break for freedom, I felt his arm tighten around me.

'Where are you going?' His eyes were still closed but his grip remained firm.

'Just to get a cig.' I leaned in and rested my chin on his naked chest. The tight hairs glinted like copper, and a smile crept across his face. I slipped out of bed and into a pair of his tracksuit bottoms; the freezing cold house was silent as I tiptoed downstairs to the living room.

I found my bag on the living room floor and was relieved to discover a flattened pack of cigarettes with five left. I pulled one out, placed it between my lips, and inhaled deeply. The warm smoke filled my lungs and I felt slightly better, but still, something wasn't right.

I trudged into the kitchen to see if there was any milk left. A trickle remained in the bottom of the carton and I hoped there was enough to stretch to two cups of tea. The kettle whistled in the background; I checked the clock on the wall.

I made two cups of hot, sweet tea and wandered back upstairs. As I passed Charlie's bedroom, I saw the door was half open – she wasn't there. The house felt abandoned. Reaching the top floor, I pushed Jude's door open with my foot. He was sitting up. I sat on the end of his dishevelled bed, handed him a mug and he nodded in appreciation. We sipped our tea in silence, allowing the hot drink to warm us.

It was his turn to smoke a cigarette. He sat back and closed his eyes as he smoked. It made me feel awkward, like an unwelcome visitor in his private place. I stretched and placed my empty mug on his chest of drawers.

'Right,' I yawned, 'I feel like a mess. I'm going for a bath.'

'OK.' Each syllable dragged; he hunkered down under the duvet and turned his face to the wall, away from me.

I left his room with a heavy feeling, wondering what had changed. I stared at my reflection in the mirror, as piping hot water gushed from the tap and the steam rose. A modest amount of mascara from the previous night lay in a fine line under my lower eyelashes. Looking at myself, tears rose up inside and soon I was in the tub, knees clasped to my chest, sobbing quietly. The pain felt so real.

When I left the bathroom, the house still as quiet as a tomb, I didn't return to Jude's room. I left his T-shirt and tracksuit bottoms folded neatly outside his door as a signal of acceptance that our encounter had been a one-off.

I felt nervy and trapped in the house and decided I needed to get out. Fumbling through the pile of shoes that cluttered our hallway, I found my pair of old, tattered trainers. I forced my feet into them without undoing the laces, noticing that my toes hurt and my ankles appeared strangely swollen. My feet felt cold, as if I were standing in a freezing puddle, but I pushed it to the back of my mind as I slammed the heavy front door behind me.

The winter sun shone down from a clear, pale sky. I decided to step outside for a moment. The fresh air would do me good and help me find clarity.

When I went back to the house, I was surprised to find Jude standing in the kitchen.

'Morning,' he said. We had already seen each other that morning, under far more intimate circumstances, and I thought his greeting was odd.

Then, the stench of rotten food came from nowhere, assaulting my nose. It smelled like death, but everything in the kitchen appeared fresh. It didn't make sense.

'I'll see you later.' I hurried past him and felt his concentrated stare burning into my back as I bolted towards the front door, deliberately slamming it hard behind me.

An uneasy feeling troubled me. Everything fucking troubled me. All I could focus on was getting to the coast. I felt the texture of the ground change below my feet and relief hit me: my survival had depended on reaching the beach. I started my descent of the slope and headed towards my golden sanctuary.

I walked slowly and deliberately, observing each step. I could feel the light on my neck.

I knew what I had to do: to hold on to my dignity, and remain true to my feelings, I had to confront Jude. Every grain of sand that passed under my feet enabled me to build my emotional strength. When I reached the large cluster of sand dunes, I felt as if I had shifted form, as if I was someone completely new.

I stood on a dune, overlooking the choppy sea. It was freezing cold and I was only wearing a thin cotton sweater. It was a beautiful day, though still damp from the heavy rainfall the previous night. I found a suitable spot and sat down. I lit a cigarette and sucked in the mixture of cold and warm air, holding it in my mouth for a while before exhaling. I took my iPod from my pocket, selected a compilation of love songs and listened to the evocative lyrics.

A flock of migrating birds crossed the sky and I wondered where they were going. I imagined a warm climate and empty

---

mountains flooded with sunshine. I longed to be there, away from the romantic entanglements that plagued my insignificant existence.

I sat on the sand for a long time, looking out over the endless horizon, daydreaming. I was awoken from my fantasy by the feeling of being watched. Turning my head, I saw Jude approaching from the distance, in silhouette. I could have picked him out of a crowd at a football stadium. He was wearing his grey jeans and a dark brown hooded sweater, and he was running one hand through his hair. I wasn't surprised to see him: it was as if I had known all along that he would come. I remained seated and watched him long enough for him to know I had seen him. I then returned to looking out over the sea, and braced myself.

He sat next to me and we did not look at each other. We sat in silence, admiring the view. He put his arm around my shoulder and I flinched, like someone had walked over my grave. I removed my headphones and turned to face him; he remained looking out at the sea. I opened my mouth to speak, but before I could say a word he was talking.

'I'd love to be on a hot beach right now. I hate the shitty cold. Somewhere peaceful, watching a sunset with a big fruity cocktail in my hand.' He paused. I didn't know what on earth he was talking about. I felt as if I had missed something. 'The thing about coming from a rich family, is there are benefits.' He stopped again. I watched as he ordered his thoughts. 'I'm going on holiday. I need to get away,' he said. His face was still turned towards the horizon. I examined his profile: the curve of his mouth, the lashes that framed his eyes. 'I have just been on the phone to the travel agents. I thought now would be the perfect time.'

My heart sank but I nodded.

'I'm going to go to a Thai island,' he said.

'Oh, when are you going?'

He looked at me. His face became very serious and my stomach knotted.

'That depends on you,' he said. 'I want you to join me.'

My jaw dropped and I looked at him in disbelief. He laughed and leaned in to kiss me. He swept his hand up my neck and through my hair, pulling me closer. The kiss went on for minutes – we could have made love right there on the cold sand. He pulled away and cupped my head in his hands.

'I fucking love you, OK? Of course I do. I always have. There, I've said it, just . . . you . . .' He gulped. 'Come here.'

I sat on his lap, facing him, with my legs wrapped around his back. One of my hands was on his shoulder, the other found its way to his neck and I stroked his hair. I kissed him again. He pulled his arms around me and guided us down so I was lying on top of him. I leaned back and looked at him again. Strands of my hair hung down, covering my face. He tucked them behind my ear and I watched his eyes while he did it. His gaze never broke from mine. We stayed like that, taking each other in.

'Jude, I . . . what I mean is, I love you, too.'

We got up and kissed again, before turning towards home and setting off hand in hand, our fingers intertwined, reminding me of a Russian wedding ring. As we slowly made our way down the hill, I was floating on air.

'You had better get your passport. Meet me at noon at the lake, by the pergola, and we'll talk about it then,' he said.

Later, at noon, as we walked towards the bench by the lake, I noticed a rainbow. Swallows darted above us and I felt the warm sun on my face. It didn't occur to me that it was unusual for December. We basked in our happiness and ambled towards our secret place.

'Christmas is going to be great. It's the time between now and then that we need to concentrate on,' Jude said. He looked at my hand as he stroked it. 'I'm not sure how you want to deal with it, I mean, I haven't really thought it through myself,' he said.

'Fuck what everyone else thinks. *We* know what we're doing.' It was my turn to be strong. It was my turn to believe that this could be real.

The next morning, I snuck into bed with Jude during the early hours. As I crept along the corridor, I realised I had never known the house to be so silent. I froze every time a floorboard creaked beneath my feet. It was exciting and frightening all at once and I felt like a child about to be caught with their hand in the cookie jar. When I reached his room and pushed open the door, he was sitting up in bed, waiting for me. We said nothing as I slipped under the covers. The darkness cocooned us and kept our secret safe as we held each other and explored each other's skin. While the dawn crept up, we talked about our adventure. I hung on every word he said as if I were caught in a dream.

I looked around his bedroom; it was like a fantasy. The furniture was all solid, antique wood. Gold brocade curtains hung in the windows and dominated the room – they had probably been there since the house was built centuries ago. It was like the boudoir of a king. It was sparsely decorated, except for two things: The first one was a huge mural of the night sky on the ceiling. It was a painting that Leonardo himself would have been proud of, although you might not notice it unless you were lying in bed, looking up at it. The ceiling was so high that the fresco managed not to encroach on the rest of the room. The second thing was a large painting that hung on the wall opposite the bed. It showed an understated English landscape, below a powder-blue sky that was peppered with silver clouds. As I lay, staring at it, Jude spoke.

'That is how I'm going to fund our trip.' He was looking at the painting.

'What do you mean?'

'I'm going to sell it.'

'Don't you like it?' I was surprised.

'Sure I do. It belonged to my great-great-grandparents.' There was something strangely familiar about the picture, and something disconcerting.

'Then you mustn't.'

'It's wasted here. It should be in a museum, or somewhere where it's appreciated.' He got out of bed and went over to the painting to examine it more closely.

'Is it by a famous artist?' I felt rather stupid.

He wiped a layer of dust from the top of the frame with his thumb.

'It's a Constable.'

I stared at the painting in disbelief.

'As in, John Constable?' I also got out of bed to look at the picture more closely.

'Yup.'

'You mean to tell me that you've had a John bloody Constable painting hanging in your bedroom, all this time, and you never told us?!'

'It's not the sort of thing you advertise, Belle.'

The pair of us stared at the masterpiece.

'It's worth millions,' he said, turning to face me, still stark naked.

'Jesus.' I puffed out my cheeks, wondering why I hadn't noticed the picture before.

'Come back to bed,' Jude said, leading me by the hand, as a band of light pushed its way through the curtains. Lying on the bed, he looked like a king, surrounded by rich fabrics; I felt as if I was living in a film.

***

Soon after Jude and I had got together and planned the trip, I called my mother to tell her about the exciting developments. She was thrilled for me and said how much she liked Jude. Will also welcomed the news and wished us well, but it was difficult not having anyone other than my family to share my happiness with.

Jude and I agreed that we would tell the rest of the house when the time was right. Nobody knew about the painting, the fortune he was sitting on from it, or our plans to disappear together. Jude suggested we share the news with them the night before our departure. He said he thought it would be easier for them to accept the idea while we were away. He believed it was best to be out of sight so the dust could settle.

The days before the bonfire party seemed distant and removed from the world I was now living in. I remembered the times I'd flinched at every brush of his arm. The few days before we left, I was so blissfully happy, the previous month's turmoil evaporated. We went shopping for things we needed for our holiday. I was eager to please: I modelled underwear for him in the lingerie shop dressing room, where we managed to sneak in a quickie. The thrill of our secret affair was exhilarating, and I was amazed that nobody picked up on it. It seemed our passion had become an entity of its own. The fact it was going on unbeknownst to everyone else was almost unbelievable.

***

I come to as my head slams down again. I am on my back, lying on something hard. It feels like wood. My hands have been bound to posts. I am in shackles. I am spread-eagled. I feel my clothes being ripped from my body. The cold, damp fabric seems to melt away. I am naked now. A bright light is above me. I am squinting. I can't see. It hurts my eyes. That pain is there still. My head thuds. My heart pounds, and my ribs feel like a cage, preventing my heart from bursting free. Am I having a heart attack? No, I am OK. Try to focus on something, anything. That sound, yes. I can hear him moving about. Why doesn't he say anything? I cannot speak. The gap where my tooth was is pouring blood again. I can feel it soaking into the gag in my mouth. Warm and wet. I am losing consciousness. The room is on a merry-go-round. Faster and faster. Here it comes. Hello darkness, my old friend.

***

'It's going to be fine,' Jude said as I returned to his world.

My head ached: the dream had been so real. Jude smiled as he lifted up the duvet and crawled on top of me.

'Wait, wait! We're not in the clear yet.' I felt panicky.

'Ah, everyone's asleep.' He kissed my neck. 'They won't be up for hours.'

As I buried the brutal images of my nightmare, I succumbed to my desires and began to take off his clothes. He pulled my T-shirt over my head, revealing my breasts. His mouth moved down my stomach and past my belly button. His tongue explored me. I was close to orgasm when he stopped and took off his boxer shorts. He entered me and I groaned. I gripped his hips; the duvet was kicked onto the floor. I wanted no obstructions. We lay exposed. His strong arms were either side of my ribcage and his hands were flat on the mattress. He supported his weight and continued to push himself into me. We were both silent, looking into each other's eyes. As I closed my eyes, he said, 'I love you.'

We lay naked in the silence and I had no doubt that it was true. I ran my fingers lightly up and down his back.

'I love you, too.'

The day before our big trip I woke up with butterflies in my stomach. I felt inexplicably cold, as if I were naked, and sick. My nerves matched my anticipation. This was the day we were going to tell the household about our relationship, and I really hoped they would not react badly to the news. The person I was most concerned about was Joanie. There was also the issue of Hunter. Although he was being brought up knowing his parents weren't together, I couldn't help feeling that I had ruined their chances of being a family. I had suffered my own family breakdown and didn't like the idea of inflicting it on anyone else.

I asked Jude to take the lead in announcing our relationship. He called a meeting in the dining room. I could tell he was nervous as he chewed his bottom lip, the way he always did when something was playing on his mind. I wondered what would be the biggest shock to them all: Jude being a multi-millionaire, the news he and I were together, or that, without any warning, the two of us were jetting off to Thailand.

Before the meeting, Jude asked me to meet him for a one-on-one chat. I felt like a school kid being summoned to the headmaster's office. I met him in the pig barn, as instructed; my breath clouded in front of me. I rubbed my hands together and watched the pigs snuffle about in the hay. For some reason, I was unable to forget the smell from the day I had seen the body of the sow. Jude came up behind me and wrapped his arms around my waist.

'So, this is it,' he said. 'Our big moment. Ready?'

'I think I might crap myself.'

He laughed.

'Don't be scared, Belle. You forget that this is my house.'

This took me aback.

'What do you mean by that?' My voice was as frosty as the weather.

'Just that, this is my home, it belongs to me. Anyone who doesn't like it can leave if they wish.'

'But this place has been built on the idea that we are a family and we share it.' I reminded him of his self-proclaimed ethos.

'Of course, to a degree. But we all know the truth. Every single person here is just a guest, really. I know it, you know it, they know it. Ultimately, what I say goes, and it's that simple. My name is on the deeds, the money from the Constable is in my bank account. None of them would dare rock the boat. They don't want to end up on the streets.'

I stepped away from him.

'How can you talk like this?' I asked with disgust. 'What about "we are a family" and everything you've said? Is that how you feel about me? If I don't go along with exactly what you want, am I going to be tossed aside, too?'

Jude could see I was irate. He decided to take another tack.

'I just meant that, if it comes to it, I *will* put my foot down. This place is built on one key thing, and that is respect for each other. If we don't receive that from any of them, I'll be forced to rethink their position here.'

I couldn't ignore what he was saying. It was the truth, but it was the first time I'd had to face it. He had never acknowledged this to me and I felt uncomfortable.

'But no one *will* react badly,' he continued, 'I am certain they'll all welcome the news and wish us well.'

'I hope you're fucking right, because if this blows up, it will ruin everything you have worked towards. Christie Hall must carry on,' I said solemnly.

'Belle, don't be so over the top. It's fine. Everything will be just fine. Now, come on, it's time. Let's do this.' He led me by the hand as we left the safety of the pig shed and walked towards the unknown.

With each step, my heartbeat quickened. Jude held my hand tightly and we made our way to the dining room. They were all there, seated, waiting for us. I saw Charlie looking at our entwined fingers. She knew what was coming. Everyone probably did.

Jude did the talking. He explained everything to them. I stood by his side with my eyes glued to the floor, terrified of getting a disapproving look from someone. When he'd finished, the room was silent. I looked up and searched each of their faces for a response. You could have heard a pin drop. No one blinked. The clock was ticking but time had stopped. My heart was in my mouth as I waited for someone to speak. Maggie was the first to break the silence.

'Well,' she smiled, 'I think I speak for us all when I say how delighted we are that the two of you have worked things out.'

Charlie cheered and banged her fist on the table. They all clapped and it was wonderfully surreal.

'Well, go on then, you two,' said Joanie. 'You've got a plane to catch.'

I was so grateful for her blessing, I gave her a big hug.

'Thank you,' I whispered in her ear. 'You're an angel.'

As I packed my suitcase, I thought about what life would be like when we got back. We hadn't yet left the country but already I was planning my return.

Once we were packed, and Jude had double-checked that he had our tickets and passports, we said our goodbyes. Wally had kindly offered to drive us to the airport. I squeezed myself past the front passenger seat and into the back, dragging my suitcase with me. Jude, by some miracle, had managed to get the rest of our things into the boot of the Nissan.

Wally started the engine and music blasted from the stereo: it was a song I hadn't heard for years and it reminded me of good times spent with friends when I was at school. Jude leaned over to turn it down and I stopped him, asking him to turn it up a notch or two. I was so excited I thought I might burst.

It was dark outside when our enjoyable journey came to an end, most of which had been spent singing our hearts out and throwing our arms around. We pulled up outside the clinical-looking airport hotel. It looked more like a car park than a four-star establishment: a tomb built for travellers in limbo.

Planes flew low overhead, their bright lights flashing, the roar from their engines echoing around us. Jude and Wally removed the luggage from the car and piled it up near the entrance, while I smoked a cigarette and hugged myself in the bitter cold, my teeth chattering. We thanked Wally and said our goodbyes, standing together and waving him off. As his car disappeared, we turned to face each other. Jude put his arms around me and pulled me close.

'Just the two of us now,' he mumbled through my hair.

'Yep,' I replied. 'You OK with that?'

He brought his face down, his mouth an inch from mine.

'I couldn't be happier.' A plane soared over us just at that moment, like a shooting star.

We gathered our bags and went into the hotel. The lobby was surprisingly nice: creamy yellow wallpaper and the furniture was upholstered to match. The receptionist greeted us warmly. Jude checked us in while I listened to a pianist playing a jazz tune in the bar. I noticed he was wearing a bow tie and I felt underdressed. We got our key cards and went up to our room.

The same decor as the lobby had been continued in the bedrooms. We dumped our bags on the floor and I went to explore the bathroom. Travel always made me feel dirty so I took a shower. Halfway through, Jude jumped in with me. We made love as the hot water trickled down our bodies. I was reminded of our first night together in the field, having sex in the rain.

Afterwards, we dressed and strolled downstairs. We held hands and it felt natural being together in public. We found a table with a leather sofa and sat down to listen to the pianist. The green leather squeaked as I moved and it felt cold against my palms. I got up and went to order our drinks. When I returned to the table, Jude had gone. I noticed him standing next to the musician, chatting to him as he played. Jude said something to the man and pointed over to me. I raised my drink in acknowledgement. When he came back I asked him what he'd been doing. He told me he had requested a song for me. A moment later 'Summertime' was playing. I took his hand and stood.

'Dance with me,' I said, smiling like a Cheshire cat.

'You're joking, right?' he replied.

I pulled him up from his seat.

'But people are watching.'

'Fuck them.' I guided him to a suitable space.

I put my arm around his waist and held his hand. He looked self-conscious.

'You're crazy,' he said.

Neither of us could dance properly so we swayed on the spot. As the song came to an end, he leaned me back, over his arm, and kissed me. We both laughed and applauded the pianist. A stuffy-looking middle-aged couple watched us with a mix of admiration and disdain.

It was nearly half past eight and the bar was filling up, so we ordered some light supper. When Jude had finished his beer and I the last of my coffee, we approached the bar to pay the bill.

The couple that had watched us dance earlier were still there. The grey-haired husband, who was slightly cross-eyed, leaned over and congratulated us on our efforts. His wife sat stiffly on the bar stool; she was wearing a floral summer-holiday outfit and reminded me of Hyacinth Bucket from *Keeping Up Appearances*. They were both a little overweight and probably in their mid-sixties. It was obvious they no longer liked each other – they hadn't said more than two words to each other all evening. Finally, the woman spoke.

'You must be on your honeymoon - I recognise the look in your eyes, my dears. Where are you off to?'

I laughed. Jude put his arm around me.

'You're right. We are honeymooning in Thailand.'

He surprised me. I had expected him to put her right. The mere mention of the word marriage sent most men running. I decided to join in with the fun.

'Yes, we've come straight from the reception. The best day of our lives, right, honey?' I looked up at Jude with exaggerated pride and pinched his bum.

'She's a keeper,' he said.

I could see he was trying his hardest not to laugh as the real married couple cooed at us.

I explained that we had an early flight and we excused ourselves. Once we knew we weren't within earshot we collapsed into giggles, tears pouring down our cheeks. For a moment I couldn't breathe. It was the kind of laughter so heartfelt that no noise is made – our mouths moved and we silently shook as we waited for the lift. The lift arrived and when the doors had slowly closed behind us, I said, 'Ever had sex in a lift?' I pushed him up against the mirrored wall.

'You are on fire tonight!' he said.

'Have you?' I undid the top button of his jeans.

'No, I haven't.' He slid his hands onto my bum.

'Me neither.' My hand was in his boxer shorts. 'Such a shame we don't have time now.' I gave him a squeeze, removed my hand and backed away with a smile.

'God damn it, woman, you drive me wild!' he said. He had a charged look in his eyes. I leaned back against him and did his trousers up.

'Earlier, in the bar, that song was the nicest thing anyone has ever done for me,' I said.

Red flooded his cheeks and he said nothing. Jude wasn't comfortable with compliments. We arrived at our floor and within minutes were back in our room, kissing while stripping off each other's clothes.

When we finally fell asleep, I had another apparition.

***

I come to. The darkness has lifted. I'm in a cellar; I can see that now. My vision is blurred. I need a minute for my sight to adjust. I am still tied up. The metal shackles around my wrists feel so cold. I cannot see my captor. He is not in the room but I can see myself in a mirror. I look at my bloody face. My blonde hair is a mass of tangles and dried blood. There is a lump on the side of my head. The blood is clotted and black. I look like a corpse: the living dead. I am so pale. My naked body looks hopeless and every bone aches. Why do I have to see myself like this? I twist my neck to get a better look. A tiny window is above the bed, letting in a small amount of light. I can see the dust particles dancing in the beam. There is a camera on a tripod pointing at me. I had detached for a minute, but the fear returns. A tsunami of terror rips through me and I start to tremble. I am fitting now. It is uncontrollable. I don't feel it, I just watch myself from above. Foaming at the mouth. Distorted limbs. I am in cruel trouble. I am going to die.

***

The next morning we woke at the crack of dawn and pulled back the curtains to reveal a dark cloud of smog. We were both shattered, but the prospect of being on a beach in a few hours kept us going. We made our way to reception and checked out, heading off in the direction of departures. This world was a man-made mess of buildings and I felt small wandering through the busy terminal, pushing the stubborn trolley. Jude fiddled about, searching for our tickets and passports.

Once we had checked in we were ushered through to the departure lounge. A little time passed before we found ourselves in our grey, carpeted seats preparing for take-off. I was a nervous flyer, having had a traumatic experience with turbulence a few years earlier on a trip to Italy. I gripped my armrests and braced myself as the engines roared and we taxied down the runway. Jude laughed and put his hand over mine – I felt reassured by his touch.

The long flight was uneventful. I noticed Jude admiring one of the female flight attendants and told him I would have made an effort to flirt with one of the male staff if they hadn't all been gay. He laughed, as did a woman nearby who'd been listening. The food was typically dreary and the in-flight movies predictably dull. For the majority of the journey, Jude slept, his head rolling from side to side; I pulled out a book from my bag and read it from cover to cover. The story scared me but I couldn't put it down.

Bangkok airport didn't leave much to be desired: it was clean and clinical inside. Some international travellers wore facemasks, a hang-up from the bird flu scare years ago. I looked outside but couldn't see past the runway, pollution hung in the air, carrying a distinctive, rotten smell. You could see the heat – it wasn't only the jet fuel that was responsible for the haze – it was also the humidity. Our journey wasn't done yet. We still had to get from Bangkok to the island where we were staying. After collecting our luggage and going through the rigorous obstacle of customs, we made our way out of the airport. Stepping out onto the tarmac in the evening darkness, we were blanketed by warm, humid air. Every bone in my body ached and I tried to shift my feelings of discomfort.

It was a chore locating the minibus that would take us to the resort, but eventually we found it and loaded our luggage on board. It was small and cramped, with few other passengers. Jude and I collapsed into our seats. The refreshing blast of the air conditioning showered our skin as the minibus pulled away.

We rattled down one of the fast roads, through the city: palm trees and exotic shrubs grew on the verges; large advertising posters separated the two sides of the bypass. Parts of the metropolis were elaborate and ornate, others grotty and downtrodden. I noticed a number of prostitutes hanging about in the shady areas. A fellow traveller told me that most of them were transvestites. I told him they made for very attractive women, and he replied that that was exactly the problem.

The air conditioning and the noise it made eventually became irritating, but we were unable to turn the vents away from our faces. Jude and I just sat for a while, not speaking, exhausted. We listened to our iPods. Our palms were sweaty but we remained holding hands. There wasn't much to see: the land was black and there were no streetlights. The movement of the bus rocked us like twins in a buggy and we fell asleep, but, when I closed my eyes, my head was plagued with images of being tortured.

I woke up suddenly, dripping wet with fear. The tiny dark-skinned male driver, who had deep wrinkles carved into his forehead, was screeching at us in an indecipherable language. We realised we had arrived at the fishing port – our destination. Getting off the bus, stretching and cracking our stiff joints, we removed our bags from the boot, and I finally felt like I was on holiday.

The busload of travellers stood near the shore, looking out at the sparkling, tropical water. Jude started singing 'Sailing' and a few passengers giggled. I felt the sun's rays tingle on my pale skin – Jude was even paler and I wondered which one of us would burn first. I suspected it might be him because of his ginger hair.

The final leg of the journey took about forty minutes by boat. We passed incredible rock formations on the way. Large towers of dark, jagged rock protruded from the sea. I became the typical tourist, snapping away at the geographical marvels with my camera. Jude teased me, but I noticed other people doing the same, and carried on. The boat docked at our island. We took our luggage from the rocking vessel and dropped it onto the soft white sand. By then it was seriously hot and the sun was high in the cloudless deep-blue sky. I admired the forest of tropical trees that covered everything past the beach. More rock formations jutted out of the landscape and were covered with the same thick green shrubbery. I had stuffed my shoes into a bag and the sand was hot beneath my feet. A petite, smiling woman welcomed us with a garland of orchids and we followed her to the hotel reception area. A young local boy was summoned to deal with our bags. Jude and I felt guilty about this. He was probably only eleven or twelve years old but the woman insisted it was his job. Jude overruled her and picked up the two heaviest bags. The boy was left to carry our hand luggage and looked extremely grateful.

We were led along a path that went through the tropical shrubs. We could hear geckos and tree frogs all around us. The strong sunlight shone through the trees, forming a spotted pattern on the ground. In the shade the air was cool and it felt good. Long wooden condos were set back from the path, spread far apart from one another. Jude told me that he had booked one on the ocean, with its own veranda.

The receptionist tried to sell us a tour of the island. She tempted us with the promise of a boat trip, followed by a 4x4 excursion. Jude and I agreed we might do one another day. By then we were desperate to get settled in and have a rest; it had been a long twenty-four hours. We were taken to the door of our hut and handed the key. The bellboy dropped our bags and quickly disappeared into the dense green foliage. Jude opened the door and ushered me in.

I was struck by the size of the room: it was airy and beautifully decorated; the bed was simply covered with white linen sheets and had bedside tables with a matching pair of lamps; a chandelier hung from the centre of the high ceiling; there was a white sofa underneath the window, looking out over the bay; a finely woven cream rug lay between the bed and a fireplace, which had a plasma screen television above it, and on the mantelpiece there were three pure white orchids.

'It's lovely, Jude!' I went to inspect the bathroom.

Like the bedroom, it was simple but beautiful. Marble tiles covered the floor and the walls were painted white – I noticed some speakers on them. There was a rainforest shower on one side and a huge spa bath on the other. I was in seventh heaven. Jude came behind me and wrapped his arms around my waist.

'I'm so glad you like it,' he said. 'Right, time to get into our swimming things. I've called room service and ordered breakfast. It'll be here in about twenty minutes, so we've just enough time for a quick dip.'

'Sounds good to me,' I said. I was determined to fight my exhaustion.

We rummaged through our bags: Jude pulled out his green patterned swimming shorts and I found my red and white striped bikini. We speedily changed and raced each other out of the room, down the sand, into the calm sea. The water was warm and crystal clear and I dived straight in. It was so refreshing that I instantly felt clean. Jude sat in the shallows, stroking the water with the palm of his hand. I swam over to him and he playfully pushed me under. We played a while, until we saw a member of staff approaching our door with our breakfast.

We made our way back to the cabin. Our tray had been placed on a table on the veranda. Assorted exotic fruits, cut into pieces, were laid out on one plate, and on the other was a pile of fresh pancakes, accompanied by a jug of chocolate sauce and one of maple syrup; the fuchsia head of an orchid had been placed on top of linen napkins, and next to a pot of coffee there were two glasses of freshly squeezed orange juice. The smell of fruit and sugar represented the sunshine beautifully. Recently I'd had an unquenchable thirst that I couldn't explain, and the sight of the food and drink left me dizzy with lust.

We were famished, and it didn't take us long to devour what was on both plates. The fruit was ripe and sweet and the pancakes were warm. Afterwards, we sat back, bellies full, to admire the view. It was now midday and the heat was growing by the minute. Jude suggested that we went indoors for a nap and I followed him in. He adjusted the air conditioning and lay down on the bed. I crawled in next to him, now fully dry but still in my bikini. I pulled the crisp sheet up over my waist. He put his arm around me and we promptly fell asleep.

***

A bucket of icy water is thrown over my naked body. I come to with a jolt and hit the bottom of my spine on the wooden bench. The water drips down my arms and legs and sits in an icy puddle on my stomach. Before I can identify where the water came from, I hear the door to the cellar being closed. My captor has hit and run, and I am left in the dark, still not able to put a face to my tormentor. My teeth chatter and my body quivers uncontrollably. I moan and beg for the nightmare to end.

When I woke up my teeth were chattering like a child's wind-up toy. Jude was sitting upright, reading a book. He said he hadn't wanted to wake me. I thanked him and suggested that we go out and explore the coast, trying to shake the fear that had embedded itself into my brain. He said he wanted a shower first, so I got up and moved towards the bathroom to get it ready for him.

I turned the knob until a lukewarm jet was flowing, and put my fingers in the water. Jude came up behind me and pulled at the string that fastened my bikini; he kissed my shoulders and pushed me into the shower. His mouth was warm on my skin. I allowed my bikini to fall and we stood under the water, exploring each other's bodies.

Some time later, we went back outside into the baking heat. As we wandered hand-in-hand along the shore, the lapping waves brushed against our feet. Before long, we came to a bustling part of the beach. Tourists and locals were sprawled out on various coloured towels, or plastic chairs, under straw umbrellas. A little way out to sea, anchored boats bobbed with the tide.

We meandered past the lazing sun-worshippers and headed towards a bar on the edge of the beach. The hum of familiar pop music floated on the light breeze. We sat down at one of the cramped tables and picked up a menu. The entire thing was in English and the bar was even called Henry's. Having already eaten a large breakfast, we ordered a small portion of chips and a green salad to share; Jude got a beer and I had a rum and coke. I watched the Australian barman pour a very generous quantity of rum into the glass, filling it a third of the way. Jude explained that the Thais didn't use European measures. I made a mental note to remember that, to avoid getting drunker than normal. For some reason, I was still shivering, and I felt very strange.

We watched a fat, young boy standing crying in the shallows, while his mother was at the bar, shouting at him to get out of the water. She wore tight denim shorts and a red T-shirt, her gold double-hoop earrings jangling as she became more incensed. Eventually, the toddler stopped sobbing and obeyed his mother. He wobbled up the sand, stopping to smile at a European couple. A muscular blond man, in orange swimming trunks, handed him a beach ball and the child's face lit up as he grabbed it and headed off, brandishing the prize for his mother to see. Jude and I laughed: we were sure the man hadn't intended on giving it away altogether.

I should have been so happy, but I couldn't shake the uneasy feeling. It was a cross between travel sickness and a hangover. But I wasn't ill and I hadn't been drinking heavily. In the back of my mind, I felt something was wrong.

After we'd finished our drinks and picked at the chips, I suggested we should leave the bar and explore the town. Jude paid the bill and we set off. The roads were narrow and dusty and few cars passed us. The popular form of transport seemed to be the moped. Modest, higgledy-piggledy buildings lined the streets. Most of them had wooden shutters that were closed to prevent the heat from getting in. Jude marched on ahead and I ambled along, taking in our surroundings. There were few shops, although there were plenty of restaurants, hostels and hotels. Some boasted that they sold English beer: the sunshine was foreign but the resources were not. As we walked on, we found ourselves in an open space. There were lines of deserted stalls; we had stumbled on the market place.

On the far side, there was a small shop that sold souvenirs. I was drawn to a rack of bright silk scarves at the front, comedy postcards were stacked up outside next to them and a strong smell of incense wafted from inside. I suggested that we buy some supplies to stock the mini-fridge and Jude agreed so we went looking for a convenience store.

Minutes later, we were lost. We couldn't even be sure we were heading in the direction of the shore, but we were unfazed. It was late afternoon, and we had plenty of time before darkness fell. I was dripping with sweat. It streamed down my back, and I couldn't shake the feeling that I was being watched.

Finally, we found ourselves on a familiar street. It was bustling with people making their way back to their houses and hotels, towels and beach gear in tow. I spotted a shop and dragged Jude in with me. It was cramped, with rows of shelves containing snacks, dried food, and toiletries. An elderly woman, with grey hair pulled back into a bun, stood in the back behind a till and watched us with beady eyes. I scoured the shelves, taking bits and pieces and handing them to Jude, who had become my human shopping basket: his arms were loaded with bags of salted crisps, bars of unfamiliar chocolate, and bottles of water and juice. As he juggled the contents in his arms, I fiddled about in my pocket for some money. Jude hurried over to the checkout and dropped the pile onto the desk. The woman rang each item through the till and dropped them into an unmarked blue bag. I stood behind Jude, resting my chin on his shoulder, watching the total add up.

'Thousand.' The woman pointed at my hand with a sun-beaten, crooked finger. I handed over the money and Jude gathered our shopping.

It took about fifteen minutes, walking along the beach, to get back to our room. Jude pulled the key from his pocket and ushered me in. He threw the shopping on the bed and collapsed on it himself.

'Ah, air conditioning,' he sighed, closing his eyes and allowing the cool air to flow over him.

By eight o'clock the sun was starting its descent. I got up, as it began to turn, and wandered onto the veranda to watch the sunset. I sat on a wooden chair, watching as the colours changed; the sky faded from blue to purple, to pink, finally settling into apricot. The low sun was huge, and rested above the clear ocean; birds made their way home to roost for the night; a stray dog pottered about on the sand, looking for scraps. I went indoors to fetch some crisps for the flea-bitten mutt, and Jude came back out with me. We threw the food to the dog and watched as the sun sank below the horizon.

After darkness had fallen and stars began to appear, we changed our clothes and headed out for a late supper. The walk along the torch-lit path through the complex was romantic. Bugs danced around the lights and crickets chirped in the trees.

We walked slowly, listening to the nocturnal sounds. I could feel the night on my skin. It was amazing how quickly our complexions had turned from pasty white to a light shade of pink. My shoulders were a bit sore and Jude's nose had a healthy red glow. We chuckled at our Britishness.

We went to the hotel restaurant, deciding to save painting the town red for another night. It was nearly ten o'clock when we entered the hotel lobby. A couple of people were checking in at reception as we made our way, past a selection of potted plants, into the restaurant: everything was painted white. Each table had a candle on it, bathing the room in a gentle light. A young, feminine-looking man, wearing a white shirt with a black waistcoat and tie, showed us to a table near a glass wall that overlooked the bay. Until then, I hadn't realised the restaurant and lobby were on a slight hill, above the beachfront. I sat down and stared into the night – I had never seen so many stars. Without pollution, the world was a different place.

I was quickly brought back to earth by the snap of Jude's fingers.

'I thought I'd lost you for a minute.'

'Sorry, sorry. What does the menu look like?'

He poured himself a glass of cold water. 'It looks OK.'

It was some time until our food was served. We chatted happily about what we planned to do on our holiday.

He saw love in my eyes that night, more clearly than he'd done before; it was the first time he had trusted that I was really in love with him. He stopped mid-sentence and smiled. His lips parted as he began to say something, but I stopped him.

'Just promise me, you won't forget,' I half-whispered. 'Whatever happens, remember this for what it is.'

He shook his head and looked out over the dark sea.

'Don't be like that. Don't spoil it by talking about the end, or any of that bullshit. You're getting tragic on me and there's no need. We'll be back here for our fiftieth anniversary, you mark my words.'

I let out a throaty laugh and he turned to face me.

'You think about stuff like that? Have plans for us, do you?' I mocked.

'This is just the beginning, my girl.' He cocked one eyebrow and sipped his drink.

'We'll see,' I replied.

A look of anger swept across his face.

'Why do you have to be so fucking pessimistic all the time? Bloody hell, can't you just enjoy this? You're so busy thinking it's all going to go wrong and I'm going to be a disappointment, that you're missing it. This is it, right? Take your head out of your arse. *You know me,* remember?' He slammed his glass down so hard that some of the water jumped out and splashed onto his hand.

'Shit!' Jude shook the liquid off his fingers. I sat back and looked at him in shock. I was speechless.

'Jesus, just let's enjoy dinner, OK?' He wiped his hand with his napkin and began to calm down.

'Do you know what, Jude?' I replied with disgust. 'Fuck you. Enjoy your dinner, I've lost my appetite.'

And with that, I pushed back my chair and walked out of the restaurant, leaving him behind and paying no attention to the nosy eavesdroppers who had been listening and now watched as I stormed out, their faces like melting gargoyles.

My heart was racing as I hurried through the reception area. Outside, I broke into a run. I scrambled along the path and almost bumped into a room-service waiter holding an empty tray. Tears streamed down my face. I was overcome with embarrassment and anger. Then I came to the water. I removed my flip-flops and wandered barefoot along the sand. The hotel beach was deserted, except for a bonfire that burned in the distance. I took a few more steps towards the sea before crumpling in a heap on the sand, which was still giving off some heat. I felt like a fool: I was mortified that he thought I was determined to fuck it all up. A million doubts filled my head.

I knew I needed to go and find him. I wiped my tears and headed to our room to clean myself up before apologising.

I arrived at our cabin to find Jude sitting on the veranda step, smoking a cigarette. He looked at me and moved over, gesturing for me to sit beside him. I did so in silence. We sat for a long time, neither of us said anything. I could feel his disappointment in me.

'I'm sorry,' I said.

He turned to face me but I wouldn't look at him.

'You have to let go,' Jude sighed. 'This is real. Let me in, properly. I can't trust myself when I'm with you and you get like that. I just . . . I don't know what to do.' There was desperation and hopelessness in his voice.

'You don't. . .,' I swallowed, 'I want to believe you.'

'Go on.'

'Oh, fucking hell, here goes. I feel like I might suffocate. I love you so much, and I feel like a bloody fool.' I stared straight ahead. 'You say all the right things. It seems easy for you, but I'm scared, Jude. I'm really fucking scared.'

'I know that. That's why you put up the tough-guy front.'

'Yes, exactly, but if you knew . . .'

'If I knew what? If I knew how scared you were? I'd what? End it? Run away?'

'Yes,' I said quietly.

'Give me some credit. You don't get it, do you? I know about your front and I can see past it: I see the real you. Please, look at me.'

I couldn't respond. My body was frozen and I didn't move. He touched my chin and I flinched.

'Look at me, Annabel,' he said again. Slowly, I turned to face him. I knew, the moment I looked into his eyes, every barrier I had ever put up would be shattered.

'Look, I'm not expecting an easy ride. I'm sure there'll be hurdles, but I'm in this for the long haul. Do you understand what I'm saying to you? I fucking love you. Every time you do that dismissive thing, it kills me. You're not the only one who's scared, you know. This is bigger than both of us. We're going to need to work at it. But don't kill it before it's even begun. Just let me in. Otherwise, what is the point? What are we doing here?' He stopped and considered what he wanted to say.

'I'm not going to leave you, like Lucy or your dad.'

The statement lingered in the air.

It was too much for me. I burst into tears and Jude held me as I cried for my past. He gently rocked me and stroked my hair. My tears subsided but we remained seated in the same position for hours, cradling each other tightly, like our lives depended on it. We had said everything we needed to. As the time passed, a feeling of peace washed over me. I knew he felt it too.

We went into the condo and decided to toast our first proper argument by opening a bottle of vodka. I had calmed down but the emotion of the evening and our discussion had taken it out of us both, so we did what people on holiday do: we set about getting drunk.

The next thing I knew, Jude was gently shaking me from my slumber on the sofa, saying my name and whispering that we should go to bed. I nodded, and he led me by the hand. I got into bed and he disappeared into the bathroom. I was asleep by the time he came back.

***

I feel his hot breath on my neck. There is a stabbing pain in my stomach, no, lower than that, it's in my groin. My pelvic muscles feel like they are being torn. His weight is on top of me, heavy on my chest, making it harder to breath. This can't be happening. He is inside me. There is a damp patch on my neck from his saliva. He is grunting. Whispering into my ear.

'You like that, I'm in your cunt. Take it, take it.' He is licking me. My groin is dry and he is pushing harder, forcing entry. The pain is so new, I wonder if it is real. My thighs are trembling, shaking. I can smell him on me. Get him off! I scream inside my own head. I can't speak: I'm gagged with a filthy rag. He smells like fried eggs and dirt. His sweaty brow is so close to my face. If I could bite him, I would, but I can't move. He pushes harder. The rhythm of my rape is slow and steady. This is the longest moment of my life. My eyes are closed and my mind is fracturing. Maybe this is not happening. I float out of myself. I am watching a film. That can't be me. I am not shackled to a bench, in a damp cellar. I am not bleeding from my head. I am not missing a tooth. My mouth is not filled with blood. I have not been lying in my own vomit. He is not inside me: his penis is not pushing into my body, his skin is not up against mine, his stubble is not grating against my cheek. Open your eyes again. Open them, and you will see this is not real. *I open my eyes and I see it in the mirror, the reflection of a monster raping me. I can see his spotty, pale buttocks and the hair on his testicles. I am going to be sick. I am going to choke. Help me. I can't breathe, stop. Someone help me. I am going to die. This is my death. Oh fuck. And then I see it: the moon reflecting in the mirror. It is so beautiful. Its pale face wobbles with my tears. I must look at it.* Focus, focus on the moon. Don't look at the other face, the monster's face. *I feel my groin fill with warm liquid. He has finished. His sperm is inside me, white tadpoles infecting me. He is just lying there.* Get off! Get off me! *I close my eyes. I hoped to die right there, beneath the watery moon.*

I woke up exceptionally early the next morning; the sun was in its first stages of rising. Beams of light pushed through the clouds and bounced off the waves. The sea was still dark, but chinks of it were turning turquoise. Jude lay next to me, asleep, snoring with his mouth ajar. I could hear the morning birds calling to one another. I lay there for a while, listening to the land slowly wake up. I watched Jude's breathing, his chest rising and falling.

I lay there, thinking about the journey we had travelled since our first meeting. My mind whirled when I realised and accepted that he was 'the one'. But I still felt strange and out of time.

Some time passed before I decided to get up and shower. I stood beneath the heavy flow, letting the water fall onto my neck and down my back. Steam rose all around me and clouded the glass walls. I wrote his name in the condensation, only to watch it disappear as if it had never existed. I reached for my shampoo and lathered my hair, inhaling the scent of rosehips and honey. As the soap flowed down my body, I was alarmed by the sight of red gushing from my crotch. Blood poured out of me and pooled around my feet, dancing around the plughole. I closed my eyes at the horror, and when I opened them again I was clean. I had imagined it. The noise of the shower had become a thud and I was suffering with a hangover. I flipped off the water and stepped out onto the cool white tiles; I slipped on Jude's cotton dressing gown.

I wandered out of the bathroom and picked up a packet of cigarettes that were lying on the bedside table next to Jude, who was still dozing. It was nearly seven and I decided to go outside and watch the day begin. I sat on the steps of our porch and listened to the world and the sounds of the ocean. I heard birds and, in the distance, I could make out a faint hum of music coming from the hotel reception. A jogger passed by on the beach as I finished my cigarette and stubbed it out in the sand. As the embers flared and died, I felt a flicker of sadness. Then I went inside and got back into bed.

Jude was still asleep as I quietly crept under the sheets and lay down. The sun was now up and shining directly through our window. A streak of light spread across the bed and highlighted his face and every hair on his head. I watched him wake up. The light had invaded his dream world and brought him into mine. He let out a yawn before opening his eyes. He smiled at me, reached for my hand, and drifted off to sleep again.

Suddenly, I felt aware of my nakedness. On the back of a chair was his pale-blue T-shirt. I felt at home in his clothes and slipped the soft cotton over my head. It smelled of his skin and I breathed it in as I put it on. It was too big for me, but I didn't mind.

I watched Jude stir and wished him a good morning. He yawned and sat up.

'Christ, my mouth is dry,' he said.

'Hang on, I'll get you a glass of water.' I sprung up and made my way into the bathroom.

'You're a saint,' he said.

I gave him the water and he took a long gulp before putting it on his bedside table. I rested my hand on his knee.

'How you feeling?'

'Pretty rough.' He reached out for the glass of water. 'I think I may need to sleep a bit longer. What's the time?'

'Quite early,' I said. I watched him drinking and decided I needed to say something important.

'You realise that, one day, when we're old and grey, we'll be able to tell our children about this place.' I stared up at the fan above our bed, slowly circling around and around. 'Maybe even bring them here.'

'You really believe that?' He sounded surprised.

'I think I do.'

He reached for a cigarette.

'Fate, destiny, whatever you want to call it, I think we're just in the right place, at the right time,' I said.

'You think this was meant to be?'

'I think we are offered the left or the right path, and whichever one we take is the one we were meant to travel. Everything happens for a reason, I'm sure.'

'It's too bloody early for this now,' Jude grunted, and pulled the covers over his head.

There was a knock at the door – room service had arrived with our breakfast. I pulled one of the sheets off the bed and wrapped it around my lower body; I welcomed the waitress and took the heavy tray. Once she'd gone, I reached for a silk cushion and playfully hurled it at Jude. I suggested we venture down to the main beach to spend some time soaking up the sun, and follow that with a leisurely walk around the market.

After breakfast, we changed into our swimsuits and went for a quick dip before making our way towards the town. The sky was overcast and the sea was rougher than it had been.

Jude stopped to pick up a stone, feeling its glossy circumference in his hand for a moment, then violently launched it out into the grey-blue waves. I watched the pebble tumble through the air and land with a splash at an impressive distance. I bent down to find him another. I found two more and offered them to him. He smiled, and again hurled them into the watery distance. I remained squatting, watching him; he stood, gazing out at the ocean, a far-away look in his eyes. I wandered up and down the shore collecting more stones, but he didn't move – he just stood with his arms folded, looking out into nothingness. After about ten minutes, I approached him and dropped my pebble collection on the sand. I stood behind him and put my hands on his upper arms. He was at least six inches taller than me and I was very aware of this as I planted a kiss between his shoulder blades. He fingered his last pebble for a moment and offered it to me.

'Here you go,' he said, 'throw it.'

I nodded as I took a step away from him, and launched the stone with all my might. I watched as it cut through the air, plummeting to a watery grave.

'Laid to rest,' I said, moving closer to him. He wrapped his arms around me and held me close, as if we were caught in a cold wind.

'Let's get going,' I suggested.

***

It's daylight. The room is still dark. The window lets in hardly any natural light. Probably a good thing. The little I can see is horrific enough. There is dried blood on my thighs. It has come from my aching crotch. It is sticky down there. I feel like my womb, my ovaries, everything has been pulled out of me. I feel so hollow, like my organs have been replaced with a black hole of pain. I can smell his semen in the air, musty, like rancid bedsheets. My knees are black and blue. My wrists throb from all the tugging I have done, trying to free myself. It is useless. I am not strong enough. It would take the strength of one thousand men to free me. I am so cold. I have splinters in my back, in my bottom, from the wooden bench. My stomach looks so flat and empty. I haven't eaten for hours. I am wasting away. My head is pounding. I am tender all over. Think, for fuck's sake, think! The room looks different from last night. I can see spider webs above me in the beams. I hate spiders. Don't think about them. Concentrate on trying to get away. *I search every inch of my prison cell. The room is bare, apart from the bench, the mirror and me. The camera is still there. Look at it. The red light is on. It's flashing. I'm being recorded. Panic floods me again.* Am I being watched? *Revulsion creeps over my skin, and I shudder. He has removed my gag. I slowly open my jaw. It's so stiff. My throat hurts. I need water. I scream, 'Help me! Pleeease', over and over. I say it so many times that the words begin to sound foreign. My throat is completely raw. I can't keep this up. I look into the camera. 'Please, bring me a drink, some water, please, I'm begging you. Water.'* Are you there? Are you watching me right now, you sick fuck? *I close my eyes. The smell of my agony envelops me again. I want to cry, but I don't. My eyes are too dry. They feel like sand. My body can't spare the tears. Dry sobs echo against my misery.*

***

134

The clouds were sparse and I could feel the sun burning down on my shoulders and neck. A lizard dashed up one of the walls as we made our way down to the beach to watch another sunset. Each one was so different; I would never get bored of seeing the light fade. Sometimes the sky was drenched with beams and coloured clouds, sometimes it was clear and gradual. At the same time every evening, just as the sun was beginning to set, the beach would empty – except for a few couples scattered along the shore, walking together, inhaling the romance beneath the vanishing sun and waxing moon.

We walked along the shore, our feet tickled by the playful waves, making our way back to our hut. The sea was bluish-purple; in the distance I saw a ship approaching. The light from it floated above the water, like an extra-terrestrial investigating the planet. I sat on our porch and watched its slow journey towards us. Jude showered. I should have been blissfully happy, but I still could not shake the uneasy feeling in my gut.

I did my best to push it away as Jude opened the door and emerged, a clean white towel wrapped around his waist. I noticed he had really caught the sun. His copper-toned skin made the darkness of his eyes stand out more than usual and I caught my breath. He rested one of his hands on his stomach. I smirked at him.

'What's that look for?'

'You'll laugh at me.'

'Belle.' Jude frowned.

'OK, it's stupid, and you'll laugh, but OK. I was just wondering what our children might look like.'

I paused, waiting to defend my fantasies.

'Your looks and my brain, I reckon,' he said with a tantalising smile.

'Ha, they're screwed then, aren't they?'

He bent down and nuzzled his face into my neck, gently biting, while he pulled at the string of my bikini.

'Oh, fuck off!'

135

He laughed and sat behind me, bringing his strong legs around my hips. I leaned into him.

'I'm a girl who has grown up on a diet of fairy tales,' I explained, 'and nothing less will do.'

We stayed there for a while, sharing a cigarette and admiring the stars that pricked the sapphire sky around the moon. He softly, and tunelessly, hummed a song. It made me smile: I suppose it's the little things that make a person who they are.

I was finally feeling relaxed, when Jude suggested we should stroll into town to grab a bite to eat and try and get hold of some weed. I thought that was a great idea, and made my way into our room to wash and dress. Jude sat on the bed the whole time, one eye on the news channel, the other watching me.

'Ready?'

'Yup.' I nodded.

'Let's make a move then.' He slapped his knees as he got up from the bed and reached for the room key.

I stretched out my hand and took hold of his as he closed the door behind us; we set off into the warm night. A light wind blew in from across the ocean and ruffled the palm trees – they shook in sync with one another, and in time with the lapping waves that crashed onto the shore and pulled the sands back out with them. I could tell it was calm beneath the waves; I imagined the marine life, swimming in and out of the corals that littered the blue oblivion.

When we reached the town centre it felt as if it had been a longer walk than usual. Light from various bars flooded the streets, busy with people chatting and laughing. A local man passed by, guiding a young elephant with him, selling rides to tourist children. Although the animal didn't seem to mind, Jude said it should be with the herd, walking free in the forest. His love of animals was another trait of his that I adored.

I spotted a cosy restaurant a few yards away and pulled him in. The barman nodded at a table and signalled for us to take a seat. I threw my handbag over the back of my chair and sat opposite Jude. The menus were already on the table and Jude enthusiastically unfolded the laminated card to inspect his options. I observed his face: I wanted to remember that exact moment. Memories are built from observations and feelings, and I wanted to absorb every ounce of him and have it carved into my mind.

I was still staring at him when a waiter appeared and rudely demanded that we order. I rapidly scanned the list of dishes and picked one out. We also ordered a couple of beers, and a jug of water to share, which were delivered to our table with lightning speed. I made a toast to Christmas as we took long gulps of the cool, refreshing beer. The bubbles swelled and slipped down my throat.

It didn't take long to get some pot and a bottle of cheap rum. Numerous men had been trying to force drugs on us from the moment we set foot out of our hotel resort. We were both aware it was risky – winding up in a Thai jail wasn't tempting – but we were fairly sure if we went back to the hut with our stash, and remained discreet, we'd be fine. We had tobacco and papers at the hotel, so, after we had securely stored the weed in the pouch of my handbag, we made our way back to our room.

We wandered onto the porch with icy rum cocktails and a joint. I brought out three candles and lined them up; we sat at the table, sipping our drinks and sharing the joint. In a place like that it was a risky thing to do. The thick blue smoke poured from the end and trailed off into the night. I took a long hit and held my breath, counting to ten in my head, slowly releasing the remnants from my lungs. It hit me almost immediately. Jude followed suit, spluttering, which set me off in a fit of childish laughter. Soon, we were both giggling uncontrollably. We took it in turns, laughing so hard that at times we had to stop to catch our breath. I suggested we take photographs of ourselves, smoking and holding up our drinks, with the backdrop of the moonlit beach. Jude stumbled from his seat and went in search of the camera. I sat, feeling light-headed and happy, enjoying my intoxication and the blurred world. He came back, sat very close to me and held out the camera. A click and a bright flash later, we were laughing hysterically again.

We absorbed the rest of the night as if we were sponges. The night closed in around us, above the roar of the magnetic waves, as the last of the candles died. The bottle of rum had speedily diminished, on a par with our self-control. Jude's hands had begun to wander and I felt his eyes on me as I stared, blankly, searching for answers to questions that I hadn't yet asked. I reached for the bottle and refreshed our drinks while he kissed my shoulders.

It was the most distant I had ever felt from him. Something was there in my mind but I couldn't put my finger on it. It was the feeling you get when you think you might have forgotten to do something – like turn off the oven. I didn't like the way it was trying to take over my senses. I did my best to disregard it and turned my concentration to Jude – he was high and drunk. I realised that I was also under the influence of an unusual high. I reached for my cigarettes, certain that, if I smoked one, I would be able to evade the panic that was trying to get a grip of me.

Jude tugged at the towel I had draped around me. I didn't really feel like sex but I kissed him anyway. Throwing myself into the moment, I let my towel drop to the sandy wooden floor, and straddled him on the chair. With my legs wrapped around his waist, he picked me up and carried me into our bedroom, slamming the door shut behind us with his foot.

Afterwards I felt better, as we lay on the bed, sharing a cigarette and staring up at the ceiling. I laughed and so did Jude. We had behaved like animals and the dirty pleasure had felt good, but for some reason my crotch was aching. We hadn't been that rough and I wondered what was wrong.

'I love you.' I planted kisses all over his face and pushed away the uneasy feeling in my stomach.

'I know you do.'

He didn't need to say it. I knew he loved me too. Just after midnight, I fell asleep in his arms, listening to the sound of his heart beating.

***

I can feel his presence in the room. He is lurking in the shadows, moving from one to another, circling me like a shark. I try not to look in his direction. I am frozen with fear, gripped by a sudden cold sweat. My heart aches and the lump in my throat is growing. I hold my breath and fear my lungs will explode. I can't bear the sound of my own breath. I am trying to hear him, to get a sense of his breathing. Why won't he show himself? Is he really a monster? Could my mind handle seeing its face? *I realise I am still holding my breath and have to gasp for air. I cough and splutter and it hurts. I am willing myself to be somewhere else. I picture another reality and try to feel something new, something good. I still hear him, though. His rough skin stinks up the room, and I am suffocating once more. He is breathing through his nose: nasal breaths rattle like snakes. I am trying to be brave. He is not a shark, there are no snakes. I feel my eyes begin to shake in my skull. I am having some sort of fit. I need to snap out of it. This is not happening. This is not happening.*

It was late in the afternoon and through the window I could see the sky turning a vibrant shade of purple. Thick clouds collected in the distance and were making their way towards the island: a storm was brewing. We'd had a lazy day, lying in bed watching television, ,and had planned to eat at one of the restaurants in town, then go to the beachfront for a night of drinking and dancing. There was only so much of the news channel we could handle, so we got out of bed and filled the bath. We slipped into the warm, bubbling water and lay there soaking, listening to the stereo. Steam had filled the room by the time we finally stepped out and began to get ready. I stood in front of the mirror and applied my make-up, while Jude dried his hair next to me. By the time we left our room the sun had begun to set and the sky was thick with dark, looming rain clouds; thunder boomed in the distance. The uneasy feeling returned, and I felt like I was being pulled from one reality, into another.

We walked through the complex and into the centre of the town, wandering the sandy streets, looking in shop windows and passing people who were sat eating in restaurants. Taking a sharp left turn, we trekked up a winding street until we reached a restaurant we had spotted the day before. The balcony was adorned with glowing lanterns and gentle music drifted out. We went in to find a number of very low tables. The air was close and it felt like the sky was about to open up. Jude chose a table near the window. There were no chairs and, having taken off our shoes, we sat on cushions on the floor.

The hostess appeared and handed us menus. We ordered a jug of water, and a beer each, before inspecting the list of dishes. I wasn't very familiar with authentic Thai cuisine and couldn't wait to try it. We giggled at the questionable English the menu was written in, and decided on green curry and jasmine rice. Modest plates of piping hot food were soon delivered to our table. They smelled fantastic and were quickly devoured. It took real restraint to stop ourselves from licking the warm plates clean.

Jude paid the bill and we left the restaurant just as it began to spot with rain. Despite the oncoming downpour, the air was still humid and close. We made a hasty dash towards the main street to find a bar to settle in for a few hours. By the time we reached cover, hard rain was falling. I smelled electricity in the air. Lightning was imminent. We got to the bar just as there was a loud crash in the sky. Tourists stood by the windows, watching in awe at nature unleashed. Jude and I quickly ordered drinks and found an empty table where we watched the storm take a grip of the island. Streaks of brilliant blue flashed across the bay. Each time lightning struck, the boom from the clashing clouds highlighted the bass from speakers in the far corner. In between the thrashes of lightning, I thought I could hear someone breathing heavily. I looked around the room for confirmation that what I was hearing was real, but found nothing. Only a strange green light permeated the room, emanating from bulbs set high in the ceiling.

The storm stopped as quickly as it had started. Jude and I watched as the transvestite prostitutes reappeared on the streets, beckoning to passing tourists, who were also being harassed by young children forcing strings of flowers around their necks and demanding payment.

We drank for a few hours before we ventured to the beach. One of the barmen told us that each night, fires were lit on the sand and rugs laid out around them. The pair of us wobbled along the slippery street until we reached the shore. There were burrowed pits in the sand all along the beach, each contained burning fires, and faded rugs were strewn out around them. It was already busy and more tourists continued to arrive. Jude and I managed to find a patch near one of the fires that wasn't crammed with people. There was another youngish couple on the other side of the fire, snuggled up together. A light breeze blew in over the now becalmed waves and neon lights made patterns on the sand.

Jude told me to stay put while he went over to one of the many busy beach bars to get us a drink, but the couple opposite made me feel uncomfortable – I felt like the guy was watching me.

He had a thick neck and cold eyes. He looked like a farmer, or a trucker, and there was something oddly familiar about his large frame.

Jude returned, balancing the drinks. He was unsteady on his feet due to the soft sand and the effect of cocktails we'd already drunk. He sat down and leaned on an elbow, stretching out a brown leg. Silence hung in the air.

There was a good twelve feet between them and us, and we quickly fell into our own private conversations. I leaned my head back onto Jude's chest and we chatted about the stars that were appearing in the sky. That man stared at me in a way that made me self-conscious. I could feel his eyes on my body and I didn't like it. Jude didn't appear to notice the unwelcome attention I was receiving.

We lay on the woven rugs by the glowing fire, which spat every now and then, sending a mass of tiny red sparks into the air around us, floating up like minute spirits.

A hawker approached, selling beaded jewellery. I wasn't bowled over by his wares, but I found myself buying a cheap wooden bracelet so he would leave us alone. I handed the trinket to Jude, who thanked me and slipped it on.

The alcohol was kicking in but I got up to get us another drink anyway. There was a string of buzzing bars and I headed straight for the quietest. When I got back to the fire, I lay down next to Jude and sipped my cold drink. We both stared in silence into the flickering flames.

Jude took a sip of his beer and spat it into the fire in a jet from his pursed lips. The fire roared and fizzled. All I could do was laugh, as he sat back looking pleased with himself.

'Silly sod,' I said.

'Oi!' He slipped a hand around my neck and pulled my mouth down to his. I could taste the beer on his warm breath. The rest of the night was lost to drunken excess. Eventually, we found our way back to the hut and we both passed out on the bed, fully clothed.

***

I am trying to work it out. Trying to understand how I got here, how it all started. The pain and the blood are stopping me from seeing it clearly. I am aching and numb at the same time. Agony has cast a shadow over my ability to think clearly. Then I think I hear him again, moving around nearby, dragging his heavy feet. Show yourself to me, let me see your twisted, horrendous face. Evil lives and breathes. Let me see what my nightmares are made of. The darkness is ready to come alive. I feel it pulsing with all that is nasty and wrong in the world. It wants to own me, to know my secrets, to make me part of it. My anguish gives it the fuel it needs. I am going to burn in its fire, in his fire. My skin is so cold but the blood in my veins feels like boiling over. It swishes around my body and I think it's going too fast, travelling through me like a train, not stopping. I can't get off this ride and I cannot see an end. I didn't ask for this. Please, someone help me. Why am I here? The shackles are pinching my wrists and his hands suddenly tighten around my throat. Where did he come from? The darkness came alive and he was born. I choke. White spots dance in front of my eyes. His hands are hot and brutal against my skin. My mouth is open, trying to say something, to beg for my life, and my tongue stabs the air looking for hope. He releases his grip and life flows back into my head. My cheeks feel flushed and warm. I can sense him grinning. I keep my eyes closed and wish myself away from that place. His hands are on my breasts, stroking them. Pinching and squeezing my nipples. I yelp and moan as he works his way back up, around my neck, and again his grip begins to tighten. I try to prepare myself for it again, but it is impossible. I wasn't ready for coping with life and I am not ready for death. He knows this and it gives him his power. He feeds off every hopeless thought I have and he grows stronger.

It was Christmas Eve. The island wasn't huge, it could have been explored in a matter of days, but we spent most of our waking hours alone in our cabin, or lying together on an abandoned stretch of beach. It was almost too perfect.

I watched Jude looking for a T-shirt. He pulled the brown and cream striped cotton over his head and reached for a cigarette. I knew he could feel my eyes burning into him as he brought the lighter to his lips and he broke the silence.

'Breakfast will be here soon,' he said. I could sense there was something else, bubbling below the surface, and he was refusing to share it with me.

'Great.' I hid my frustration. He smiled reassuringly and turned on the television, pretending to be interested by whatever drivel it was spouting. I knew there was something on his mind but I bit my tongue. Women talk too much, and men never say enough. Jude and I were no different.

A while later there was a timid knock at the door. Jude jumped out of his seat and sprinted to answer it.

'Yes?' he said, opening the door. A shy-looking bellboy stood holding a tray.

'Please put it down over there.' Jude pointed to the table on the porch.

I pulled my hair into a bun and left the cool, air-conditioned space to join him outside. Jude sat at his usual breakfast place, but the look on his face was far from normal. He presented the tray to me with a proud flourish. On it, there was a vase of red orchids, a bottle of champagne and two delicate flutes. The assorted fruits had been arranged into a heart and the pancakes had been cut out to match. I was speechless, which was a rare occurrence.

'Do you like it?'

'Well . . . I . . . yes,' I faltered. 'What have I done to deserve this?'

'It's Christmas, isn't it?'

'Yes, it is, kind of.'

'Champagne, my lady?' He cocked a glass and let the sparkling bubbles fill it.

The whole holiday had gradually become more like a fantasy. His dark brown eyes sparkled like they must have done when he was a boy.

We tucked into the food. The fruit somehow tasted sweeter than it had before, but then I choked on some pips. I hastened to catch my breath and, as sweat stung my forehead, my eyes searched Jude's face for help. He remained motionless, looking out over the ocean. I was still choking, desperate for breath: I thought I was going to die. Eventually the tightness in my throat released and I could breathe again. Strangely, Jude didn't seem to notice.

'I've got a special day organised for us. It's a surprise, but we are on a bit of a timetable, so get yourself organised for a day out,' he said, as he piled our plates onto the tray in a half-hearted attempt to clean up. His urgency encouraged me to get a move on. I wondered why he seemed so flustered, but I was touched by his thoughtfulness and attention to detail. Excitement rippled through the room as we threw our belongings into a khaki bag. I had no idea where we were going, or what he had planned, but the anticipation was exhilarating and I was overcome by the eternal battle my mind faced. Inside, my body was awash with nerves.

As we stepped into the sunshine, he took my hand and led the way. We walked barefoot, our toes sieving through the fine sand. It was still early – despite the air-conditioning, we had been woken up by the rising heat. Jude led me along the beach into town. I had to fight the urge to ask where we were going.

Eventually, we reached a shack that was surrounded by mopeds for hire. Jude went in and returned holding a set of keys and two helmets.

'I'm driving. All you have to do is get on the back and hold on,' he said. He threw his leg over a pale blue moped.

'That much I think I can manage.' I clambered on behind him and put on the helmet. Feeling claustrophobic, I wrapped my arms around his waist and gripped him firmly. He started the engine, which grunted loudly before settling into a repetitive chug.

'Right, here we go.'

I was nervous: we zipped through the bumpy streets, passing a buzz of shops, tourists, locals and the market. We passed a residential area we hadn't seen before and finally got out of town, weaving our way through the dense shrubland. The road wasn't anything more than a dirt track and we had to manoeuvre around large potholes. The bike grunted with resistance as we climbed a hill. Thick trees lined the road and I half expected to see snakes dripping from the branches.

As we made our ascent, the breeze became more noticeable. We had climbed one of the steepest roads, and were able to look down over the town. The sea was a true blue and sparkled as if it had been sprinkled with diamonds. We were far above the rocks that burst from the seabed and had looked so huge from the shore. We gazed down on our hotel and the people lying on the beach – they were as small as ants.

We drove for about fifteen minutes until we reached the top of the highest peak on our part of the island. Jude pulled over onto a flat stretch at the side of the road and we got off. I quickly removed my helmet and it became instantly easier to breathe. A breeze cooled my sweaty brow.

'Look at that.' Jude pointed at the view below us.

'I know, incredible.' I crossed the road and stood next to him at the edge of a sheer drop. We stood in silence for a long time and surveyed what felt like our kingdom. Then, as if from nowhere, a white cloud appeared and covered the sun. The land was under a giant shadow until the light found a chink to shine through.

A thick beam of light was projected onto one of the smallest, empty bays. It was almost like witnessing a divine intervention. It was stunning.

'Holy shit. Do you see?' I said.

'Sure.'

'That almost convinces me there is a God.'

'There's something there, something bigger than us,' he admitted.

'You're a big softie under all of that bravado.'

He smiled and said nothing.

'Let's go there,' I suggested, pointing at the bay.

'Good idea. We'll have a picnic on the beach. Come on then.' Jude went over to the bike and put his helmet on. I climbed on the back and adjusted the strap on my helmet, squeezing his ribs as we set off.

To my relief, there were no more hills to navigate, it was all downhill. We bobbed along the uneven road and soon were lost. Every bay we came across was the wrong one. It felt like being trapped in the twilight zone. We must have made at least three wrong turns before we finally found the right place. As we had hoped, the bay was unoccupied. Jude parked the bike up against the cliff, where we could keep a close eye on it. We wandered onto the sand: it was our own private beach and it felt like being ship-wrecked. Due to the shape of the island, and the position of that cove, we were unable to see the town or any other evidence of human existence from there. It was deadly quiet, except for the sound of the waves unfolding onto the shore. I kept rubbing my wrists. They were throbbing and sore. They had been bothering me for days. As I looked down, I noticed rings of bruises forming around my wrists, like red and purple bracelets, and I wondered what was happening to me.

Jude dragged our bag to a spot near the rocks and spread our towels out next to each other. I took off everything except my bikini bottoms. He sat watching me. I decided to move into the shallow water. He stayed on the beach, staring at me. I dunked my head under the water and flicked my hair out of my face, sending a spray of tiny droplets flying. I swam out a little further, until the water was up to my waist. I turned, and watched him watching me. He had propped himself up against the hot rock, his legs were stretched out in front of him and his arms were crossed over his ribs. He had a strange smile on his face and his head was slightly tilted.

'Come in! The water's lovely!' I called out.

He nodded, took a sip of water, and stripped down to his swimming shorts. He reached into the bag, removed two sets of snorkelling gear and waded into the water. I waited until he was inches away from me and launched myself at him, wrapping my legs around his torso. He let go of the snorkels and they drifted down to the seabed. He picked me up and threw me into the water. I sank like a stone and had to fight panic. When I came up we both laughed, then he dived under the water to retrieve our snorkels. We swam further out until there was about twelve feet of water below us. Jude passed me one of the sets of goggles and a snorkel. We linked hands and gently dunked our heads.

We saw a radiant underwater world: we passed shoals of rainbow-coloured fish, of all shapes and sizes, which swam about us aimlessly, unaffected by our presence in their domain. The seabed was littered with various rocks from which bizarre creatures would appear and potter about. Suddenly, Jude let go of my hand and dived to the bottom. The fish made a hasty dash out of his way as he glided through the turquoise water. I saw his hand reach out to retrieve an uninhabited shell from the sand, then he sprang up through the water like a rocket. We met again at the surface and removed our blowholes so we could speak.

'Look at this!' he exclaimed, holding out the clean pink shell for me to examine.

'It's amazing.' I stroked the smooth surface.

'For you,' he said, with pride, like a caveman returning from a successful hunt.

'Thank you.' I hugged the shell to my chest. 'I shall treasure it.'

We had been in the water for a long time. I followed as Jude powered his way through the water towards the beach. It was a struggle to keep up and my shark phobia was starting to take hold.

Ten minutes later, we trudged out of the water, limbs tingling and aching.

Jude walked over to the towel and lay down, wiping his wet ginger curls from his face. He looked so different like that. Beads of salt water rested on his chest, and his shorts clung to his groin and thighs. I stretched out beside him and put down the shell. I could feel the sun evaporating the water on my skin, leaving a fine layer of dry salt. Jude suggested we had our picnic.

Once our bellies were filled, we spread ourselves out on the sand to sunbathe. We remained securely planted on our island of towels. I sat with my legs tucked up to my chest and looked out: the bay couldn't have been more than forty feet across, and on the opposite side, a piece of driftwood sat on the sand. It looked like a small bench, ideal for two.

The sun shone on us for an hour, before it disappeared behind the vast rock face we had settled near. As the day wore on, we watched as the tide went out, farther and farther away with each wave. The sky became a beautiful shade of peach that faded to blue, our figures eventually becoming silhouettes against the backdrop of the sunset.

The journey back into town was effortless, and we drove along a road that followed the coastline until we found a landmark we recognised. The road gleamed like a mirror with the low light. I sat, holding on to Jude, watching the sunset develop. A mild breeze came in with the evening air.

We returned the bike to the rental shack, settled our bill, and headed to our cabin. The last crescent of sun sank below the watery horizon as we walked along the beach. The ghost moon was already in the sky, close to being full; it was enormous and the craters were visible. Seeing both the sun and moon at the same time wasn't that unusual, but the sheer size of them both made me feel insignificant. It was the perfect end to a lovely day.

We got back to our room, I threw the keys on the bed and Jude went to run a bath. I presumed we would be spending a quiet night in. He called out that he had booked a table for us at one of the restaurants overlooking the bay. I would have happily settled for room service and a pay-per-view film, but I gave in to his enthusiasm, fighting my inexplicable exhaustion, and hopped into the bath with him.

He spent an unusually long time getting ready, running wax through his hair and making it crunchy. Since he was making a special effort, I slipped into a pair of high heels and an emerald green strapless dress. As I pinned my hair up and applied some make-up, I noticed that the bruises around my wrists were bluer than ever. I wondered why Jude hadn't noticed them. They throbbed and I felt strange all over.

He spent ages perfecting his hair and trimming his beard. When he had finished, he smelled fantastic and looked wonderful. He wore a pale blue and white striped shirt, with jeans and a belt.

By the time we left our cabin it was nearly nine o'clock. A perfect night's sky greeted us. Stars littered the rich blue backdrop and the moon looked down on us from her cosmic throne.

'It's almost Christmas day,' I said, as we walked through the complex, under the dark cover of the trees' silhouettes. Every now and then we would catch a glimpse of the jealous moon, watching us through the thicket.

Jude had arranged for a taxi and, despite a bumpy journey, every moment in the car was worth it when we pulled up outside the restaurant. The building was elaborately built from wood, exquisitely painted in red and gold. The establishment was large and it looked old; I wondered if it was a former monastery.

A woman in traditional Thai dress greeted us. She bowed her head and we followed her inside; she appeared to float along the floor. Jude offered me his arm as we entered. The hostess led us through a long, wide corridor towards a room that was lit entirely by candles. An ornamental fountain sat in the middle of the room, and finely detailed bamboo had been painted on cream silk hangings on the walls. There were only twelve tables in the restaurant, all evenly spaced around the fountain, and five of them were occupied.

The room had a subtle smell of incense, and gentle music floated from some speakers. We were shown to a table on the far side of the fountain. A waitress came and placed a champagne bucket on the table, bowed, and backed away from us. Jude poured us both a glass and made a toast to Christmas, and to us. I raised my glass and smiled in appreciation, taking in the view: we were high up on a cliff edge. Below us, the bay curled round and the street illuminations looked like flickering lighters at a concert. The sea was calm and as black as the night.

Soon, the waitress returned to explain there was no menu, and customers were served the speciality of the day. I was eager to discover what culinary delights lay ahead.

Jude and I sipped the champagne and chatted while we waited for our undisclosed starter to arrive. I was starving, as if I hadn't eaten for days. It wasn't a hunger born of greed, it felt more like a basic need. My stomach was rumbling and I felt suddenly very thin.

A platter laden with various items arrived at the table. Pieces of tempura, skewers of chicken satay, sizzling king prawns in spices, and a variety of sauces in ceramic bowls were spread out over our table. We started to eat the mouth-watering morsels; I binged like a creature possessed.

The next course was a mildly spiced crab soup – it was fresh and tasted of the sea. Seconds after our soup bowls had been cleared away, two new plates were brought over. They contained pieces of tenderly cooked pork in a mild sauce, with crispy, spiced vegetables. It was heaven. Every ingredient tasted and looked beautiful. Dessert was fruit served with sticky coconut rice. The more I ate, the hungrier I felt. I couldn't explain my bizarre appetite. My desire to eat was matched only by my unquenchable thirst. I put it down to having spent too long in the sun.

We spent at least two hours enjoying our dinner, and in that time we unwittingly put away a bottle of champagne and a bottle of red wine. Jude paid the bill and we got into a taxi, feeling light-headed as we made our way back to the hotel.

We heard a band playing indoors and were drawn towards the cocktail lounge. The room was brimming with other tourists, all drinking and celebrating the imminent arrival of the festive hour. We joined them, and found a vacant table near the plastic token Christmas tree – there to accommodate the Western travellers. Purple and pink baubles hung from its branches, among a mass of bright, flashing fairy lights. It was wonderfully tacky.

It had been a long day, and we slowly rocked in silence on the dance floor. Wrapped around each other, we swayed to the familiar tune of 'Have Yourself a Merry Little Christmas'. Then Jude took his cheek away from mine and looked me in the eye, staring, as if he was searching for a lost possession.

'What's wrong?' I asked.

'Nothing's wrong. Nothing at all.'

'Good. Same here.'

The song continued; the disco lights shone over us in snowflake patterns. We rocked for a minute longer before he said, 'Marry me.'

My immediate reaction was shock, and then I decided I must have misheard him. I looked up with uncertainty.

'I mean it,' he half laughed, 'will you marry me?'

A blur of thoughts shot through my mind as I searched his face. He let go of me and got down on one knee.

'It's simple,' he said. 'We are meant for each other. Marry me.' He held my hand. The stupid lights danced around him on the floor.

'Yes. Yes!' I pulled him up from his knees and sniffed back happy tears. 'I can't believe this!' The enormity of the moment began to sink in as we walked back to our cabin.

Jude came out of the bathroom and dimmed the lights over our bed. Sinking into the sheets next to me, he pulled a small, faded velvet box from his pocket and stared at it, fixedly.

'This belonged to my grandmother. It's a family heirloom, a tradition. Now it will belong to you,' he said.

I stayed quiet as he opened the box and removed an antique diamond ring. He took my hand and slipped the ring on my finger: it was the perfect fit, but I was reminded of cold metal shackles; I pushed the feeling away as we held hands and looked at it. There it was: tangible confirmation of the evening's events, something solid that meant how we felt, and what we said, was real. Outside, a meteor shower lit up the black night.

'It's beautiful,' I said.

'Just like you.'

We lay on the bed and slowly undressed each other. He kissed my neck and I grasped his hair. We made love, savouring every movement, every sensation: taste, smell and touch. It played out in slow motion. Afterwards, we shared a cigarette and held on to each other in the darkness.

'I feel like I should wake up now to find this has been a dream,' I said, as I drifted into another restless sleep.

***

He was standing over me and I watched as he picked up the hammer and held it by its head; without any warning, he thrust the handle into my burning groin. I squealed like a lamb being slaughtered. He pulled it back and thrust harder. Every time my muscles would tense, and every time it hurt more.

I opened my eyes and watched this new type of rape take place in the mirror. Everything was covered in long shadows, and out of the darkness I found the moon again. I forgot to think about the pain and just lay there, my eyes fixated on the lunar brilliance. I was so transfixed by the iridescent glow, I didn't notice him remove the wooden-handled tool from my bruised parts. Out of the corner of my eye, I saw his reflection in the mirror as he raised the hammer above his head. I turned, just in time to see him bring it crashing down on my kneecap.

The noise it made was unlike any other I had ever heard: it was a crack and pop rolled into one. The reflex sent uncontrollable vibrations up and down my leg. My eyes bulged and my vision was pricked with bright white spots. It felt as if a million shards of glass were digging into my knee, scraping against my skin and bone. It took a few minutes for my sight to return to normal and for the awfulness to sink in. I couldn't bring myself to look at the damage but I knew I had to. A morbid curiosity crept through me. I felt like the driver who stops to look at a fatal accident on the motorway, only this time, I was the victim as well as the voyeur.

Looking down at the mess, my mind began to somersault. Where the bump of my knee had once been, was now a dented crater of bloody tissue. White splinters of fractured bone stuck out at various angles. An icy coldness punctured me. I watched as my leg jerked and twitched; the nerves in my knee were mangled beyond repair. I continued staring at it with such revolted concentration, I didn't notice my torturer leave the room.

Part Three

The reflection of the sun in the mirror blinded me. I winced, and tried to turn away but it was hopeless: I was still trapped. Once my eyes had adjusted, I looked around the room: this wasn't where I was meant to be. I squinted, trying hard to replace the image with a happier one. I closed my eyes and counted to ten, but when I opened them I was still in that place. I was in the cellar. I looked at my hand, searching for the ring, Jude's grandmother's ring. It wasn't there. *Oh my god, he's stolen it.*

'Give it back!' I screamed out. 'Give it back to me!'

I pulled on the chains so hard that I thought I might snap my wrists. Suddenly, I found some strength. Sweat trickled down my face and the stale smell of fear flooded my nostrils. I stopped tensing and lay back on the bench. I knew I needed to calm down, get a grip of myself, and try to think rationally. I took some long, deep breaths and exhaled slowly. I repeated the process until my heart rate returned to a steady pace.

I scanned the room. Every shadow had a familiar feel; each brick, each cobweb, now looked more real than before. This dream was becoming more terrifying by the minute. The muted feeling in my head had subsided, but the hunger in my belly and my unquenchable thirst were getting more unbearable by the second. I looked in the mirror for a very long time. I inspected every wrinkle, each little graze and bruise – I looked strangely real. My hair was so dirty it would have been impossible for anyone to tell I was blonde. My eye make-up had formed dark, muddy rivers down my face. The reflection staring back at me looked confused and lost.

'I am not meant to be here,' the image said. 'Get me back to Jude. Wake up, please, just wake up.' But nothing happened. I tried so hard to get back to that place. *I will wake up, when it is time. Just ride it out until then, like you have been. You'll see, it will all be fine.*

But this time everything was different. I scrunched my eyes shut and tried hard to picture the beach and our hut. The harder I tried, the further I felt it slipping away. All my recurring dreams had felt like scenes from films, but this felt real, too real. I shuddered at the vivid memory of being raped. *Thank goodness that wasn't real*, I thought to myself, as I lay there in the cold light of day, trapped in the cellar: his victim.

My thoughts went back to the missing ring: my captor must have taken it as a trophy. I was so dehydrated, I had become delusional. It does not take much to understand how quickly this situation would affect my sanity. I was still not able to see the wood for the trees, the two realities had become so blurred, I was unable to work out which one was the dream and which was real life. They melted together and I was left to float in the greyness. The spiders' webs began to unravel, the silky threads weaved their way around the beams and down through the crumbling red brick. The spiders that inhabited them metamorphosed into luminous hummingbirds that buzzed around the room, singing in chorus. The flashing red light from the video camera grew and grew until it was a large, orb-like planet, floating in the air. The spiders' webs were now on the dusty wooden floor, flooding towards me. They spun together, like a translucent chiffon blanket, and began to embalm me.

The fear was too much to cope with and I passed out. When I regained consciousness, my head was still muddled. *How could I be there? Why hadn't I woken up on the island?* I was sandwiched between two universes; I couldn't tell fact from fiction. The pain in my body felt utterly real but this couldn't be the real world . . . I didn't understand any of it.

I ran through everything in my mind: *Jude was real, wasn't he? Yes, Jude was definitely real. My dear, lovely, wonderful Jude.* I hadn't imagined him. That felt like a good starting point. I felt a bit better already. *Now, Annabel, look in the mirror again.* I stared at myself and I began to remember my nightmares more clearly: the boot of the car, my pain and misery, the humiliation of my nudity, the rape, the monster who was keeping me there.

Next, I focused on the other life I had been living, on the island – the romance, the sunshine, the warmth and happiness. The harder I tried to hold on to those things, the faster they slipped away. Thailand disintegrated until it was nothing more than sand, sieving through my mind. I was desperate; I wondered if I was dead. Perhaps neither world existed. Maybe I never existed. *I couldn't have got it all so wrong, could I? This was the nightmare, wasn't it? How could someone mistake a dream for reality?* It all seemed so unlikely, but there was a niggling voice inside me, whispering, telling me this *was* what had happened. Lunacy took a grip of me and I thought I might combust. My body and mind felt caught in a supernova.

I screamed so hard that a migraine struck my head like a thunderbolt. It seemed like a million currents were running through me. I twisted and contorted in my shackles, trying to escape the agony. I could feel myself losing consciousness. At last, I would get back to where I belonged, away from this nightmare. I let the violent pain in my head and the hyperventilation cocoon me, as I drifted off once more. *I'm on my way, Jude, hold on, I'm coming . . .*

***

When I came to, it was sunset and I could see streaks of peach sky in the mirror. For a moment, I thought I was back on the island. Then my peripheral vision kicked in and I knew I was still in the cellar. I began to believe that this was my reality: Thailand had just been a beautiful dream. The fog had lifted but I still needed answers. I resigned myself to lying there, not struggling. The little energy I had left, I would need to conserve, ready for when the monster next appeared.

In the distance I heard footsteps. I turned my head towards the bolted door; I could hear keys jangling. *He* was coming back. I closed my eyes and tried to imagine myself back on the beach, wrapped in strong arms, safe, with the warm sun on my skin. I opened my eyes and there he was: my grotesque monster.

He was holding a bottle of water and a hypodermic syringe. I didn't bother trying to speak. I was too overwhelmed to find the words or get them out. That was the first time I had properly seen him. He was in his forties and dishevelled. He looked like he worked on a farm, mucking out pigs, shovelling shit. I could picture him no other way from that moment on. He smelled of dung and death. I tried to describe his face but it was difficult: he was like a fantastical nightmare. I doubt I will ever know if what I saw was real. Perhaps my mind was twisting the image. He stood about six feet tall. He had stubble and dirty grey whiskers that spiked out of his double chin. If I hadn't been a prisoner in his house, I might have suspected he was homeless. His hands were large and rough. They looked as if they had spent a lifetime working. When he looked at me, he gave a satisfied smile and I saw his uneven teeth, stained with nicotine. He wore grubby overalls with a terracotta shirt beneath, and around his waist he had a tool belt.

He started to approach me and I noticed he had a limp. His large boots were caked in mud and I watched dust particles move out of his way as he shuffled in my direction. He reached my bench and took hold of my chin, forcing my mouth open. He poured the tepid water into my mouth. I forgot my nakedness and vulnerability as I sucked down the clean water. *Life.* Then he pulled the bottle away and watched as I lay there. Goose bumps appeared on my skin: the water had spilt down my chin and sprayed my naked chest. I felt a current of cold and was reminded of my nudity. I looked at him, calmly, for the first time. He had cold, dead eyes. They were brown with no warmth in them. I spoke to him directly, also for the first time. 'More,' I whispered hoarsely. 'More water, please . . .'

He put the bottle on the floor, near the door, before turning to me and saying, 'After.'

Dread filled me, and I thought I might regurgitate the water I had just drunk. He walked over to me and injected me with the syringe, then turned and left the room, slamming the wooden door behind him and locking it again. I was on a roller coaster of relief and terror. I had escaped any further abuse, for a while, but his reply echoed around my head, taunting me. *After what?*

I had to get out of there. Right there and then, I swore to myself that I would break out of that dungeon. I concentrated on trying to free myself from the iron restraints around my ankles. I pulled and pulled until my feet were swollen and blue. I attempted to twist myself out of them. I approached the problem as if it were a puzzle I needed to solve. I tried to stay calm and tackle the issue with scientific detachment. My skin was blistered and split, and fresh blood trickled down to my toes. My feet looked like joints of meat on a butcher's table – I suppose that's what I was.

And then, minutes later, the drug began to take effect. It ripped through my veins like wildfire; it was heaven and hell at the same time. I didn't know if I was going to pass out or have a euphoric out-of-body experience.

If possible, I experienced both at the same time. It was like looking through a kaleidoscope: everything I saw folded over and became a thousand more images of itself. The half-empty bottle of water on the floor was an oasis. It was like being trapped in a room full of mirrors. Each new picture bore another, and went on into oblivion. I could feel myself reaching the end of the trip, the chemicals had control of me and my psyche couldn't cope with any more. Seconds later, I was lost again to a deep, dark, dreamless sleep.

When I woke, I felt burning in my legs. My head was heavy from the drug and I tried to shake off the sleepiness. I looked down at my limbs and saw *him* standing over me. He had a nail and hammer in his hands. My legs were covered in neat, bloody holes. Before I'd had a minute to adjust to what was happening, he lowered the nail to my thigh and brought the hammer down.

The miniature metal spear entered my flesh like a knife through butter. I could feel it inside me: he'd hit bone. He smiled briefly, turned the hammer on its head and pulled the nail out. Dark blood surged out of the perfectly formed wound.

It snaked down my white skin, past the dried blood from my healing injuries, and disappeared out of view. He prodded the hole, making it bleed harder. His mouth was agape and he ran his gross tongue along his bottom lip. A trail of spittle sparkled in the dusk light. The nail hovered above my leg, two inches away from the latest gash.

'Nooo,' I slurred.

Like a robot, his head slowly turned to face me, the rest of him spookily still. He put down his tools and dusted off his hands, slowly shaking his head. Then his hand formed a fist that came crashing down to my jaw – it was my turn to dribble. Blood and spit mixed together in my mouth; I will never forget the metallic taste on my tongue. I was too shocked to react. I lay on the bench, my face turned away from his, as he hocked a large ball of spit on me, just before I passed out.

***

He turned his attention back to the hammer and nails. This time, he decided to concentrate on my feet. In turn, he hammered a nail into each toe, shattering the bones, breaking my spirit. I wondered how I would be able to escape after this. With each bang, I felt him chipping away at my hope. I looked down at what had once been my feet. I pictured my toes, digging into warm sand. That was my convalescence. It lifted me out of the misery, and for a millisecond I was back on the beach. When I next looked at my toes I noticed my chipped coral nail varnish. I found myself thinking I needed to touch them up. It was another fractured consideration that allowed my mind to be elsewhere. The relief didn't last.

It seemed like each foot now had nine toes. I kept counting, trying to make sense of the numbers. One, two, three, four, five, six . . . and then I realised, all, except my big toe, had broken in two from the force. My toes had been replaced with bits of chipped bone and bloody gristle. The strangest thing was that it didn't really hurt. I had passed the pain stage, and entered a new realm; I suspect surgery with a local anaesthetic must be very similar. I was watching my body being mutilated and it was painless.

I dragged my eyes away from my feet and ended up fixing my gaze on his mouth again: white globules of saliva had gathered in the corners. It was the only fresh thing in the room. I admired the newness of it. The idea that anything could be born in that room gave me drop of hope. I don't understand why I was drugged and suffering the most intolerable cruelty, but that's what I learnt about the human condition: we hope. It is what we do best.

When the monster had finished demolishing my feet, he stood back and admired his work. He wiped his mouth with the back of his hand and tucked the hammer into his work belt. His animal eyes glinted with pride and insanity. I almost laughed. The madness was so tangible it was airborne. He cocked his head to one side and I could see the cogs of his disturbed mind slowly turning.

He hoisted himself onto the bench and straddled me. Broad, powerful thighs pinned me down, lest I try to escape. I had neither the energy nor the will to attempt such a thing. He cracked his neck and, interlinking his fingers, proceeded to pop his knuckles. I lay limp and detached under his weight. All I could think about was the ring I was missing: the ring I never had, from the man I met once.

He roughly grabbed one of my breasts and twisted it until I yelped. With his other hand, he gripped my throat and squeezed; my airways narrowed and my eyes bulged. I could feel the blood flowing to my cheeks. This was it, my death. I tried to get some air but it was pointless. Darkness pricked my eyes and the light faded until all I could see was him. Just as I thought that was it, he would release his grip enough for me to take a sharp breath, before choking me again. He repeated this over and over. Each time, he would take me to the edge of unconsciousness and bring me back again. I found a distorted comfort in the rhythm; familiarity is a strange thing.

The bulk of his body felt heavy, like setting concrete. The longer the mass was there, the more of a strain it became; I thought my ribs might snap. His fat frame pushed down on my hipbones. Among all that awfulness, there was his penis – I saw the stiffness prodding against his trousers. My rape had only just begun. I let my eyes roll back into my head, and allowed myself to be swallowed by the iniquity of it all.

***

I came round when he had finished brutalising me, and watched as he removed an ageing banana from his pocket and broke off pieces for me to eat. He was playing good cop/bad cop – I felt something that resembled gratitude and hated myself for it.

After I'd eaten the banana, he uncuffed me, hoisted me over his shoulder and put me down on a stool. The cold, smooth wood felt hard against my bony bottom. I was free, temporarily. I looked around the cellar, desperately searching for a weapon, anything would do. I was weak, and the only thing I could see was out of reach. He would snap me in half before I made it over to the plank of wood leaning up against the far wall. Think, god damn it! He bent down and tied my ankles to the legs of the stool with old rope that burned and cut into my flesh.

While he was hunched over, tying knots, I folded my hands together and brought them up over my head, bringing them crashing down on his thick, heavy skull. He tottered backwards, holding his head, and I could tell his vision was blurred. He was cursing and bent over. His body looked like a huge mountain.

Without thinking, I tipped myself over onto the ground. My elbow and shoulder crashed onto the brick floor, sending a tremor through me. It felt like the start of a small earthquake, vibrating through my body. He was still doubled over and I knew, if I could just wriggle free from the rope, I'd stand a chance of escape. And then I realised my hands were still free. I struggled with the rope, like an animal caught in a trap, until finally, miraculously, I loosened them enough to slip my battered feet out – and he hadn't noticed.

Out of nowhere I got a burst of energy that allowed me to get up to my feet. As long as I focused on the door, my escape remained a possibility. Lunging forward, I grabbed the handle and twisted. The adrenalin running through my body had become a force of its own - I was no longer in control. Instinct took over. Hot and cold flushes took it in turn to batter my quivering form.

As the door opened and I felt the breeze coming down the stairs, he grabbed hold of my shoulders. With one violent tug, he pulled me back into my prison, as if I was weightless. My spine made contact with the rough brick wall and I squealed in pain. He stood before me, grunting and huffing, his eyes dilated with fury, and I waited for a barrage of punches. Instead, he picked me up and threw me back on the wooden bench, shackling me once more. My escape was over. I was back where I had started. Wailing sounds rippled around the room and I realised they were coming from me.

The moon was there, again, smiling at me. She was shrinking now, getting farther away. I wish I had been able to gaze at her properly: it was only her reflection I could see. There was no way of knowing if I was seeing the real thing. She was there nonetheless, my bright and distant heroine. As long as I could see her in the glass, *I* was real. Daylight was agony, the blackness was my home. I searched her silver face for familiar craters. I could see the looming clouds, lingering in the sky, dark and threatening.

As a midnight cloud covered the terrestrial goddess, I was struck by a sinking feeling: I needed to look at my body again. It was time to embrace my reality once more and prepare for the nightmare ahead. I think I groaned – an animal growl went right through me, down into my feet, vibrating my broken toes. Instant sickness returned. It was as if I had a belly full of wine. I wasn't sure I was a woman anymore. It was the beginning of an exhausted forever that had no destination.

I wondered how long I had been there, in *his* cellar. Had it been hours, or days? I couldn't be sure. I tried hard to remember the events that had led to my imprisonment. When and from where had he grabbed me? It seemed a veil had been pulled over my mind. The only thing that had felt real was Jude and our time together on the island. *The mind can play tricks on itself.* I had found a happy place, a dream world in which to immerse myself, to lock out the horror of what was actually happening. Everything began to make sense, but now I was faced with the truth. I had so many truths to come to terms with; I was dealing with something like grief. It was worse than the pain caused by the monster. My heart was broken. And then I remembered the moment I was taken. Everything since then had been fantasy. My troubled mind had invented it all.

It struck me again and again, like waves in a storm. I was being hit from all directions and I had to fight to breathe. My brain started to implode. I was travelling at a million miles an hour but was glued to the spot.

The wild wind blew and I saw the branch waver in the breeze. I cried for yesterday. I couldn't look at myself. Vanity clawed away at my temples. Maybe it would be best if he just came and killed me, there and then. But I still had a bit of fight left in me. As long as I could see the door, the exit, I would not give up hope.

I realised there was no chance of freeing myself from the chains. I tried to think laterally: he was my only hope of escape. *He had the keys*. I didn't have a plan, but I had the start of an idea, and that was something. All I had to do was hope he came back. I didn't allow myself to think too deeply about it – fear would have paralysed me and I would have buckled. Instead, I went back to watching the moon. She was my timepiece. I watched her work her way around the circle of time and soon found myself back at home, in my delusions once more. I was floating on a cloud above tiny, perfect islands. It was grotesque bliss, a strange and beautiful picture.

I was brought back to earth when I realised I was lying in a warm puddle. For a split second, I thought I had been raped again, but that wasn't it. I was lying in my own urine. I had wet myself. My crotch was stinging. Agony made my acquaintance once more.

Behind closed doors, women talk about the indignity of childbirth. Discharge, bladder control, episiotomy, are all associated with the wonder of giving life. I was giving birth to something, but it was no miracle. The pain began to take on a life of its own. In the dead of night, my shame became its own deity, then the door handle started to turn. *He* had returned.

Embarrassment and horror gripped me and tugged at my sanity. I wriggled in the yellow wetness, trying to get away from the stench of ammonia – he would see it and he would know. His large frame appeared, a silhouette against the light, as the door burst open. I couldn't see his face, but I felt his twisted grin and his eyes burning into me. The open wounds on my legs ached with the memory. He came over to me and stood admiring his work.

Then he snorted in a deep breath and hocked up a large amount of gluey phlegm onto my face like before. For a moment it felt warm on my cheek. I roared and screamed, writhing on the spot like an animal, unable to wipe the filth from my face.

He chuckled and used a grubby finger to prod one of the holes he had made earlier. To my surprise, my feet were still intact. Had I dreamt that? Was I now destined to be trapped inside nightmares instead?

I moaned and closed my eyes, trying to ride out the agony. Then he picked up the water bottle and offered me a drink. I slurped hard, enjoying the cleanness in my mouth, washing away the stale spittle and taste of blood. Gratitude and violent hatred mingled together in my head, making me feel dizzy. My monster was also my lifeline. Placing the bottle back on the floor, he pulled a crumbling biscuit out of his overalls' pocket and held it to my mouth. As I bit down, a current of pain ran through my gum. The dry, hard texture dug into where my tooth had been, and sent a stabbing pain into my head, but I knew I had to eat. With each bite the throb in my skull increased. When I'd finished the last mouthful, I felt exhausted again.

Without a second's warning, he slapped my face, hard, filling my mouth with the taste of blood again.

'Say fank you, you fuckin' bitch,' he spluttered in anger.

My eyes pricked with tears from the shock and hurt that rumbled through my cheekbone.

'Sorwee, sorwee, dank yaw,' I managed through my swollen gums, tongue and lips.

He had his back to me and I couldn't tell if I had pleased him. I hoped I had. I wondered what he had planned for me, as I looked down at my punctured legs. When he turned to me, I saw he had the hammer in his hand. I thought I was going to be sick; a familiar tidal wave of nausea returned. I searched his other hand but it was empty. He came over to the bench and put the hammer down near my feet. I froze, like a deer in headlights. Then I felt his fingers inside me, pushing hard, forcing their way in like the nails had done to my flesh earlier. Only this time, the pain was different; his searching fingers were coarse and rough against my insides. I was unable to move. I don't know how long it was before he pulled his hand away and put his fingers in his mouth, making a loud sucking sound.

Then, a strange thing happened to me – I had an unfathomable urge to smoke. I hadn't thought about cigarettes during my incarceration, until that point. The desire was so intense, I almost forgot about the aching pain. I just needed to smoke. I lay there for a moment, trying to remember the feel of a cigarette between my fingers. I imagined the silver smoke snaking into the air and became hypnotised by the fantasy. I started to see amber lights glowing around me, like a thousand smoking cigarette tips. I would have suffered any pain to get my hands on a cigarette. I screamed into the night, my frustrations ringing through the silence. That was when I thought I might lose my mind altogether. The violence alone hadn't been enough to tip me over the edge, although it should have been. I had smoked since I was a teenager – it was an intrinsic part of my character – to have my craving denied felt like the final straw.

It wasn't the last time during my ordeal that I would feel that way; nonetheless, it was the first time I had reacted to that specific frustration – they say you always remember your first time. I felt as if my predator was crushing everything I had to nothing, slowly picking away at the pieces of me that no one should ever have been able to reach.

I allowed myself to believe that I might be able to have a cigarette. It was easy to picture my captor smoking. I invented a scenario in which he put a lit cigarette between my lips and allowed me a long, luscious drag. The fantasy was gone too quickly and I found I had tears pouring down my cheeks. I sobbed until I could not cry anymore, every last drop of energy had been spent, and I was left static in my own disenchantment.

I wallowed in my nicotine mourning until I was too tired to think; exhaustion got its claws into me and my eyelids became too heavy to hold up.

***

When I woke up, after another bad dream, I felt bitterly cold: my body shook uncontrollably and my teeth chattered. I found it hard not to stare at the mess that had once been my legs. The blood was clotting and the craters looked like a mass of sticky jam. A fly landed on me and began to eat. Had I been able to move, I would have swatted it away but instead, I was forced to watch as its disgusting tongue fed on my suffering. In a twisted way, I was glad to see it. I watched as it walked around on my cold, pale leg. I was able to forget my restraints, the blood and the horror. The fly pottered about freely, unaware of my presence. I stayed totally still, terrified I might frighten it away. At that moment, I could have been anywhere. I could have been on a beach.

My dreams came flooding back to me, and that uneasy feeling returned with a vengeance. I looked at my hand and searched for the engagement ring. I knew it wouldn't be there, and that it never had been, but half of my mind had returned to the fantasy and refused to let go. Panic surged through me; thoughts of my family and friends returned. I had been so wrapped up in my situation, I'd been unable to think of anything but my own basic survival. It wouldn't have been possible to cope with thoughts of the people I held dear. Until then, I couldn't afford that luxury, but all of a sudden, I was unable to contain myself.

I thought about my mother and Will. I wondered how they were coping. *Did they think I was dead*? Maybe they believed I'd run away. Maybe they were at home, none the wiser, watching telly. *Was anyone looking for me*? Sickness returned to my empty belly as I relived the fantasy conversation with Jude and felt my heart breaking all over again.

Images of friendly faces whirled around my head on a carousel - people I hadn't thought about in years reappeared. It was as though my life was flashing before my eyes. They passed through my mind with such speed I was left with motion sickness. My body shook and taunted me with the urge to urinate. *What did it matter anymore*? I wondered, as I wet myself for a second time. Only it was a very different experience. This time, I noticed the flood of red that seeped out of me. I whimpered like a dog, the sting was too much to bear. I remember the sound I made, and the noise of the dribble falling from my bench to the hard floor below. I listened as it slowed to a drip, but in the rhythmic patter I found little solace. I began to realise what Chinese water torture must be like. That thought led me to think about food: I would have drowned in a vat of noodles, had I been given the opportunity. I was so hungry, I could see my ribcage expand and contract with every exhausted breath. My skeleton still had plenty of bones for him to break.

***

He had come and fed me twice, shoving biscuit crumbs into my mouth and bite-sized pieces of fruit. Sometimes he brought me a glass of cold milk. It was so surreal. That was the only glimmer of gentleness I saw from my captor.

It had become clear by then that I had little chance of escape. My shackles remained as steadfast as ever, and my body and mind continued to deteriorate. Desperation expanded and changed like the colours of my bruises. My injuries offered me a morbid fascination – similar to watching changing skies – as the shapes and hues faded and moved. I saw varying shades of green, yellow, pink, purple, red and blue over the course of some days. It was almost wonderful.

I began to think my only hope for survival was to befriend my kidnapper. I'd read stories about young girls who had been taken and kept in captivity for twenty years or more before escaping or being discovered. I couldn't see how I might survive twenty days, let alone years, but still clung to the instinct to live. I fought an internal battle. I debated whether it would be better to die or remain in that state. As long as I wasn't undergoing the torture, I could see hope, but the moment he appeared and the pain started again, I found myself longing for a quick death.

In the moments I was alone, in the silence of my prison, I could dream. I could just about remember the rough details of the romance I hadn't lived. I pictured the faces of my family – they remained crystal clear. I imagined conversations with those I missed most. It was easy to conjure up dialogue between my mother and myself; I knew she would tell me to hang on, to fight; that I was strong, that life was precious, that he wasn't going to win. A list of clichés, but they were what I would have needed.

In between thinking about people I loved, I dreamt of food. My hunger made it easy to imagine delicious feasts. There were a few things in particular that I thought about: a freshly made, thin and crispy pizza margherita; chocolate fudge cake; Chinese food, and curry with all the trimmings from my favourite curry house.

My desire to eat was so intense that I could smell food being cooked. The fantastical odours became so real that I cried out, begging for a taste. Unfortunately, the mirage didn't last long, but I still thought there was a chance that this reality was the dream, or rather the nightmare, and I would soon wake up, happy and sun-kissed, on a perfect, white sand beach.

As had been the case so many times, that didn't happen. I lay, confined to the bench, and inspected my body. Had it not been for the gross injuries I had suffered, I would have liked my figure: I was stick thin. How ironic life is. I hadn't dared glance at my face in the mirror for a few days, and had found a way to look at my reflection without really seeing myself. I had become invisible to my own eyes, and this was for the best. Vanity provided me with blindness to the suffering, and for that I was grateful. It's amazing the form self-preservation can take. Even then I didn't understand the lessons I was learning were to be of no consequence, for in the next few days, things were going to get much worse.

I was ruined to his satisfaction. He stopped brutalising me in that sense, but his attention became focused on a relentless routine of rape. He had done it so many times that I no longer fought - I would simply lie there and close my eyes. The pain was more excruciating each time; with each new invasion he irritated my raw parts – it was as if my insides were on fire, or suffering from intolerable carpet burns that were being pressed and rubbed up against. It seemed I would never heal. I bled every time, and I knew he had taken away any chance I might have of bearing children.

I spent a long time mourning the loss of my future. Never mind the physical similarities to a miscarriage, emotionally I was suffering the same thing. I grieved for my lost children. Their ghosts were all around me, in every shadow of the room. I saw them in the mirror, in my reflection, and they were beautiful. They hid during the daylight hours and came out to greet the moon. Only when the light shone at night was I able to identify my comfort and sadness.

I conjured up pictures of their faces in my head. With every rape, I lost another child. I was surrounded by so many of them. Their spirits played all around me. I felt the echo of their laughter envelop me, and in it I found solace. I was reminded of my own childhood; I remembered how invisible I'd felt when I was little. My individuality was still in its foetal state, trying to find a space where it could grow. But now I was fully formed I wished to go back to that time of innocence. I was glad the younger me hadn't known what was in store.

I hoped my Mother didn't know I was suffering, and would never know. If I suffered at the loss of my *imaginary* children, I wondered what it must be like for her. Enough time had passed for people to be aware of my disappearance. I envisaged the news coverage:

Young woman missing. Appeals for information

That was when the penny dropped. The young women and the murders that had been happening around Southwold, I was one of them. I was now part of that story. *Why hadn't I realised before?* It was *so* obvious. *How could I have been so stupid? Why hadn't I made the connection?* A whirlwind of information swept around my head as I put together the pieces of news I had heard and read: Three dead, no suspects, serial killer, victim, brutalised, naked, murdered, dumped.

Then I vomited. The small amount of food that was in my stomach came spilling out of my mouth. Since I was unable to move, I began to choke on my own sick. I gasped for fresh air with a mouthful of lumpy mucus and bile. I bucked like a horse being broken in, and eventually managed to clear my throat enough to gulp down some clean air. Once I had calmed down properly, and my breathing had returned to normal, I spat out the remaining lumps of vomit as far away as I could manage. My body was sweat-ridden and I felt it clinging to the creases in my skin. I felt so naked.

I knew my brain wasn't working properly. The monster had invaded my dreams as well as my days. I was as ill as I had ever been. I had fallen down again, only this time it wasn't clear if I would ever get up and walk away. Instability had stolen my youth and this monster was about to finish the job. I thought my sadness would get bored and go away, then I realised that I despised myself. The worst thing was that it felt like I was out of luck this time, and I deserved to be. Outside, the world had closed its shutters and the void I felt inside made me sick again. My throat was in indescribable pain; my soul ached. It was too late to fix myself. My body remained tied to the prison bench, but my mind had gone. When that happened, I became free of all the septic infection that had crept over me.

Before I could adjust to my new state, the door creaked open again. He lumbered in and stood over me. He had a bottle in his hand. The liquid inside was like wine, sloshing against the glass in a repetitive tidal movement. I was transfixed by its rhythm. It glinted in the light and reminded me of Ribena and my childhood. The purple contents were rich and fruity looking. I thought he had brought me a drink.

My monster loomed over me, inspecting my healing wounds. His icy glare lingered over the parts of me that remained uninjured. I could see he was making plans. He grunted and walked over to the wooden workbench. It seemed he enjoyed mental torture as much as the physical pain he inflicted. He put down the unidentified bottle and removed a clear plastic container from his pocket. He had his back to me and I noticed the width of his shoulders. I felt smaller than I had ever felt before.

I was still caught up in my own ambivalence, struggling to cope with the newness of my emotional state, when he turned to face me. His right eye was looking in a different direction to his left: he was cross-eyed, which I hadn't noticed. He looked even crazier than I first thought. My stomach ached and the familiar throb of pain had returned.

He picked up the bottle and approached me as he unscrewed the cap. I didn't bother to wriggle or plead, the fight had left me. His dry, flaky top lip curled in a twisted smile to reveal yellow teeth. He was enjoying himself, but I didn't get the joke. He slowly lifted the glass bottle above my thighs and dribbled the purple juice onto my legs. It only took a second of agony until I realised what was happening: the liquid was vinegar. The smell was unmistakable and the burning sensation excruciating. Fire ripped through my limbs and they flailed uncontrollably. Blood erupted out of each and every hole he had made. It was fresh and fluid, almost volcanic. If I was screaming, it was silently. I noticed disappointment in his face. He had enjoyed the anticipation more than the reality. He put down the bottle and wiped his mouth with his sleeve. Then he began to undress.

My eyes rolled with the pain. After the initial surge had passed, I was able to focus again. I saw him standing there, nude. His rough, hairy skin looked grotesque in the moonlight. I searched in the mirror for the moon, but she wasn't there. That night, she hid. I felt abandonment blanket me. I prepared myself for another violation but he remained totally still, eyeballing me. He licked his lips; his tongue reminded me of a slug. The only thing I could do was close my eyes.

'Open ya eyes, ya bitch, or I'll get the vinegar again,' he hissed.

I did as I was told. It was a more disgusting sight than looking at my battered legs. Then the strangest thing happened: I started to laugh. Standing there, he looked utterly pathetic. It was tragic. Here was a monster – my monster – naked, and it was funny. The harder I laughed, the faster his erection waned. I was winning. Tears rolled down my cheeks as I shook with hysterics. The laughter hurt, but the more it hurt, the harder it was to control myself.

'You are fucking pathetic!' I screamed at him between chuckles.

He froze. He let his penis go flaccid and he stared at me. His expression was one of disbelief.

'Look at you! You're a freak, a tragic little freak. You are disgusting. Didn't mummy love you enough?' I spat at him. 'You wouldn't dare pick on someone who could defend themselves, would you? You gutless fuck!'

A split second later he had reached for the bottle and was drenching me in vinegar again. But I was so angry I almost didn't feel it. My fight response had finally found a voice.

'Take that,' he hissed.

I gathered a mouthful of phlegm and spat it at his face. He stopped and began to smile. The spit slowly made its way down his forehead. His eyes were twinkling.

'That's right,' he said, wiping his face with his hand. 'Keep fightin', my little pussycat. I like it when you fight.' He lifted his hand, made a fist and brought it down on my cheek. I blacked out.

In my unconscious state, I found myself in an unfamiliar world; it was like walking through fog in a derelict land – the world was covered in a silver-grey shroud. It felt like I wasn't alone. I called out, but no one replied. I walked for a long time. The quiet surrounded me like a bubble. Through the mist I could make out the faint outlines of bare tree branches. I tried to walk towards them, but they stayed the same distance in front of me.

I put out my hand and tried to feel for something, I didn't know what. My skin was translucent and I could see all my blood vessels, my muscles and bones. I thought perhaps I had died, then I thought I heard something in the distance. I stopped and listened, carefully. It came again: a muted noise like a tiny voice. The air around me felt cold and empty. I strained to hear the noise again. It was like a dying echo.

Something moved. It darted across my path in a flash. I couldn't see what it was. I froze, and became aware of my own heavy breathing. Something brushed against my shoulder. It was so light and gentle, I might not have noticed had it not been for the stillness of the unknown realm. I turned around and saw it again, but it darted back into the fog before I could identify it. I tried to run away but I couldn't make any ground; I was running on the spot, unable to escape.

A voice sounded through the dense air, clear as a bell. I looked left and right, trying to see where it had come from. Before I knew what was happening, they appeared in front of me: the faces of three young women. They were in a state of decomposition and stood in a row like broken angels of death. Their hair was matted and clung in streaks to their pallid faces. Their bloodshot eyes stared at me, unblinking. They were as grey as the world they inhabited. I should have been appalled, but I felt no fear. I reached out to touch them but my hand passed through them like a sword through silk. They spoke with one voice, 'You are coming home. You will be with us soon.' Then they disappeared and everything became black.

***

I woke up in a puddle of blood and sweat. It was a long time since I had felt hot. I had got so used to the cold that it had become my home. The sunlight came pouring in through the window and I squinted. One of my eyes ached and was swollen shut. Once my good eye had become accustomed to the brightness, I examined my prison again. I was alone for the time being. The bottle that had contained the vinegar lay callously on its side on the workbench, empty. I was so thirsty. I swallowed hard and my throat felt like sandpaper. Looking up at the window, I was able to make out a spider's delicate web, across the panes of glass. It twinkled and glistened in the light. A fat spider sat in the middle, guarding its kingdom, waiting patiently for a victim. I hated spiders but I was glad of the company. I lay still for a while, watching it, until I became aware of a strange sensation in my legs.

I looked down at my raw, bloody limbs, and noticed that the surface of my skin appeared to be moving. I shook my head and did a double take. At second glance, I saw the same image. My skin had a life of its own. It looked like a rippling carpet of red and I couldn't understand what I was seeing. I craned my neck and took a closer look. My legs were crawling with hundreds of maggots, they were basking in my blood and wriggling in and out of the cavities in my flesh. Now I understood why he'd made the holes so small, and why he hadn't just smashed my legs to pieces. I remembered reading somewhere that maggots were used by hospitals, to eat away the dead and dying skin on the wounds of amputees. Apparently, it was a safe way to ensure that gangrene didn't set in. *Could this be my monster's twisted version of kindness?* I doubted it. Watching them squirming about was intolerable. I strained as far forward as my restraints would allow, and blew furiously on my legs. I thought I might be able to get them off but it was no use. Although I knew it would be agony to move my leg, with its broken knee, I had to remove them. I bucked and shook myself and a few fell off, but the majority remained, clinging to my skin, enjoying their meal.

After twisting and turning I was exhausted, and resigned to lying back and letting the maggots feast. I could feel each and every one of them creeping over my skin. I felt their tiny mouths sucking on my raw edges. Mostly they were content to focus on the source of food, but a few got distracted and began to crawl up my thighs, towards my genitals. The humiliation and pain I had already felt at the hands of my captor was bad enough, but the thought of maggots invading me was too much to bear.

I broke down. I don't know how long it lasted, but for a good while madness belonged to me. I breathed it in like a poison that took hold of my imagination: I was falling into a black hole, I was in a state of vertigo. My mind became an entity in its own right. My spirit went astray; my heart dissipated and any trace of the person I had been, dissolved, as I quit being. I became something else; I became all that would remain of me. My mind had fractured and any remnants of hope had died. Then came the realisation that there was a solution to my situation; it became clear that life consisted of one choice: what you do. Clarity came to me like a light being switched on and I felt suddenly drenched in calm.

I pulled my right arm as close to my face as it would go, my mouth touched my wrist and my skin felt icy cold against my lips. My blue-green veins stood like hills in the landscape. I looked around my prison one last time, hoping to see something new, something different, but everything remained the same. I opened my mouth and dragged my teeth across the skin on my wrist. Before I had a second to think about it, I bit down as hard as I could. My mouth filled with warm, fresh blood, and I bit again. My monster would not kill me, I would not let him. I would kill myself before that happened. All I had to do was sever my artery and I would bleed to death. I would fall asleep as life seeped from me and never wake up. I bit harder and scraped my canines against my flesh. It hurt like hell, but it was the only way I could take charge of the situation and regain control of my life. I carried on trying to gnaw through my arm for a while, but I couldn't go through with it. No matter how hard I tried, I didn't have the stomach to finish the job.

By the time I had given up, I was so drained that even sobbing was impossible. My chewed, limp wrist looked like discarded roadkill that even crows would pass up. I felt as pathetic as I had accused my monster of being. Death was all around me but not yet close enough to touch. It hung in the air like a distant thunderstorm, threatening to break. It was so tiresome, even the thought of it seemed ironic, like the lines from a really bad song that refused to stop playing.

I tried hard to think of happier times – I'd had plenty of them. My childhood should have been a haven for daydreaming, but it was lost to me. I couldn't remember my parents, my brother, how I'd felt, what I'd done – nothing. It was all an empty shell. I had been a fortunate child but it was too far away from me now. I couldn't summon it up. I might as well have been born into this state as everything that went before seemed unreal, as if it had never happened. I could only live in the morbid present; I was a leech, at home in the swamp, and my monster was my god.

If only I could recall something else, something concrete and true, surely I would be able to confirm I existed. Life ran on a loop that was caught somewhere between slow motion and fast forward. That was it. I was on stage, playing a role. It seemed like I was due an interlude, but life is not theatre or that convenient.

I remembered how hungry I was. It was the kind of hunger anorexics must suffer; my body was too frail to gorge on anything truly tasty, but my mind fantasised about it. At the same time, there was a sick satisfaction in starvation. *Control, control, control: an eating disorder's best friend.* It reminded me of something, a feeling from my youth, maybe. Some teenage girls flirt with the idea of bulimia, or something similar. Bulimia is the beginner's hurdle. If you like food, which most people do, the idea of giving it up altogether is horrifying. Bulimia gives you the best of both worlds: eat but stay thin. Fill your face with biscuits and chocolate but avoid thunder thighs – it's almost cheating. Maybe if young girls stopped seeing it as romantic, and saw it as a swindler's answer to mirroring the models in magazines, it would lose its appeal. Or maybe not. During my school years, a girl was only worth something if she was fucked up enough to stop eating, or spent hours huddled over the loos with her fingers down her throat. I'd spent many hours thinking up new ways to get thin quickly. I was fourteen at the peak of my dieting obsession, and that seemed to be the only thing I could remember about my past. I was unsure if I'd been popular. I couldn't recall if I'd had any real friends. Shakespeare had said, 'Nothing is so common as the desire to be remarkable.' Hindsight should have answered those questions, but it was too much of a blur. Reality, fantasy and delusion had all become so tangled that the truth had been completely lost. I couldn't begin to try to sieve through it all. It had been swallowed down like a bitter pill. Deep in my subconscious I hoped that someone, somewhere, knew the truth about me.

The shackles were gone. I looked down at my now tiny wrists and saw that I was free. My bruises were fading and the gashes in my skin were slowly healing. The cellar looked different; it was warmer. I sat up, a free woman, and wondered what had happened. My body was sore and felt tender. I was weak and didn't trust my legs but I knew I had to get up.

My legs hung over the edge of the surface I had been tied to and I noticed the chipped nail varnish on my toes. It seemed, if I could just paint them, everything would be alright, my life could return to normal.

He'd changed his mind. Something had happened to alter my fate. I felt hope return. It was like ice melting in the sunlight. My body was on the mend. It was unclear when everything had changed but I didn't stop to question it. I got up and gingerly made my way towards the cellar door. I remained stark naked but I didn't feel cold. It was daylight and, in the mirror, I spotted the smiling crescent of the moon in the blue sky. She was with me as I reached the door and tried to turn the handle. I felt a screaming heat in my palm and watched as my hand crumbled into a pile of ash.

I woke myself up, crying and screaming. It had been a cruel dream. But then I noticed something was different.

I was lying on my belly, cuffed. He must have turned me over. I didn't know when he had done it; I couldn't have been awake, but it hadn't happened by magic. The new position felt alien – I had spent so long on my back, the familiar position had become a sort of comfort. I was lost again, left floating in a strange, deep space. My view was altered. *Where had the moon gone?* And then I realised it was morning. I could still see the mirror, and therefore, when I needed her, I knew my lunar goddess would reveal herself to me.

My chin was so uncomfortable, rubbing against the wooden base of the bench. My ruined toes and knee were pressing, wounds down, into the hard surface. The bitter scent of my faeces and urine infested every sense with unforgiving intrusion, making my eyes water. I could taste my own filth. I was living in a sewer. I wriggled for a while. I must have looked like a worm, or a beetle on its back.

The day passed slowly and the light started to change. The onset of night grew imminent. I hoped my moon would be there. I watched the sky through the glass as it turned from blue to grey to blue again; veins of purple crept in, and finally, peach, amber, gold and silver. It was a long time that I gazed upon that sapphire-blue blanket, before tiny pinpricks appeared gleaming through. They were my lost children, and I knew they dared not come out without their mother.

Before the clear beam of light could shine on the mirror, I heard the lock of the cellar door click. I strained to free myself, with more gusto than I'd had for a while. This new, uncompromising position had shaken me. I was still struggling when he came in. I bent my neck as far as I could, to see if he had any vinegar with him. His hands were empty, but his obtuse smile held a promise of its own. He slapped the side of his thigh, as if he were about to participate in line dancing. I held my breath and waited. Nothing happened, but I knew the show wasn't over. I longed for the strange, lucid drug he had given me just like an addict returned home to the indulgence, it was rectifying.

My hollow skeleton pushed down, into the wooden table, finding strangely familiar grooves. He approached the bench and slapped the area where my healthy bottom had once been. It was now nothing more than an empty discarded sack. If he had hit a fraction harder, I was sure he would have broken me; that was what I hoped for. Instead, his greedy, fat sausage fingers pulled at my baggy flesh, like a dressmaker pinching cloth round a mannequin.

I don't know when, or how the moment came about, but in a blink he was on me. This time it was different. I felt like a bull in a rodeo. I bucked and did all that I could but he was too strong. My insides felt like they were being pinched and pulled. It was similar to a cramp; I was sure I would die. My dignity had already been shattered and I was nothing more than a missing shadow; my lost children would have thought of Peter Pan. *How many times can someone die?* Nietzsche had said, 'And when you stare for a long time into an abyss, the abyss stares back into you.' Suddenly, I understood what he'd meant.

When he had finished with me, he climbed off. It stung so badly. He walked round to stand in front of me. I kept my face pressed to the wood and didn't look up.

'You dirty little whore. You fuckin' bled all over me,' he said. I stayed perfectly still and refused to look, there was no point. He chuckled to himself and firmly patted the top of my head, before pulling up his trousers and leaving the room.

***

My lost childhood hung about, taunting my memory and trying to rise from the dead. It threatened to introduce itself, like a perverted stranger, but never actually stepped forward. It remained, lingering in the wilds of my mind, observing, but never stepping out of the shadows. I didn't know what I should have remembered, but I knew that something should be there. The empty space bothered me.

I was left holding on to a void. My mind wronged me cruelly. Even my unspoken name felt unfamiliar. I could only live between the lines.

I listened to the silence and found my family: my mother and Will and the complicated harmony we'd shared. She would torture herself with guilt, and he would find a home in anger. That saddened me more than any of the physical abuse the monster dished out. I knew them so well and could see them in the future, a future that didn't include me. I ached for them and was thankful they couldn't see me. I had already gone, they were all that was left. It felt like the end was getting closer and I could only ponder it. It was such a strange sensation: not far from being suicidal or terminally ill, whichever was worse. I knew death was around the corner, I could hear it approaching. It tiptoed with creaking footsteps and was relentless.

Then I began to ponder something new: was there a heaven and a hell? I had always been sure that we ended up a pile of bones, nothing more. I wish I could tell you that I suddenly found religion, and everything lost its gloom, but that wasn't the case. My situation only backed up my beliefs. If there was a great divine power, how could it allow such misery? If there was a god, surely it would be brave enough to take responsibility for its creations? I found no divinity in a lack of responsibility. If I'd had a child, would I have believed that free will meant it was on its own, and I was free from any responsibility? The answer was a resounding no, and I could see it no other way. What the faithful fail to realise is that atheism is a belief in its own right. I found relief and comfort in my beliefs, or lack thereof. The only time I suffered from conflicting thoughts, was when I thought about my captor. Only then did I wish that God and the Devil existed. My logic suggested, if they did, he would surely spend eternity burning in hell.

It didn't take long for me to rectify my thinking. I did not wish hell upon him, not really. I wanted fate to step in. I wanted him to pay for what he'd done. It was too simple that he should only face consequences in the afterlife. I hoped that he would rot in prison – ostracised to begin with, ultimately forgotten. I believe that you only truly die when you're forgotten. That was the penalty I wished upon the murderer I had been unfortunate enough to cross paths with. Love is fickle, and it dies quicker than the memory of it, or so I believed. I would float on, in some minor form, and that was OK.

I tried not to think about how I might eventually die. I had suffered unimaginable cruelty and my mind boggled when I contemplated how he would finish the job. I tried hard to remember the details about the other bodies that had been discovered, but I came up blank. The papers had been very vague about the particulars. Perhaps because they were not privy to the information. I hoped that was the case. But I couldn't help but wonder whether the truth was so vile they were unable to publish it. Based on my experiences so far, that didn't seem far-fetched. It was irrelevant now: my death warrant had been signed, and my execution seemed a mere formality.

Time spent focusing on my family, made up for not thinking about my imagined friends and Jude. It was a relief, after the long period I'd spent pining. The imaginary world I had immersed myself in seemed so far away, like the dream it had been. That moment I had woken up and found myself panicking about the lost ring was a lifetime ago. I searched my bony hand for the ring, just to check. It no longer felt naked. How ridiculous that I'd spent time fantasising about a fairy tale that never was. It seemed to be part of my genetic make-up, a pre-programmed default that made little sense but just simply was. I had found a way to see him again, and to rewrite history. I would always have that.

Fate had led me down a dark path. The gritty, honest love I had for him was all an illusion.

It had started as a figment of my imagination and became what could make me happy, the only thing I would need. For someone who believed in fate, I hadn't been any good at letting it take its course. Unwittingly, everything I'd imagined he'd done, everything he'd said, had helped me on my journey down that path. All I'd ever really shared with him was the same sky. I don't know how many times that sad thought occurred to me.

My stomach rumbled and I was brought back to earth. Lying there in a crumpled heap led me to a number of realisations: I was on my way to becoming something else and, no matter how much it sickened me, I had a bond with the monster now and he would always be with me. The growl inside me echoed around the room with the violence he had bestowed. The sound penetrated my eardrum with aggressive velocity; I felt like a new-born thrown out into the world, unprepared. I had to get out of there.

I hadn't noticed the pad of his feet coming down the stairs; he appeared at the door, which opened smoothly like the curtains in a theatre. I did not turn my face to look, his image was ingrained in my mind. I would be better off dead. I just needed him to let me go. I wanted to go back to my dreamland.

He didn't say anything as he approached the bench. He stood in front of me and began to unpeel a blackening banana. Without a word, he held it close to my mouth, offering me a bite of the grey-beige flesh with its phallic curve. I had become so accustomed to the scent of my own body – the blood, the fear, the piss and the shit – that this new smell was wonderful. It transported me to a different world. I was reminded of supermarkets and the summertime. I don't know why, but I thought of ice cream. I took an unforgiving bite and slowly chewed the flesh; it tasted even better than it smelled and I almost thanked him for his kindness. I was too busy eating to talk, though. As pleasing as the food was, I found it near impossible to swallow it while lying on my front. I felt like a snake, slithering on its belly, trying to consume an animal twice its size. The difference was that I lacked the ability to dislocate my jaw, or hunt successfully, unlike my predatory keeper.

When I had finished, he left the room without a word, which only added to my diminished feeling of self-worth. It wasn't that I wanted him to pay attention to me, but if I was no longer there to be abused, I was as pointless as dust. Oddly, it made me smile. I was at peace with my surroundings. I was the spider in its web, invisible, waiting for something that might never come. It washed over me like a gentle wave, preparing me for my death, promising that the future was insipid. I knew I would not see the sun again, and that the next time I saw the moon she would not look at me; her light would pass over me. My ghost introduced itself and I was glad to finally make its acquaintance. It had spent too long in the background. You learn a lot about yourself when you have to be on your own – I learned I was no good at being alone. And I had no idea who I had been. My existence was predictably relentless. That was all there was to it. Life was stubborn. I suppose that is why mankind still rules the planet, and watches while other species go extinct.

The banana sat in my belly like a rock and I quickly regretted eating it. Nausea returned and battered me like a ship in a storm. I rode it out again. The body I had once inhabited was simply a vessel now, nearly abandoned and close to sinking into the blue. Like a bubble floating over shards of glass, I came close to bursting. My purging led me to be punished. I was reminded of the maggots, their disgusting pink bodies feeding off my pain. I wasn't even sure if it had happened. Nothing seemed real anymore. I'm not sure it ever did. I knew I should forget, but it was all I had to cling to, and cling on, I did. My escape attempt remained at the forefront of my mind. I'd failed, but an opportunity had presented itself and from that I took hope. There would be another chance, there had to be. Hope returned and my stomach churned with it.

The lumps of freshly consumed banana reappeared without an apology. I could not escape them. They were accompanied by a thick, slimy river that oozed out of my mouth and gathered in a swamp-like puddle near my chin. I thought I might drown in it. Everything ran in slow motion and seconds felt like years.

I have no idea how long I spent living that moment, but my mind was strangely stimulated. My head became full of open doors that welcomed me inside. Behind each one was a memory. I almost remembered my favourite song, but not quite. I could hear songs that reminded me of good times in my life, like a soundtrack from a better place. Then it became obvious that I was actually hearing music, it wasn't my imagination.

Listening to the distant hum of an unfamiliar tune, playing in the room above me, made me cry. I hadn't imagined I would ever hear music again, and I was so thankful. I cried for the lovely sound, and I cried because I was unable to clean up the puddle of lumpy vomit that was where I wanted to rest my head. Happiness and sadness danced together, round and round, waltzing inside my gut with strange fluidity.

I cursed myself for crying because the sound of my sobs was drowning out the music. But that made me cry harder. Feeling the tears stream down my face felt shockingly good. It was the closest to being clean I could experience. I can't count how many times I've imagined myself in a bubble bath, or standing under the steamy flow from a shower head. By the time I had stopped wailing, the music from above had ceased. I strained to hear more, hoping it was just an interlude between songs, but after a few minutes had passed, I had to accept I wouldn't hear any more. My heart was in my throat as I tried to come up with a solution to the lake of banana sick that was shimmering beneath my chin. I had been craning my neck for a while and it was beginning to ache. It was inevitable that I would end up resting my jaw in it, but I was determined to avoid doing so until I absolutely had to. I kept my head awkwardly suspended for a long time. It was strange that, in the end, I was looking forward to putting my head down in the vomit. The strain on my spine was agonising: it felt like shards of glass were sticking into my neck in between the vertebrae. I finally succumbed to the pain when my exhaustion took over. I turned my cheek and slowly lowered it into the icy, cold puddle. It felt disgustingly slimy against my skin and I had an urge to lift my head again. I was too tired, though. I had no choice but to stay put, and I gradually drifted off into an uncomfortable sleep.

I could no longer see myself. My role was limited to being the one who looked into the mirror and gazed at the world through it. It was a world built of reflections and it felt safer that way. I stopped looking around the room. It was slowly driving me mad. I was ill. A fever gripped me and with it came hallucinations that were a welcome break from reality. The dull, flat world I inhabited was suddenly psychedelic and beautiful. Orange butterflies, as big as my hand, fluttered around the room leaving rainbow trails. Flowers grew from the cracks in the floor. It was so real, I swear I could smell them. The faint scent of roses replaced the vile smell of my rotting legs. In the corner of the room, a waterfall of stars appeared, glinting like diamonds. Hummingbirds hovered nearby and drank the nectar from the flowers. The best thing about the delusion was that I didn't exist. I was a mere particle of light that hung in the air between the fantasy flora and fauna.

Amid the hot and cold sweats, I slept for long periods of time. Any dreams I had were reserved for waking hours. My sleeps were restless and left me feeling more tired than I could have ever imagined possible. My brain and body had become utterly incompetent. In my previous life, the life before the cellar, I had always been able to rely on my imagination. It had been my favourite hiding place, but it didn't have anything left to give. All its energy was reserved for surviving. It kept me alive, but I couldn't understand why. My heart kept on beating. The thump against my ribcage was like a ticking clock counting down the hours.

My body began to get accustomed to my surroundings. The lack of movement left my skeleton in a brittle, diminished state. I was stick thin as a result of the starvation and pain but, to compensate, my senses were heightened. My hearing in particular had improved dramatically. I picked up on every noise within a wide radius. When it rained outside, my head felt like it was being battered. The noise was so loud it shook my brain. The windowpane was pelted and the rhythm reminded me of tribal drumming. It would have been soothing were it not for the volume. The rain was a new form of torture, although I longed to be out in the deluge. I wanted to stand under it and let it wash away everything that had happened to me since I left my friends on the winter beach that night.

I became consumed with thoughts of my Jude. He was back with me again and it was as if we had never been apart. I could feel his arms around me, telling me it would be all right. I could remember the feel of his breath, the way it had a slight smell of chocolate. I was back to being in love again, and with it came a heavy sadness.

I was sure my fate was to be the same as the other women. With acceptance came relief. At the same time, the rain ceased and a beam of hazy sunshine came through the window. It felt like a sign.

That was when I finally knew what to do. I let go of Jude and took a step into my bleak future. I hoped that everyone who knew me would be able to let go of me, too.

My mother would be able to get on with her life and focus on Will. He was the best of us all, and he deserved a calm, normal life, free from the troubles I'd brought. I imagined him as a grown-up man: happily married with a good career and adorable children. It made me smile. I pictured my Mother with a new partner. Someone who could make her laugh and take care of her. She would be freed from the responsibility my illness had brought.

In truth, we were probably responsible for suffocating each other. I saw how hard she had tried with me and I felt pain in the core of my soul. I realised that going to Southwold would always have led me to this moment.

Whatever the monster had in store would pass over me. Death was around the corner, lingering with the smell of my demise. I was resigned to saying goodbye to my family and friends and, in my head, I spoke to each and every one of them. I told them that *he* couldn't get to me anymore, I had already gone.

It was as if I'd just received news that I had a fatal condition. The monster was the cancer, eating me alive, and I needed to accept my fate. I dived into the reality of my situation and swam in the calm waters of acceptance. It felt like a weight had been lifted. When I next craned my neck to look at my battered body, it seemed of little consequence. My mind felt free, and it was waiting for the opportunity to escape the useless, earthly form that kept me in that place.

He appeared in the room again, like the Grim Reaper. I smiled at him and the muscles in my face flinched in response to the unfamiliar movement. He was unaware of my inner harmony. Nothing I did could spoil the fun he was having. After running his cold eyes all over me, he approached his workbench and began banging at something. He had his back to me and I couldn't see what he was working on, although I was certain it would not be pleasant. I readied myself for another onslaught. It had become clear that his timetable had evolved, and the periods I spent alone were becoming less frequent. He was building up to the grand finale. I could feel it.

When he turned around, he had a baton in his hand. One end was wrapped tightly with barbed wire and had nails sticking out of it, like teeth. I gave a long sigh and closed my eyes, resting my forehead on the bench I was spread-eagled on. He gave a throaty chuckle that set off a rasping coughing fit. I heard him hock up phlegm from his chest. Again, I smiled, although I knew what was coming and he relished the terror he held over me.

A moment later he brought the club down onto my back. The spikes dug into my flesh and tore chunks out of me when he pulled it free. I screamed like an animal caught in a snare. He did it again. This time it slammed into my neck and shoulder. He tugged hard, but my hair became tangled with the metal and wood. He pulled harder still and I gave out a long, guttural groan. He kept on tugging until I heard a rip. I saw a chunk of my scalp and a bloody mass of hair attached to his weapon. I felt liquid running down my back and ribs and realised it was my blood.

My breathing was so heavy I thought my lungs were going to collapse. He did it again, this time ripping up the skin across my lower back. I whimpered and moaned as he continued whacking me. I heard the ribs on one side of my body crack beneath the unforgiving barrage.

I lay in a heap of broken bones, bloody and torn. He had exerted himself so much that he was left panting. His chest heaved up and down as he sucked in the air he needed to breathe. Strangely, I took no joy from his discomfort. After his breathing had returned to normal, he threw down the club and limped heavily out of the room; blackness enveloped me and I was lost to unconsciousness.

***

I lay perfectly still, terrified of the pain. It felt like the temperature in the room had been turned down. An icy breeze skimmed across the ruined, bleeding skin on my back. My scalp ached and I felt so dizzy I thought I would lose consciousness. Unfortunately, that didn't happen. Before I knew what was happening, the monster had come back into the room brandishing a can of fluid and a lighter. Without a second's hesitation, he squeezed the fuel over my shredded back. It stung, and my eyes watered so much I was temporarily blinded. But my ears were working and I heard the click of the lighter. The noise rang through me like aftershocks in a tsunami. I had just enough time to suck in a large breath before he lowered the flame to my skin and lit the petrol. I roared like a lion as the fire was born. I felt it licking me and making my skin bubble. Then my hair caught alight.

I choked on the smell of my own burning body and knew what it was like to be in hell. The arsonist leaned down and retrieved a rough woollen blanket from under my bench. He shook it out and threw it onto my smouldering shell. The remaining flames sizzled and hissed as they died. He stood back and wiped his dripping nose on his sleeve before removing a set of keys from his overall pocket. He approached the bench and unlocked my shackles. Had I been stronger, and able to think clearly, I would have seen my chance to escape, but instead I lay there, helpless. After unchaining my hands and feet, he swept me up and turned me onto my destroyed back. I squealed like a pig. I felt my spine tear through the burnt shredded layer of skin that remained. My ribs gave another loud crack and one pushed its way out of my red transparent casing. He roughly pulled my arms and legs into place before locking them in the iron cuffs again, and I felt his erection pushing against my side. It sent a shiver through me. Then he left.

I lay there, consumed by the new, excruciating level of pain. I could feel the raw muscles in my back, grinding against the hard wood. My skeleton felt so heavy in its skin. Breathing was impossibly difficult. The scent of burnt flesh was in the back of my throat, and my broken rib was pushing into one of my lungs. I began to convulse, and the harder I shook, the worse the agony became.

***

When I woke up, the light that poured in through the small window blinded me. It bounced off the mirror and straight into my eyes. Had I been a believer, it might have felt like a religious experience. The light was so clean and felt hot against my hollow face. Quickly, my vision adjusted and I was able to look around the room. I was still there. Nothing had changed. From the corner of my eye I caught a glimpse of something red moving in the mirror. I slowly turned to look more closely, and saw only my own reflection. I was greeted by a lump of bloody meat, but my hair remained.

I stared at myself for a long time. My brain was unable to comprehend what it was seeing. It was as if I had woken up in someone else's body. What I saw in the mirror wasn't me. It looked dead already, like a corpse in the early stages of decomposition. I tried to move my hand to my face to touch it. I needed confirmation that I was real, that *it* was real. Before then, part of me had been able to imagine escape, but looking at what remained of me brought the reality screaming home. He had not burnt me – my own imagination was aiding him in destroying my sanity.

Looking at my shredded back and my reflection, I was reminded of the graphic images I had seen in history books, of the bodies of prisoners at Auschwitz. I tried not to think of my mother having to identify *these* remains. She would never have believed it was me. It occurred to me that the families of his other victims had been subjected to that gruesome experience already, and I ached for them. I cursed him for extending the terror to those who were left behind. The gap left in their lives from the loss would be filled with horrific images. I doubted any of those people would ever be the same again. How could they be?

I battled with my reflection for many hours. I fell in and out of time. It felt like I was wandering around in the dark, searching for a light switch that didn't exist. I was a needle lost in a field full of haystacks. I began to feel at home in the maze of my mind. Before long I realised I would rather dwell in the darkness – the daylight was cruel. It showed me horrors I could never get to grips with. I turned my head away from the mirror and knew I would never be able to look at it again. That action took the most, but meant the least. It was time for me to say goodbye to the moon.

I longed for night to fall; I needed her blackness to consume the image of what I had seen. It seemed unlikely that the stars would ever shine again. I felt like I was being pulled out by the tide and I knew I would never return to the shore again. A swell of fury surged through me. I was angry that I was alive. I wanted to scream and shout and pull at the shackles. Cursed self-preservation stopped me. My skin felt tight and fragile and like it might break at any moment. I knew my scabby back had moulded itself to the table. Had I moved, it would have ripped. It was not a pain I was prepared to inflict on myself, the monster had done enough of that already. I would conserve my energy and prepare myself for his next visit.

I focused on the glimpses of memories flitting around my head. Images flashed rapidly through my mind. It was as if I were flicking through a photograph album. Snippets of my childhood appeared, vanishing into my subconscious. Strangely, I became obsessed with trying to remember my brother's eighth birthday party. I knew it had been a happy day but was unable to see it clearly. Colours whirled around in a cloud of blue smoke and I was kept from dreaming. It remained just out of reach.

Only Jude was clear. I wanted him to evaporate too, but he would not. So, I did the next best thing, I rewrote my end. I pretended my life was a book and I formulated a happy ending.

I tried not to think of the fantasy world I had lived in with Jude. I needed something more realistic. I pictured myself living in a cottage near a wood. Life would be uncomplicated. There would be chickens to feed and vegetables to look after. I would have a few apple trees. I imagined walking in the sunlight in the orchard, reaching up to pick ripe red apples. I could feel the warmth on my skin. Jude would be there, in the centre of it all, with our shaggy dog standing faithfully by his side. Our children would be playing on the swings: a girl and a boy. The boy would be the spitting image of him.

It didn't seem that much to ask for. All I'd ever really wanted was something simple. Sometimes, what you want and what you need are two very different things. During that moment, they were intertwined – freedom in whatever form it came.

The truth was, I was so tired. I had reached breaking point and hadn't anything left to fight on with. I could feel my body eating away at itself. Hunger was all-consuming and my breathing had become so shallow I thought my lungs might pack up at any moment. My thoughts crept like dying animals trying to pull themselves out of the gloom. It had been so long since I had been a human being, I could scarcely remember what it was like.

I was going to die like an animal and that seemed to make a poetic kind of sense. When you scratch the surface, that is what we are, after all: animals. Our televisions and smartphones are props we use to create a facade that we are more than that. I had always believed that to be true, but had never appreciated the relevance of my faith in that belief, until then. It turned out I did believe in something, after all.

I suppose it was predictable that I found myself indulging in distorted philosophical mantras, but I had to do something.

Lying there was actually fucking boring. In between the pain and self-pity, my time was empty and dull. It was similar to being in hospital. Time went more slowly than I'd thought possible. I wished I could have spent my last moments enjoying the pleasures of just being alive, but the truth is, I get bored very easily. I wondered if I should tell the monster that I was bored. Surely that would take the wind out of his sails. I am sure it wasn't something that had ever occurred to him – he would have been too busy enjoying the horror he had created. It saddened me that I was going to die emotionally broken. The physical pain, I could just about bear.

I had made a promise to myself, upon leaving Redwood Psychiatric Hospital, that I would fight my illness and never become an emotional mess like that again. I was gutted that I couldn't keep my promise, that was the worst thing of all.

It is a funny thing, having to address your mortality. I hadn't thought about how I might die, any more than anyone else my age – setting aside the period I had spent feeling suicidal, which is different. When the idea did enter my head, I'd presumed I would be old and, if I wasn't lucky enough to live to see my twilight years, that my life would be cut short by something like cancer, or a heart attack. You never think that you will die at someone else's hands. It wasn't too difficult to consider I might be blown up while travelling on a plane, but this, being there with the monster, I never could have imagined.

As children, we are taught to be careful when crossing the road. Parents teach their children to beware of strangers, and women know not to walk around in the dark on their own. I had chosen to ignore all the fundamental things I'd learnt about being safe, and that had landed me in the cellar.

I realise it was bad luck that led me there – I could have been any young woman walking along in the rain that night. He saw the opportunity and took it. It wasn't personal, I was simply in the wrong place at the wrong time. Again, my belief in fate was reaffirmed, although I cursed the universe for doing this to me.

The next time my monster paid me a visit, things were different. He came into the room as usual, but this time he seemed angry. Previously, he had been happy to see me: there had been a glint in his eyes, excitement about the next chapter of torture. This time he looked uninterested, like a child that had grown bored of playing with its latest toy. After a few minutes, he spoke.

'What's ya name?'

I was taken aback. It hadn't occurred to me that he didn't know my name. He knew my body so intimately, it seemed odd that we fundamentally remained strangers.

'Annabel,' I said in a whisper.

He grunted and got up from the stool. I readied myself, but he turned his back and left the room. I struggled to understand what had just happened, but the sound of my name had felt good. I said it again.

'Annabel, my name is Annabel.'

Just that word brought me a tiny bit of freedom. I was a person after all. I had a name and a family and a life. I had a past, and at one time thought I had a future. It was clear my name didn't matter to him, but I wondered why he wanted to know. Curiosity, I suppose. It might not have been important to him but it gave me a feeling of worth, strange as that may seem. Thinking about my name made me think about my family again – my name was synonymous with them; they were entwined.

I glanced into the mirror and, ignoring my own hideous reflection, gazed at the grey sky framed in the image of the window. The world looked dull and fitted in perfectly with how I felt. When I was little, and the weather was bad, I would sit with Will, eating popcorn and watching Star Wars films, over and over again. I remember the feel of the blanket I'd curled up under. It was large with beige squares, made from a soft fleecy fabric. My brother would sit at one end of the sofa and I at the other. Quite often we would have our guinea pigs on our laps, telling them to pay attention. I lost count how many times we watched those films.

In fantasy games, he would be Luke Skywalker and I was Princess Leia. We would take it in turns, swinging from the rope that hung from the chestnut tree in our garden, pretending we were battling Storm Troopers. Long sticks made good lightsabers, and our dog that followed us around, wagging its tail, became Chewbacca. The memory of this made me smile properly for the first time since my incarceration.

Lying on the bench, I began to hum to myself. I tried hard to remember the various tunes that John Williams had composed for the films. I couldn't remember them all, but while I hummed I felt content. I had found another happy place.

My thoughts were interrupted by the sound of the creaking ceiling. Heavy footsteps limped around above me – it had to be the monster. It wasn't possible that anyone else lived in the house. My screams would have been heard. I realised the house must be in the countryside somewhere. I hadn't thought about it until then, but I hadn't heard the sound of the city or roads.

It left me wondering what the house was like. It had to be old. The cellar had old beams in it and the floorboards were aged and worn. Even the air smelled ancient. The stale, musky stench of damp lingered like fog. I hoped the rest of the house shared the smell. I liked the idea of the monster living somewhere offensive to the senses. I pictured the rooms of his house being cluttered with filthy objects. It was easy to visualise him living in a dusty room with no windows. I wanted his existence to be miserable and hollow. My tired eyes scanned the room, looking for confirmation of my suspicions, but the cellar was empty and offered me no clues.

I heard him coughing and spluttering. For a moment, I thought he was on the stairs, making his way to the cellar, but he was still in the room above. It was hard to picture how he might fill his time, when he wasn't busy brutalising and killing. *Did he have a job?* Maybe, but I found it hard to care. It made no difference to my situation. I imagined him doing a labouring job, something physical that required strength, *like kidnapping, raping and killing.* I didn't want to spend another second thinking about him.

I focused my thoughts on Wookie, how his brown tail wagged backwards and forwards like a pendulum. It never seemed to stop. His slow and deliberate wag was reassuring. I wished I could see his large, kind eyes. He'd always made me feel safe – he had a knowing look. If ever I, or any of the family, were feeling blue, he would be there, sitting loyally by your side, his head resting gently on your lap. Stroking his solid head was calming.

It was strange how quickly my body had adapted to the new pain I was suffering. My skin felt dry and stretched too tightly over my bones like a covering of eggshell. I knew, if I moved, it would crack and bleed. I was sweaty. My back and legs throbbed endlessly. The pulsing tenderness felt like a hot blanket wrapped around me; it made a change to the cold feeling I had grown used to.

It was best not to concentrate on that, though. If I allowed myself to think about how my body was feeling, the ache increased tenfold. I understood that my pain was temporary, but it seemed the heinous nature of it was going to stay with me for eternity.

Slowly, the hours passed, and I watched as daylight faded. There was an orange glow in the room at sunset. The wooden beams looked warm and homely under the soft light. I pictured a beautiful sunset in my mind and allowed the colours to flood over me. I felt consumed by the pastel warmth and hoped it would last for a long time. But gradually, the sunset faded and darkness crept into the room. I realised I had been alone for a long time. This meant I should expect a visit from the monster soon. Adrenaline rushed around my body, like cars on a racetrack, and the familiar buzz of nervous anticipation left my body shaking. It hurt.

I heard him coming down the stairs and braced myself for the unknown. He came into the room and flicked on the light. The sudden brightness made the world I was trapped in seem stark and uncompromising.

'Annabel.' My name sounded wrong on his tongue. It didn't belong there. My stomach began to churn. From his pocket, he removed a chunk of dry bread. He approached me and held it to my mouth. I took a bite and chewed it for a long time, before swallowing it with difficulty. The bread was too dry. It caused more discomfort than it did me good. I no longer saw the point in eating anything.

'No more . . .' I croaked, turning my face away.

'Please ya self.' He put the bread in his pocket and turned his back. I thought he might be about to leave the room. From behind, he looked like a mountain; his bulky form seemed to eclipse the light from the single bulb that hung from the low ceiling. My blackened body felt like a vacuum.

Still with his back to me, he said, 'I saw ya mum on da telly. Nice lookin', ain't she?'

The horror of it left me speechless.

'Pleadin' she was. Wants to know where ya are, wants ya home.'

He turned to face me. He was enjoying himself. 'Fing is, da bitch'll see ya soon. May not recognise ya, but she'll see ya, for sure. Once I've finished, course.' And then added, 'Thought you'd like ta know.'

My heart was in my throat. *Not like this*, I prayed to the universe, *please, do not let her see me like this*. I imagined her in front of cameras. Lights flashing as photographers captured her agony. I felt sick at the thought of the monster looking at her, and panic began to bubble. Until then, I hadn't imagined I could feel any worse, but fear for my family brought with it a whole new level of dread.

'Don't you . . . just . . . leave her . . .' I struggled to speak.

'Old birds ain't my fing. Surely ya'd know dat by now. Stupid bitch.' He spat and muttered to himself. The disgusted look on his face told me that he was telling the truth. Relieved tears streamed uncontrollably down my cheeks. If he noticed, he didn't say anything. The swell of emotion surprised me – I'd thought I had no more tears left to cry.

As I began to get control of myself, he approached me and balled his hand into a fist. He punched into my stomach, three times, leaving me breathless and gasping for air. Then he rubbed his knuckles, smiled gleefully to himself, turned out the light and left the room.

I was left reeling. The blows had knocked the wind out of me with such ferocity that, once again, white spots danced about in front of my eyes. The familiarity was sickening. My mind didn't know whether to focus on trying to breathe, or trying to clear the stars from my vision. It took me a little while to calm down, but once I had I noticed my breathing was raspy. There was a thumping pain in my empty stomach. My intestines had been pounded and felt as if they were tangled up. Gurgling and growling noises echoed from my tummy in protest. This could not go on much longer. Surely the end was near.

**

The next time the monster returned I was ill, vomiting large amounts of bitter bile, tainted with blood. I knew I had a roaring temperature, and I was unable to control the liquid faeces that was pouring out of me. I remained lying in my own stench and filth for hours before he arrived. When he came in, he recoiled at the putrid odour and looked at me with contempt. It seemed it was all right for me to wallow in filth, provided it was a result of his handy work. He grunted and pulled the door closed. I thought my revolting state had put him off but, a minute or two later, he reappeared with a metal bucket. I could see water sloshing about at the top of it. It glistened and sparkled; it was the loveliest sight. Everything about it looked clean. I wanted to bathe in it. A second later, I got my wish.

The monster, whose top lip was curled in repulsion at the sight of me lying in my own excrement, took a step back from the table to which I was shackled. As if in slow motion, he threw the water over me like he was putting out a fire. I let out a high-pitched shriek. It was ice cold and my body was instantly covered in goose pimples. The feeling of the freezing water on my burns was almost soothing. After I had recovered from the shock, I began to enjoy the feeling of being clean. He hadn't meant to do me a favour, but that was how it felt. The tight feeling of my skin, which I had grown so accustomed to, was considerably relieved. The cold had been worth it; I felt the sweat from my fever being sluiced way.

Once the joy of the experience had faded, I noticed my teeth were chattering. I didn't know whether it was a result of the icy water or the fever.

'Disgustin' whore,' I heard him say to himself as he placed the empty bucket in the corner of the room. In the mirror, I noticed the sun was very low. The fever had left me disorientated and I couldn't tell whether it was dawn or dusk. The sun gleamed, like a large soft peach suspended in a marshmallow sky. It was stunning and I was lost in the beauty of it.

I looked at him, watching me with confusion. My face was almost happy, something he hadn't seen before. It brought me crashing back into reality: the sun may be lovely, but I was still in the cellar, I was still his.

***

He examined the new, cleaner version of me with curious eyes before deciding what he was going to do next. The monster walked over to his workbench and began to rummage through his toolbox. I felt my pulse quicken. I held my breath and tried to prepare myself for the next phase. I strained my sore head to see if I could get a glimpse of the implement he intended to use. I heard him suck in a nose full of snot – every noise that came from him was vile.

When he turned around he was holding a Stanley knife. The handle was faded blue and grubby but the blade shone with sharpness. I wished he would just cut my throat and be done with it. His revolting tongue came out of his mouth and wrapped itself around his fat pink bottom lip. The monster walked over to me and leaned down low so he could whisper in my ear.

'Ready?' I wanted to close my eyes, but I couldn't tear them away from the silver blade. With a firm hand, he pinned my elbow to the table so I couldn't move, then he sliced through the skin and muscle of my upper arm. The blood ran out, clean and new, like a red gushing waterfall. It stung to begin with, but then the pain was gone. He made three long cuts, which stretched from my armpit to my elbow, in my right arm. The blood that flowed looked vivid red next to my pale skin. I gritted my teeth but couldn't look away. I was transfixed. It was like watching someone else's autopsy. I felt utterly detached. When he had finished with my right arm, he moved around and made a start on my left, repeating the same cuts.

I could feel the warm blood seeping onto the table, soaking my back. When he'd finished, he stood back and admired his handiwork. Of all the things he'd done to me, this was the least painful. I suspected I might bleed to death – I felt dizzy, I had lost so much blood. He wiped the knife on his jeans and put it away.

'Back in a minute,' he announced, leaving the room.

Despite my light-headedness, I recalled the incident with the vinegar and wondered if he had gone to get some. When he reappeared carrying a bulging pillowcase, I thought he meant to smother me. Instead, he tipped the contents onto the workbench. The room filled with soft white feathers. They blew around in the air, carried by the slight draft that came in through a crack near the windowpane. The smaller ones floated about with the dusty air, before gradually finding their way back down to earth. It was almost beautiful.

He began to arrange the feathers into three neat piles, according to their size. It took him some time to finish the task, and once he had, he turned triumphantly to face me. I was still feeling giddy, but I sensed he hadn't finished with me. He scooped up a pile of the largest feathers and brought them over to the bench. Carefully, he removed one and ran it across his chin. The look of pleasure on his face was grotesque. With his free hand, he used his fingers to open up the knife wound on my arm. That hurt. He took the quill end and pushed it into the cut.

A rush of blood poured out, soaking the white feather and turning it scarlet. He repeated the process, over and over again, until he had put a number of feathers in my right arm. He moved to my left and did the same on that side. When all the large feathers had been used up, he stood back and tilted his head. He checked his work: it seemed he was pleased with it.

The monster went back to his toolbox and removed a long, thin needle and some dark brown embroidery thread. It didn't take a genius to work out what was coming next. He pinched the raw, cut skin together, and started stitching the feathers into my flesh. I squealed and wriggled; he slapped me hard across the face and put a rag in my mouth. The rag was dirty and oily. It smelled and tasted like petrol and it made me gag. I tried to spit it out but it was wedged in. With each new stitch, I bit down harder into the fabric. A guttural noise came from my throat and my breathing quickened. My chest heaved up and down. I noticed how sallow and flat my breasts had become, not unlike empty balloons. I was starving to death.

When he had finished, he tied a clumsy knot in the thread before cutting it. He repeated the process on my other arm. It felt right that he had turned me into an animal and I had been like a caged bird since he had abducted me. Now my body reflected my mind. The symbolism seemed fitting.

He stuffed the medium and small sized feathers into my remaining gaping cuts and sewed them up too – he had given me wings. The feeling of faintness stayed with me all the while. By the time he'd finished, I was too drained to protest anymore. He took a mobile phone out of his pocket and took a picture of me. The flash hurt my eyes. He squinted at the screen with his crazy eyes and examined the photograph.

I was repulsed. I wanted to scream and curse at him, but the gag was still in my mouth. My jaw was aching. I was breathing heavily through my nose and the smell of my blood mixed with the petrol rag was putrid. I gave a helpless moan and he removed the rag from my mouth.

'God isn't here,' I managed to get out at last.

He chuckled. 'I know dat!' he boomed. Then he left the room. The sound of the lock being turned, echoed around the damp walls as I lay there, helpless, battered and done for. I was as broken then as I would ever be. Whatever happened next didn't really matter. He had already won.

***

After that, he left me alone for about twenty-four hours. I was mangled inside and out; my body was numb. I no longer felt the pain like before and the feathers had been a figment of my imagination. Another nightmare blurring the lines between reality and hell. But it made a twisted sense: I wanted freedom and I'd pictured myself transforming into an angel.

Madness had become my home and I accepted it – the way you learn to tolerate the cold in winter. I would never feel the satisfaction of comfort again, but I didn't mourn it. It was such a distant memory I could barely remember what it felt like. It was no more than a lost dream.

My death felt closer now than ever before. I was already dead in a sense, just my useless body was holding on to life, refusing to give up. I cursed the survival instinct that is ingrained in us all. Again, the human condition turned out to be flawed. I was tired of seeing the negatives in being alive and I was tired of living, of *thinking* about living. I wanted my mind to be as numb as my body. I wanted something inane to concentrate on, so I focused on the pattern in the cellar beams.

I examined every crack in the wood, the rings and the knots. I began to see the subtle different shades in the brown. I wondered what the trees had looked like before they had been hacked down to build the house that the monster, and those who had gone before him, lived in. I tried to work out how old the house might be, maybe sixteenth or seventeenth century? I had no idea what size it was. The cellar wasn't huge, but I had a feeling the house above me was much bigger.

I wondered if the monster had money. It wasn't impossible. I doubted the house was rented – he couldn't risk the interference of estate agents, or a nosy landlord. I was reminded of my room at home, which would now be sitting empty. My things would still be there, scattered about on the chair and other surfaces. A half-empty glass of water probably remained on my bedside table, gathering dust. *Had people been through my belongings, searching for a clue to my whereabouts? Had the police been there?* It seemed likely. I felt hollow at the thought of never seeing my room again, or gazing upon the photographs of my family and friends; I wouldn't get to play my vinyl records or flick through any of the books I owned; my skin wouldn't feel the fabric of my clothes against it. They would be put away in boxes and most likely stored in my mother's attic. That was where she kept Lucy's belongings, to this day. She couldn't bear to part with them.

My life would be packed neatly away, and stored in the darkness until eventually someone decided it was time to let go of me, or I was forgotten. It was a solemn realisation: I missed my life. This wasn't living, it was surviving.

Out of the corner of my eye, I saw a flash in the mirror. I turned my head with lightning speed to see what had caused it. What greeted me was my own reflection: I had forgotten about myself, the vision never failed to appal.

My skin was pallid, where it wasn't raw. My hair was thinning like dry grasses in the desert. My eyes were so sunken, I looked sixty years older than I was. My mouth was dry and my lips were cracked and pale. I felt a surge of emotion - I wanted to scream and felt I might have found the energy to do so. I let out a long blood-curdling yell.

It seemed to go on for a very long time. Once I had finished, and the noise and pain from inside had been expelled, I slumped back. My ribcage was heavy on my organs and my lungs felt stretched by the outburst. The release had done me good, though. It had exorcised some of the hatred that had been building up inside me.

I had begun to fear that my monster's spirit was infecting me, that his rage and deep-seated loathing was contagious. I was learning what it was to hate. I had begun to find satisfaction within anger.

He had done his best to ruin me physically, and I was horrific to look at, but he wasn't going to have my soul.

I heard the thud of feet directly above me. The ceiling vibrated with each footstep and I could tell exactly where the monster was standing. I prepared myself for his return. I listened intently to the noises coming from above. I thought I heard the scream of a kettle; I heard banging, what sounded like pots and pans, cupboards being opened and closed. It was easy to imagine him going about his daily business, tidying his kitchen, *pretending to be human.*

I wondered what had made this man a monster. Had he been born like that or had life twisted its knife into him? There was no excuse for what he had become, but I lingered on the debate of nature versus nurture. I had always been a firm believer in nature – I accepted that events can result in us adjusting our behaviour, but I had always felt that people are born to be who they become.

Lying in that prison left me feeling doubtful. It was too depressing to think that the monster was always going to end up killing and torturing. I found no comfort in that answer. It would have been easier to believe he had once been good, and life had dealt him a shit hand that had ruined him. I needed there to be an excuse for the monster, any excuse. I couldn't fathom the idea he was born that way.

I looked around the cellar. It seemed smaller than it had before. Everything looked to be under a shadow, and not a glimpse of natural light could be found. It felt like late afternoon and the small world I inhabited was a chilly shade of grey. I examined the reflected view of the window and was transfixed by the sight. Perfect, white flakes floated down from the sky; it was snowing and I wallowed in the vision of purity, but the season was irrelevant in my dungeon – I'd lost all concept of time.

My urge to be out in the snow was almost unbearable. I would have killed to feel the icy cold crystals land and melt on my skin.

I knew I would never again feel snow against my palms, or flakes landing softly on my nose and face. I would never again put on gloves or a hat and wander in the fields. Or hear the crunch of fresh snow beneath my boots. I remembered what it felt like and my head filled with childhood memories again. For a moment, I was happy. I relived an afternoon spent with Will, hurling snowballs at the barn roof. Throwing them in the air for our dog to jump and catch.

The next time I saw the monster, he burst into the cellar with an enthusiasm I hadn't seen in him before.

He hummed a familiar tune as he examined me. The madness in his eyes only reflected my own. This was a man who should never be allowed near people should have been locked up in a zoo and studied by scientists, or fed to hungry bears.

My dread returned in spades, and nervous anticipation made it much worse. I couldn't bear the wait. It was a cruel game he had invented to extend my turmoil. I tried to relax and made an effort to slow my thumping heartbeat, which felt like it might burst out of my chest.

I looked back at the snow-covered ground I could see in the mirror's reflection. It was glistening under a gentle sunlight. It looked pure and clean. I felt my pulse slowing down and gradually got a hold of myself. I marvelled at the tiny, glittering ice crystals that caught the light and seemed to shine with all the colours of the rainbow. I was so enraptured by the sight that I temporarily forgot *he* was in the room with me. He caught my attention again by thrusting his face close to mine and coughing, 'Hello.'

It made me jump, and a sharp surge of pain coursed through my body. My spine felt like it was broken in a thousand places, and the bones in my pelvis throbbed with the discomfort of movement. I turned my face away from his. My dry throat filled with the familiar taste of bile. I wretched but nothing would come out. My stomach was completely empty. I could feel his warm, sickly breath on my cheek and I closed my eyes. I needed to escape the horror of having him so close. It was then that I felt his dry tongue lick my bruised cheek. He whispered in my ear, 'I got a special present for ya. Somefing real nice, bitch. It'll clean ya right up.'

His words echoed in my ear and I smelled booze on his breath. The sweet scent of cheap whiskey turned my stomach and made me want to throw up again. I was tired of his clichés. Did the psycho think he was starring in a film? I didn't respond to his vicious mockery.

He walked over to his workbench and searched around in his toolbox. I listened intently to the noise of the tools bashing and scraping against each other, trying to decipher what it was he was handling. When he turned around to face me, a twisted grin on his ugly face, he kept his right hand behind his back, hiding the instrument from me.

'Dis is gonna hurt.' He was relishing the power he held over me. Slowly bringing his hand forward, he revealed a set of secateurs. I was horrified. I suspected my fingers were at risk and tried to prepare myself for their removal. He put the cutters on the surface I was tied to and slowly ran a chubby finger down my torso, starting at my protruding collarbone and ending at my pelvis. His fingertip felt rough against my thin, dry skin and it sent terror through every nerve in my body.

His fingers lingered in my pubic hair as he played with the wiry coils. My body began to tremble, fear took hold of me. Without any warning, he roughly grabbed my chin between his fingers and moved his face close to mine.

'Stay still for dis bit, if I were ya,' he hissed, and his mad eyes bulged.

I did as I was told. I focused on a spot on the ceiling. I didn't want to witness what he was going to do. His hand moved back over my private parts and his fingers began to search me. I held my breath and closed my eyes, knowing what was coming. I heard the snip of the garden cutters and agony surged through me, swiftly followed by a warm, wet flood. I knew I was screaming but I couldn't hear myself. He had circumcised me.

My scream went on for so long I had to gasp to catch my breath. I opened my eyes but refused to look at the area he had just decimated. I could see the monster had returned to his workbench and his broad back was turned to me. I felt as if I had wet myself but I knew this time it was blood, and that was when I allowed the darkness of sleep to consume me.

***

When the monster turned, he was holding a jar with a yellow-tinged transparent liquid in it. In the other hand, he held the metal lid. I didn't want to face him but I couldn't look away: I was gripped with a fascinated disgust. He was looking at me with a crazed closed-lipped smile. Slowly and deliberately he opened his mouth and allowed his fat tongue to come out. On its tip sat a small, bloody lump of flesh that had once been part of me. My mouth hung open as he held the fleshy morsel loosely between his teeth.

His shoulders moved heavily up and down as he silently chuckled to himself. He moved the piece of me between his lips, and half dropped, half spat the grisly lump into the jar of fluid. There was a splash as it broke the liquid's surface before it floated to the bottom, leaving behind it a red cloudy trail. He held the jar up to his face and proudly examined the contents.

The glass and its contents distorted the shape of his eyes and nose. His face looked like it was being pulled in all directions. One eye was large and bulging, the other was stretched sideways and appeared magnified. His eyelashes looked like thick, dark spiders' legs and I could see that, like me, he was dead inside.

***

The next time I looked into the mirror I saw a torrent of rain battering the small glass window. The world outside was cold and grey and the downpour drummed loudly on the panes. The snow had been washed away and dirty, icy lumps remained clinging to the limp grass. I lay there sweating. The moisture that poured from my skin reflected the weather outside. I felt hot and cold at the same time. It was as if my body was fighting poison. My veins burned under my skin and I couldn't focus.

At the same time, I realised I could no longer feel anything below my knees. My legs were swollen, and marbled in a variety of colours – mainly blacks, purples and blues: they were riddled with gangrene, which stank and was slowly creeping up towards my torso. My legs looked like dark stoneware pottery, tinged with green and yellow. I viewed my rotten limbs with detachment, as if they had nothing to do with me. I felt like a pathologist in a morgue.

A fresh surge of anger rose in me. I could just about accept that the monster had ruined me, but I was livid he had inflicted pain on my family.

My fractured mind kept coming back to the same thought – as if every idea I had was for the first time. I was living in a world of déjà vu. Somewhere in my synapses I was aware I had thought about these things before. The fever had a tight grip on me and I knew if the monster didn't kill me, the poisonous infection coursing through my body soon would. I wanted the fever to be responsible for my death, to take the opportunity away from my captor. It offered me a glimmer of hope. I longed for the grotesque man to find my corpse and realise that his final sick enjoyment had been snatched away.

***

I attempted to find my way back to the dream world I had inhabited so happily. Reality had returned to me with such a vengeance, it had severed all ties to the fictional place I'd once found solace. I suppose it would have been too much for my mind to cope with – I would have been unable to suffer the transition from heaven to hell without causing myself more damage. To splinter my mind further would no doubt have been the final straw, and the damned human desire to survive would not allow me to self-destruct.

I watched my breath cloud - it was the only tangible evidence that I still existed. I noticed how strained my breathing was, and the rattle that echoed in my chest with each breath. My ribs felt like a cold, concrete cage, imprisoning my lungs. I listened to the wheezing from my chest. The noise became almost soothing and held a hypnotic quality. I found myself drifting in and out of a feverish consciousness and still the sound remained a constant. At the same time, I could feel the pulse in my wrists and neck. The rhythm of the beat was in time with my shallow breaths. My body and its clock had begun a countdown, I could feel it.

The door to the cellar swung open with a loud thud. I hadn't noticed the sound of his footsteps on the stairs. He shuffled into the room and pulled the stool into the corner, shyly sitting on it, trying to balance his large frame. He sat there, awkwardly, looking at the floor. I had never seen him like that and this new side of him left me feeling uneasy. Naively, I had come to believe that the monster could no longer surprise me. I was wrong.

I noticed his mouth was moving and he appeared to be whispering to himself. His voice was so quiet that I couldn't hear what he was saying. I strained, but his tone was indistinguishable from the distant rumble of thunder. I couldn't tell if he was talking to me or to himself. He remained on the stool, muttering, for at least five minutes, before slowly getting up and inching towards me. He was furiously chewing the nails of his thumbs and was finding it difficult to look me in the eye. He stood a few feet away from my bench, half of his face hidden in the shadow. He looked almost childlike, but as mad and monstrous as ever. Again, he murmured nonsensically. A tear ran down my cold cheek as I turned my face away from him and closed my eyes.

I heard the jangling of keys and spun round to find him coyly fiddling with my shackles. The locks were stiff and it took some force before he was able to pop open the first one, on my ankle. I stared down at my damaged but free foot in disbelief. The monster shuffled to my other side and released my other ankle's shackle. Then he backed away and returned to the shadows. A moment or two later, he spoke.

'Now ya can go. Dada says it's time for ya to go home now. You has learnt ya lesson.'

I blinked a few times, questioning whether what I'd heard was real. Unable to speak, all I could do was look helplessly at the restraints around my wrists. *How did he expect me to leave if I was still attached to the wooden bench?* He eyed the metal cuffs and chains that held me prisoner. Apprehensively, he continued.

'Ya mustn't fight or wiggle when I unlock dem. Dada says you is to be a good gal, alwhite?'

My mouth was too dry to utter a single word. I nodded my head so violently that it brought on an instant migraine. He seemed satisfied and returned to his task of freeing me. With the final click of the last lock I let out an exaggerated breath; I hadn't moved but already I felt free. I almost smiled at the monster – almost. He too, seemed pleased.

'Well, now you is free. Fly away, lil' birdie.'

He put the keys on his workbench and turned to leave the room. My heart began to race and panic surged through me. *Don't leave me!* I squealed like a rabbit in a snare and he looked at me with confusion plastered across his face. I extended an arm in his direction and silently pleaded for his help.

'Nah, nah, gal,' he said. 'You have to take the step yaself. Free yaself is what Dada always says.' He left the door open behind him, before beginning his ascent up the creaking stairs.

I lay there in stunned silence. *Could this really be happening?* The excited rush of blood to my head made me feel dizzy. I looked around, frantically trying to work out how to exit my hell. I stared at my legs and wondered how to get down off the bench.

Slowly, and with immense effort, I lifted my right arm across my body. I didn't have the energy to move quickly. I lay back, gasping for air, trying to steady my breathing. I felt light-headed and needed to compose myself. I had to focus on my next move. My mouth was so dry. I searched the room for anything to drink but found nothing. I heard the familiar footsteps in the room above me. My heart leaped into my throat and I realised I had no time to waste. I needed to get out of there before the monster changed his mind.

With a low groan, I managed to turn my body onto its side. My bones cracked in protest and my sores throbbed. Determined to overcome my physical state, I forced myself to swing my diseased legs over the side of the bench and sit up. It took all the energy I had. Blood rushed to my head and I felt very sick. I looked down at my thighs and the small amount of flesh that still clung to my skeleton. The room span around me and I gripped the edge of the bench to steady my fragile frame.

Once the feeling had passed, I hurled myself onto the floor. There was no way I was going to be able to walk out of my prison. I would have to drag myself out. I landed with a hollow thud and the vibration of the hard floor rippled through me. The ground felt so cold against my brittle skin, which had cracked on impact in some places and leaked red. My bony hips were the cause of severe agony, but I pushed on. What choice did I have?

I gritted my teeth and dragged my body along the floor, away from the cellar, using the small amount of strength I had left in my arms. My injuries scraped along the floor and opened up where they had started to heal. A burning sensation gripped me.

My progress was slow but steady as I dragged myself to the bottom of the stairs. I rested there for a moment and looked up at the daunting task ahead of me. The stairs seemed to go on forever. I could see light through the open door at the top, but the staircase itself was dark and smelled musty.

I tried to pull myself up, but my legs scraped against the edge of the stairs and the agony was too much to bear. I stopped and allowed the pain to flood me for a moment, then decided to change my approach. If I was unable to move forward, I was left with one option: go backward. I flipped myself onto my back and my spine creaked in complaint. Taking all my weight on my buttocks and elbows, I slowly started the climb again. Thankfully, it was easier. Watching the cellar get farther away with each step was a wonderful and surreal experience. I started to believe I was going to make it.

When I finally reached the top step I was limp and breathless. I rolled onto my front and allowed myself to rest. With a determined push of my left hand, I managed to open the door enough to get through. The door was heavy and my fingertips were numb. I squinted and turned my eyes away from the light. I had become so used to dull darkness that the brightness hurt; It was like waking up in sunshine. I shielded my face with my arm as I tried to adjust to the light. Cautiously, I surveyed the house before me.

It wasn't what I had expected. In my imagination, I had envisioned the monster living among filthy piles of old newspapers, the windows thick with dirt and dust. I'd thought rats and mice would live with him, side by side.

It wasn't anything like that. The home he lived in was neat and tidy and old-fashioned; the floors were polished oak. It belonged back in the fifties and looked like my grandmother's house. Even the paintings on the walls were from a bygone era.

The mention of his 'Dada' was beginning to make sense. Perhaps the monster came from a long line of depravity. My pulse quickened at the thought, and I decided not to hang around deliberating any longer.

I searched left and right for an exit. My instincts guided me right. I followed my nose and dragged myself through the dated sitting room, desperately trying not to make a sound. My senses were on full alert as I focused all my attention on the door that led out of the room. I slithered past two high-backed armchairs, upholstered in embroidered floral fabric. An ancient television sat on a teak side-table. On the mantelpiece there was a porcelain Victorian vase, which was white, with hand-painted posies of flowers on it. My mother would have liked it.

I struggled on, refusing to look back. I felt the floorboards against my skin but was no longer conscious of my nakedness. When I got within arm's length of the closed door, I flopped to the ground and allowed myself a moment's rest. I thought I heard a sound behind me and spun my head around to investigate. Every movement was painful. I noticed the bloody trail of skin and sweat that I had left behind me – a slippery path leading back to my dungeon. Claustrophobia returned in an instant. I reached up to the door handle and turned it. The action was agony.

When the door opened I discovered my instincts had led me in the right direction. There was a hallway, with stairs leading up to the first floor and a front door leading outside. I was nearly there, I could feel it.

As I groped my way along the terracotta-coloured rug on the floor, I noticed a picture hanging, pride of place, next to an old, round ship's clock. The time was ten past three. In the frame was an old black and white photograph of a family. From their clothes, it looked like it had been taken in the seventies. In the picture there were two serious parents, and one plain-looking boy of about four years old. The father stood, glaring at the camera, unsmiling. He had his hand firmly on his son's shoulder. The mother, standing a foot away from her husband and son, looked meek and sparrow-like. I realised I was looking at the monster as a boy with his parents. *How could such an average-looking family have given birth to that amount of pain and suffering?*

It occurred to me that the boy, my monster, may not have acted alone, that his father could have been his accomplice, his guide. I felt sickened by the idea. His father would be an elderly man by now. I imagined him, bed-bound and barking orders at his simple son. The pair of them had probably been murdering for years.

My head whirled with gruesome images and pictures of violence. The fear and revulsion returned and my body shook uncontrollably. Vertigo took hold and I was unable to move. The walls closed in around me and it felt as though the ceiling were coming down. Breathless with terror, I frantically scrabbled around on the floor. I didn't have the luxury of time. The more I thought about it, the harder it was. In the end, I had to let the panic attack take its course. The harder I fought, the worse it got; but, as I succumbed, I felt my mind and body let go. After a short time, I lay still and lifeless on the floor of the monster's hallway.

When I came to I felt a bitterly cold breeze against my skin. I heard the sound of my teeth chattering and was acutely aware of my nudity. I couldn't open my eyes at first. My brain thumped against my skull. I knew the light would do more harm than good. I tried to shake the heavy feeling. My mind gradually kicked into gear and I remembered where I was. My eyelids sprang open and I scanned around for signs of danger. I was alone, escape was still a possibility. The icy breeze was coming from a gap beneath the front door. I looked at the clock on the wall and saw that only ten minutes had gone by.

I pulled myself a little closer to the door and stretched up towards the handle. I tried to turn it a number of times, but it was stiff and I had no luck. I slumped back down on the ground and took some deep breaths before making a second attempt. I had to summon up all my might and anger to release the bolt that held the door closed. Eventually, the door flew open and the wind came sweeping in, dancing on my flesh. I hadn't felt fresh air for a long while. I would have relished it, had it not been mid-winter. It felt abrasive on my fragile skin.

From the front door I could see an open space, in the centre of which stood a cherry tree. A rusty, old army-green jeep was parked up near a straggly border. The sky was grey and thick and darkness was beginning to get its grip on the land. The threat of night lingered in the air with oppressive force.

Looking into the distance, I tried to get a glimpse of another house or building, but found none. This house, wherever it was, was on its own. I looked at the ground outside and saw it was frozen. I doubted my body would be able to withstand the icy temperature. As luck would have it, I was within reach of a hat stand that was covered with men's coats. I pulled down the warmest looking one and slipped my skinny, bruised and broken frame into it. It was a huge, woollen-checked number that felt itchy and foreign against my skin. I tried to ignore the fact that it belonged to the monster.

I had no idea how far I would have to travel before I'd reach civilisation, but I was determined to make it – despite the weather and the creeping darkness. I did not look back as I tugged myself over the doorstep and out into the cold. I felt a spot of rain on my head and looked up at the sky. It looked ready to break and I opened my mouth and stuck out my tongue, hoping to catch a raindrop. No more came. I longed for a drink and clung to the idea it might be just around the corner.

I pulled myself a few metres across the driveway, getting closer to the grass island and the tree. I felt small and insignificant beneath its sprawling naked branches. The sensations I had were conflicted: I felt safe and under threat at the same time. I made it to the thick gnarled trunk. I lifted myself up and rested my back against it. It was so nice to be sitting upright. Again, I was aware of a light drop of water landing on my head and running down my neck.

The light was fading fast and I felt scared and exposed. I had become accustomed to the small space in which the monster had kept me. The temperature was also falling and I could see a frozen layer covering the grass; the murky puddles of melted snow had a film of ice on them. I was repulsed by what the coat represented, but was glad to have it.

I set off again, slowly dragging my useless frame. Escape was on the horizon. The world was silent, apart from the noise of my body on the stones of the driveway. There were no birds - I was truly alone.

Then, from behind me, came a low chuckle. I froze – I recognised that laugh. I picked up the pace and tried to put more distance between us, but I heard the crunch of footsteps approaching from the house. He was gaining ground and there was no escape.

I saw the man I had hoped I would never see again. He fixed me with his cold stare and took the last few steps to reach me.

He stopped, inches from my head. His large Timberland boots were grubby and the laces were fraying. I looked up at him. His expression had changed. He was no longer the shy, retiring creature I had last seen in the cellar. Before me, stood the familiar animal I was well acquainted with. He stood silently over me for some time. I didn't try to speak or move. I thought if I stayed still, he couldn't see me.

Eventually, he bent down, and said in a husky voice, 'Where da ya fink you is going?'

He wrapped one of his large hands around my throat and pulled me up. With no effort, he flung me over his right shoulder and began stomping back towards the house. I moaned and tried to speak.

'B-but you-your Da-da,' I managed to hoarsely whisper, stopping the monster in his tracks. He shrugged me off, onto the ground with a thud. I felt my ribs crack and I screamed like a child.

'What ya sayin about Dada?' He bent down low and shoved his face into mine.

I was breathless and winded from my harsh landing. It took a moment or two before I could respond.

'Y-you . . . said . . . he . . . s-said . . . l-let . . . m-me . . . go . . .'

The monster sat down on the ground next to me and shook his head in a matter-of-fact fashion.

'Changed 'is mind, he did. Says ya is a wrong 'un, and I need to see dat da rubbish gets put out.' He dusted off his hands and stood up. 'It's time na.' He grabbed me by my right wrist and dragged me along behind him. I tried to put up a fight but I was too weak. I was no match for the strength of the man who was going to kill me, my screams were half croaks; he was unfazed by my attempts, they were of no significance to him.

Effortlessly, he pulled me back into the house and into the kitchen. He released his grip and I collapsed in a heap on the cool tile floor. The kitchen was vast with a cream Aga and a pine kitchen table and chairs. It was a homely, country kitchen that might have belonged to a normal family. The monster flicked on the kettle and pulled up a chair. Without any warning, he picked me up and sat me on it. My head slumped forward with the pain that travelled through every inch of my trembling body.

Next, he bent down and opened the cupboard beneath the ceramic sink and I listened as he rummaged about. The kettle whistled and I watched as a cloud of steam poured from the spout. I had a vision of myself leaping up out of the chair, reaching for the boiling kettle and pouring it over his fat head. The thought made me grin inside. As I wondered if his inventive nastiness was rubbing off on me, he turned around, triumphantly brandishing a length of coarse rope. He slid across the floor towards me and began to tie me tightly to the chair. The rope burned my skin and dug into my injuries, sending fresh waves of agony through me.

Once he had checked and double-checked the knots, he made himself a mug of tea, as if having a dying woman bound to a chair in his kitchen was perfectly normal. I was as astounded as I was horrified.

He sat in a chair on the opposite side of the table and gulped his tea. I could smell the sweetness and my mouth began to water. He noticed the desire in my eyes and shrugged as he drained his cup. At the same time, I noticed the distinctive smell of a pie cooking. The scent of crusty pastry and gravy filled my nostrils and set my head spinning. The smell was too much for my mind, it took me back to happier times – lunches spent in cosy pubs, my Mother's cooking; the food represented comfort. It was something I longed for.

I hung my head, and felt saliva swish around my mouth for the first time in days. I had become so used to my lips being dry, the moistness felt alien. I heard the chair legs squeak against the floorboards and sat bolt upright. The monster opened a cupboard and removed a packet of bourbon biscuits. *Tea and biscuits, how quaint.* He removed a biscuit and wafted it under his nose, teasing me. I turned away, it was too much. The small things seemed to bother me most.

He grinned, revealing his uneven teeth, and took a large deliberate bite out of the bourbon. He swallowed it without chewing, and I watched as the lump of biscuit travelled down his throat. A few crumbs clung to the whiskers around his chin and I was reminded of a scene from Roald Dahl's *The Twits*, in which Mr Twit's revolting beard collects various scraps of food. It was such a vivid image from my childhood; I was grateful that my mind had found a way to belittle the monster.

'Better get on wiv it, den.' He wiped his mouth with the back of his hand and the crumbs tumbled to the floor.

In one swift movement, he picked up the chair I was tied to, and carried me out of the kitchen as if I were weightless. He set me down in the hallway while he retrieved a heavy chain from a cupboard underneath the stairs. He pulled the long, thick metal links over his shoulder, picked me up, and left through the front door.

It was almost dark. The sky was a purplish blue and soft charcoal clouds gathered together. He took me over to the jeep and put me in the open back, along with the massive chain that clunked to the floor. The monster slid into the driver's seat and started the engine. The jeep spluttered into life and accelerated away from the farmhouse. About forty metres from the house there was a field with a gate. My monster left me in the car, with the engine running, while he got out and pushed open the gate. Moments later we were bumping over the grassy field, heading into the darkness. I considered screaming but my throat was too sore.

The wooden chair creaked and bounced in the back and I thought it would topple over. The scent of hay was mixed with the familiar scent of the sea.

The 4x4 rattled along for a few moments, its headlights guiding the way. I strained my neck and tried to make out where we were going. Soon, we came to a halt near a dune. The monster turned off the engine but left the lights on, shining in the direction of the shore.

Grunting, he slid out of the jeep and slammed the door behind him. The whole jeep vibrated and I was reminded of his brute strength. He walked over to what appeared to be a gravestone, stood with his hands on his hips, and looked at it for a long time. I listened out for a sign of help but heard nothing. I was trapped by the deadly silence. Panic set in and I tried to wriggle my right hand free from the rope. The harder I fought to free myself, the more the fibres rubbed and cut into my skin. I had been concentrating so hard on trying to escape, I hadn't noticed the monster return. Then I saw his face, watching me. Shaking his head, he opened the door with a tut.

'Now, what ya finkin' of doin'?' He sounded disappointed. 'Can't ya see, ya ain't goin' nowhere.' He reached in and pulled me towards him as I began to sob.

'No use crying, bitch,' he said as he lifted my chair out of the jeep and dragged me, and it, across the ground. I could see little ahead of me, only blackness, then something glistened on the ground under the headlights. He set me down and left me while he returned to the car.

It took a minute for my eyes to adjust. Eventually I could make out the waves; we were close to a shabby-looking jetty. My heart sank. *Was this where my body was going to lie?* The lump in my throat felt like concrete.

The monster returned, cheerfully, with the chain and a number of bamboo garden torches. He stuck four of the torches, set about a metre apart, into the sandy ground and lit the wicks. The flames looked magical against the blackness of the night. He stood back and admired the scene. I held my breath, wondering what to expect from him next. He removed a quarter bottle of whiskey from his inside jacket pocket and sipped it in silence.

Now that I could see better, I turned my attention back to the grave. The light from the flames had revealed two of them. The mound on the right appeared to be much older and had long grass growing out of it. I read the headstone. There was one word, coarsely carved: Mummy. My eyes darted to the more recent-looking second stone, which read: Dada.

My mouth hung open as I tried to make sense of it all. Then, like a lead balloon, all the pieces of the puzzle fell into place. The monster was watching me work it out and he interjected.

'Is all for 'im. He tells me which gal to get. Dada knows best, and now ya gunna get it, just like he wants ya ta.'

He dragged me, still bound to the chair, onto the rickety deck of the jetty. In the ripples of the water I saw the moon's reflection; she was low and not quite full. I marvelled at her. *At least I get to see you one last time.* I gazed at the pearly orb as the monster cut the ropes that were keeping me strapped to the chair. I fell to the floor.

The monster unwound the dense chain, before fiddling with a rusty padlock. It clicked open and the echo travelled over the sea. With the noise bouncing off the water, came the knowledge that this would be my final prison. He tugged at the chain to make sure it was secure and removed the bottle of liquor from his coat to take another slug.

He moved me to the edge of the jetty. I was inches away from the water and I felt its coldness dancing around my legs. I held my breath. I knew what was coming. The monster nodded in the direction of the graves and said, 'Time to meet Dada.'

As he turned his back to fetch the chain that would help me sink, I closed my eyes, let my head go floppy, and rolled myself into the icy wetness.

I wasn't prepared for the bitter cold. The freezing stab of the water made me open my eyes and I started to panic. I struggled and took in deep breaths of black, salty water. I felt myself sinking, and the further down I went, the colder it got. After a few metres my body made contact with the silt on the bottom. I could see nothing in front of me and my lungs began to hurt.

My life didn't flash before my eyes. I felt darkness embrace me, as the last bubbles of air drifted up and escaped my body. The last thing I thought of was Jude. In a dream, he would have dived in and breathed life back into me. But this wasn't a dream. With hapless ease, I finally stopped living. The second before I left my body, I felt like a bird, singing after a storm.

Then I saw the wobbly moon through the water above me, and a feeling of calm came over me. I sat perfectly still, allowing fate to take the lead. The moon smiled down at me and promised me freedom. As I drowned beneath her spotlight, I believed her.

Epilogue

I wish it had been different. I wish I'd had more foresight. I wish, I wish so many things. It is hard to know where to begin. I wish most of all that death was how I had imagined it to be: empty, numb and painless, but it was not that kind. Death exists like a shell. It is the shadow of the living. I remain here as I am. I am not the person I was before my murder. I am no longer a person at all. All I am is the feeling I was at the moment of my death – the outline of a woman. The broken bits of my soul flit between the realms of reality and non-existence. I am not a ghost but I share the world with them. The haunted are with me and I watch as the restless walk the earth.

I would like to be able to offer you a neat ending. It would be better if I told you that the world is a kind and gentle place, and dreams do come true. I don't doubt that may be the case for some people. Neither should you. But I can only tell you *my* story, and that is how it went. I am sorry if you are disappointed and would like to know what happened to the monster. I wish I could tell you he was caught, or karma stepped in and played her hand. The truth is, I don't know, and I never will. I have only the memory of my grievance.

Maybe he will pay for what he did, maybe he will be caught. Maybe not. I don't know if the people I love will ever be able to bury me. Perhaps my body will never be found, perhaps it already has been. I only know how it feels to be swallowed by the black satin night and how heavy eyelids can feel – like final veils of concrete. I am the feeling of calm acceptance. Death made me a bride. I am nothing more than I was at the moment of my death.

The ghost of myself lingers now, haunting me. It whispers on the salty breeze and taunts me with the promise that my death has only just begun.

My light is dark
And dark is my night.
While my noble madness rocks
Backwards and forwards.

The shadows on my wall dance
Tormented by the song
That plays tirelessly inside my head.

And then the mania arrives
And the looming thunderclouds part.
They retreat in the psychedelic beams of hot light
Which take me to another place.

Then the sadness arrives
And refuses to leave
Weighing me down like cement.

And when that burden has lifted
Creeping elation grabs me by the throat
Tightening its grip,
Promising to never let go.

What is worse?
The cold dark or the fire?
They are lovers taking turns
Of raping my mind.

And yet,
I would never be without them
And they could not exist
Without me.

THE END

Acknowledgements

First of all, I would like to say a heartfelt thank you to Jasper Joffe. Jasper gave me my big break and without his help and faith, I would not have the career I do today.

Secondly, I would like to thank Alexina Golding for all her help reworking the book. Your input was priceless – thank you.

To Joanne, who helped knock the book into shape, I am extremely grateful for your input, and to the proof reader who had the difficult job of tidying up all my typos, I am in your debt.

To my family, my friends and all the people who encourage me to keep going, I would be lost without you.

Finally, I would like to take a minute to say that this book was intended as a nod to the suffering that goes on inside the heads of people who have mental health issues. Some make it back from the brink; others don't. This is for everyone who has seen the darkness and stepped back into the light.

Book club questions

1. What did you like best about *Broken?*

2. What did you like least about *Broken*?

3. Have you read any similar books?

4. Have you read other books by this author and how did this one compare?

5. The author uses graphic descriptions of torture as a metaphor for mental health problems, how effective is this?

6. What do you believe was real in the novel?

7. Why did the author blend fantasy and reality in this book?

8. If you could hear this story from another character's point of view, who would that be and why?

9. How did *Broken* make you feel, and did your emotions change as you read it?

10. What do you think were the main points the author was trying to make?

11. Did any themes emerge in *Broken* that surprised you?

12. The ending was ambiguous – do you think it was the ghost of Annabel telling the story, did what the protagonist tell the reader actually happen or was she still alive and imagining her death?

13. What do you believe actually happened to Annabel?

Lightning Source UK Ltd.
Milton Keynes UK
UKHW041156090219
336887UK00001B/74/P